BATTLE SCARS

JANE HARVEY-BERRICK

HARVEY
BERRICK
PUBLISHING

Battle Scars

Copyright © 2017 Jane Harvey-Berrick

Originally released in serial form 2016-2017

Cover design by Sybil Wilson / Pop Kitty Designs

ISBN 978-1-912015-87-0
Harvey Berrick Publishing

DEDICATION

To Erin Spencer, who asked for a short story and got 20 chapters ♥

CONTENTS

Chapter One

A BAD START

2016

Two hours later and my hands were still shaking.

I'd been sitting in the cafeteria, fingers pressed against a cup of coffee that was now lukewarm. I could still smell the faint scent of soap and sweat as the man's hands tightened around my waist and pulled me towards him, the scream dying in my throat.

Another shudder ran through my body. *If he hadn't been there ... the other man...*

My brain refused to consider what could have happened next. He *was* there—and I was thankful for that. I'd been in the wrong place at the wrong time. He hadn't.

Working as a foreign correspondent wasn't as glamorous as it sounded. I spent my time in harsh climates, trying to talk to people who were too scared to have their words reported, too intimidated to have their photographs taken.

It was important work—I thought it was important. My friends didn't disagree, but they worried about me. And after everything that had happened today, it seemed they were right to worry.

I couldn't help replaying the afternoon's events in my mind.

My guide and interpreter, Omar, had taken me to a small, mudbrick house on the outskirts of the tired-looking village of Washir, trapped in the war torn land of Helmand Province, Afghanistan.

We'd been careful. Omar had borrowed a rickety, beaten up-car from one of his numerous cousins rather than risk being seen in the modern American Jeep that I had access to. Then I'd been covered from head to toe in a blue *burqa*, seemingly indistinguishable from every other Afghan woman, so I couldn't guess how we'd been spotted.

But ten minutes into the interview with Anoosheh and her family, there was a loud thump against the door, then glass showered onto the floor as a large rock was hurled through the window. An angry mob was gathering, and they were threatening to drag me outside. Omar wouldn't tell me what else they were planning to do to me.

I could guess. An unwanted Infidel woman. My chances were bleak and I was terrified.

With no escape route, no backdoor, and no plan, my fingers trembled helplessly as I used my satellite phone to call the emergency number I'd been given upon arriving at Camp Leatherneck, the former USMC base where I'd been living for the last week.

These days, it was run by the Afghan Army, but a small USMC detachment was still based there in a support and training role.

Thank God they were still here. Help was on its way, but the noise outside began to grow louder, uglier, and more windows were smashed. I cowered into the back of the room with the other members of the frightened family as Omar and Anoosheh's father piled furniture against the door, their eyes wide and panicked.

Suddenly, I heard shots outside, the distinctive sounds of a semi-automatic weapon firing. I thought I was going to die, and I prayed for the first time in a long while.

The door exploded inwards and one of the children screamed. Then I saw the most beautiful sight in the world: US Marines, armed and deadly.

The leader grabbed me by the hand, yelling something I couldn't hear above the gunfire, clamor and noise. Then he wrapped his arm around my waist and pulled me toward the door, his men clearing a path to the waiting Jeep.

Anoosheh and her family followed quickly, and we sped away in a cloud of yellow dust as the furious mob rained down rocks on us.

Omar insisted that we leave him and the family I'd been interviewing at his uncle's house. I pulled out my wallet and gave him every dollar I had in there. It wasn't much, but it would help them flee Helmand. I hoped.

The Marines stoically ignored me as they drove back to Camp Leatherneck. They'd checked I wasn't injured, but they had nothing to say to me. I could sense their dislike.

Once I was safe in the compound, I was debriefed by my liaison, Captain Luis Fernando. He offered to make an appointment for me with the Base's counselor. I just wanted to take a hot shower and wash away the fear and grime of the day.

When I finally felt clean, I forced myself to the cafeteria, but my stomach churned too badly for me to risk eating. Thankfully the coffee was drinkable. Okay, it tasted like crap, but coffee helped. It was a normal thing to do, ordinary, nothing scary here.

Until one very large and very pissed off Marine came marching over to me.

"You don't belong here, lady," he snarled, standing next to my table, his broad, tanned hands resting on lean hips.

"Excuse me?"

"You nearly got yourself killed today. I had to risk *my* men to come and get your ass out of a sling. You risked lives: yours, ours, that Afghan family, your terp. For what? Another damn story about how badly the US fucked up in Afghanistan!"

"I don't! That's not what…"

"I'm not finished!" he snapped, and I couldn't help flinching away from his obvious anger, from the raw power locked inside his muscled body.

"We're supposed to be winning hearts and minds out here, but your dumb stunt has set us back weeks—maybe months. You don't belong here. Go home and leave the real work to us."

My mouth hung open, moving uselessly as I tried to reply.

He shook his head in disgust, his dark blue eyes flaring with anger.

My own fury ignited at the sight of his broad back and arrogant lift of his head as he marched away from me.

I called out loudly.

"Do you have sisters, Sergeant?"

He stopped and turned slowly, his eyes narrowing as he decided whether or not to answer my question. His eventual reply was grudging.

"I've got a younger sister."

"That's nice," I said flatly, my eyes flicking up and down his tall body. I guessed he was in his late twenties, so a younger sister would be … what … early twenties? "What's her name?"

"Why do you want to know?"

"Just interested."

I could see him examining my question, searching for any danger areas, any way in which answering would show weakness, anything that could be twisted and used against him.

He licked his lips, then answered.

"Lucy."

"That's a pretty name. Did Lucy go to high school?"

"Of course she did," he scoffed. "She's in college now and…"

His words cut off when he realized he was coming close to having a conversation.

"That's nice," I said again. "Good for her. The girl I went to interview today is fourteen. Her name is Anoosheh—it means 'lucky'. She'd like to be a doctor, but that's not going to happen. I know you won't ask me why, so I'll just tell you. Her family has been told to take her out of school or she'll be killed. For wanting an education. And it's not just her—the same thing is happening all over Afghanistan."

I saw a muscle in his jaw tic as he clamped his mouth shut.

"Schools for girls have been burned down and teachers educating girls have been threatened or killed; girls have been attacked walking to school and even at school. So education is unsafe for them—it's rare to find any females educated past elementary age.

"Anoosheh is an exception—was an exception. Her school was burned down so she doesn't go anymore. Eighty-five per cent of Afghan women are illiterate*."

The sergeant frowned, his full lips thinning as he pressed them together. I had his attention and I was on a roll.

"Maybe you read about Malala Yousafzai, a young Pakistani girl? In 2012, when she was just fifteen years old, she was shot in the head by Taliban gunmen because she spoke up for the rights of girls to be educated. Or maybe you read about the 276 girls who were kidnapped from their school in Nigeria by Boko Haram—their crime was attending school. Many are still missing. Does any of this sound familiar, Sergeant?"

He nodded, a staccato tilt of his chin.

"Well, that's why I do what I do, because I believe that we in the West need to read these stories. We need to keep fighting for what is right because otherwise we let the darkness win. That's why I'm here. And that's why I'll continue to do my job."

"Fine," he said, his dark blue eyes glittering in the harsh lighting. "You do your job, you go save the world. In the meantime, poor slobs like me have to save you from yourself!"

"What's that supposed to mean?" I bristled.

"You come here, to a fucking war zone, and think being a liberal do-gooder is going to save you? Well it won't. People like me, people with guns are going to save you. You're so naïve and ill-prepared, but you think that you have the right..."

"I am not ill-prepared!" I snapped back. I certainly wasn't going to have this asshole tell me that I didn't know my job. "I do my research, Sergeant, just like you."

It was true: I'd read up everything I could find about Helmand Province—correct behavior, local customs, even a few words of the Qu'ran to use in an emergency. Although I had to admit none of that preparation had helped me today.

"Just like me," he mimicked, an ugly smile on his handsome face. "So with all that research, with all that preparation, how do you think they found you today? You think it was just an accident that a mob turns up outside the house where you're conducting an interview—a mob with the intention of dragging you out and stoning you to death? Probably raping you first."

I felt faint as every drop of blood rushed from my head, leaving my body cold and shocked. For a moment the asshole sergeant looked chagrined, but then the stormy expression returned.

"I didn't know," I whispered.

When he spoke again his voice was still stern.

"Your footwear," he said. "In Afghanistan, women don't wear white socks and white sneakers: your research should have told you those are banned, because the Afghan flag contains white, so wearing white shoes would signify walking on top of it." His voice was acid as he sneered at me. "You were seen. So much for your preparation. You should stick to reporting from the Bronx—it would be safer."

When he walked away this time, I didn't stop him.

I sat stewing for another hour, alternating between fury at the way he'd spoken to me, shock at how close I'd come to dying today, and the danger that I'd put myself in along with Omar and Anoosheh's family. And then the shameful realization that I hadn't even thanked Sergeant Asshole.

He was right: he and his men had put their lives on the line for me.

I felt small and ashamed.

I left the cup of cold coffee and went to speak with Captain Fernando again.

He looked irritated when he saw me standing at his door for the second time that day.

"Yes, Miss Buckman, what can I do for you now, ma'am?"

There was a slight emphasis on the word 'now', as if he really meant, 'why are you bothering me again?'

"I wonder if you could tell me the names of the men who came to my rescue today, Captain?"

"For the purpose of?"

"I want to thank them," I said simply.

He looked surprised.

"Anything else?"

"Well, I'd offer to buy them all a drink, but seeing as alcohol is forbidden here..."

He smiled.

"You don't need to do that, ma'am. I'll pass on your thanks to the men in question," and he turned back to his paperwork.

"I wonder if I could thank them in person," I pressed gently. "It would only take a moment—it would mean a lot to me."

He sighed, but nodded and stood up.

"This way, ma'am."

We walked through the camp, sweating in the relentless heat, despite the long shadows cast by the setting sun. He led me past rows of military vehicles and featureless temporary buildings, until we arrived at a long, barrack-style tent, and heard the sound of men's voices.

"She sure got you chasing your tail, Jack," someone laughed. "Not that I blame you. Man, that pretty little journalist is a sight for sore eyes."

"I don't care how smokin' hot she is," came the reply. "That stupid bitch risked her life to..."

"'Ten 'hut!"

One of the Marines lounging by the entrance had noticed us. Captain Fernando risked a quick glance in my direction then clearly decided it was better if he pretended neither of us had heard that last sentence.

The only giveaway was the dull flush of red beneath the handsome asshole's tanned cheeks as his voice cut out, the words 'stupid bitch' dying on his lips.

My own cheeks were equally red, not just because of what he'd said, but because he was standing bare-chested in front of me, a t-shirt dangling from one hand as if he'd just yanked it over his head.

His skin was smooth and tanned golden by long hours in the sun. I could see the muscles of his chest and stomach, an eight-pack with light brown hair leading downward, before I tugged my eyes up to his strong chin, ruthlessly shaved, and those intelligent, heated, dark blue eyes.

"At ease, men," said Fernando, clearing his throat. "I think most of you know our resident reporter. Miss Buckman, this is Sergeant Jackson Connor, the man who led the extraction party today. Men, Miss Buckman has got something she'd like to say to y'all." Then he turned to me. "The floor is yours, Miss Buckman."

I looked at each of the men in turn. The oldest couldn't have been more than 30; the youngest, a teenager who barely needed to shave. But they all had hard bodies and the flinty expressions of men who'd seen too much.

"I didn't get a chance to thank you before," I said, my voice carrying across the length of the long canvas dormitory. "You know, what with all those distracting bullets flying around and the angry mob out for blood." There was a soft murmur of laughter, but I had to close my eyes briefly as the feeling of terror began to crawl up my throat again. I swallowed twice before I could continue. "So, thank you—all of you—for saving my life." My eyes locked on Sergeant Connor. "I mean it—without you guys, I wouldn't be here now."

I'm not sure if I imagined it, but his hard expression seemed to soften slightly.

"I'm flying home tomorrow," I continued. "Someone told me that the Bronx is safer than Lashkar Gah..." I paused as a few more laughs echoed down the room, and even Sergeant Connor cracked a small smile. "But the next time any of you are in New York City, I'd love to buy you a drink. I work for the *New York Times*, a great big building on Eighth Avenue, so I'm pretty easy to find."

I looked across at Captain Fernando.

"That's it," I said softly.

As I left the room, I could feel Sergeant Connor's dark blue eyes burning into my back. I squared my shoulders as I walked away. The bastard had called me a stupid bitch; but he'd also saved my life ... and said I was smoking hot.

I'd been back in NYC for three months. I'd tried several times to find out what had happened to Omar and Anoosheh's family, but so far—nothing. They'd disappeared into the chaos of a country still at war after more than a decade of intervention.

I kept thinking about what Sergeant Connor said to me: had I made things harder for the troops still out there? I'd had such a strong belief that I held the moral high ground, but now I wasn't sure. I certainly hadn't improved things for Anoosheh, but my articles about the plight of women's education in Afghanistan and elsewhere had garnered plenty of publicity, and several charities had benefitted by receiving substantial donations from the public. So maybe it had been worthwhile.

My musings were interrupted when Allison, my PA, put her head around the door.

"Hey, MJ, you've got a visitor waiting for you in reception."

I frowned at her.

"There's no one on the schedule?"

Besides, it was after six on Friday, and most people had already left for the day.

She shrugged, a mischievous look on her face.

"Nope, no one scheduled, but you'll want to make time for this one, I promise."

"Well, who is it?"

She rolled her eyes.

"You're the reporter—go find out!"

Irritated but intrigued, I rode the elevator down to reception, scanning the lobby for my mystery guest.

My breath caught in my throat when I saw Sergeant Connor leaning against the wall, his arms folded and an amused expression on his face.

He wasn't in uniform and he looked far more relaxed than I'd seen him before. He was dressed in worn blue jeans and a plain gray t-shirt stretched over his broad chest and shoulders. I remembered that chest all too well, especially as it had starred in several erotic dreams.

The automatic doors slid open bringing a gust of air toward me, along with the faint scent of soap and something more masculine.

I realized that I was still staring, and the corners of his mouth lifted in a smile.

"Sergeant Connor!" I choked out. "This is a surprise."

I held out my hand and he shook it.

His tanned hand was large enough to completely cover mine, and the palms were rough. His grip, however, was surprisingly gentle.

"Jackson," he said. "My friends call me Jack."

"Mine call me MJ. So what are you doing here? Can I help you with something?"

"Waal," he said, a slow drawl in his voice, "I met a journalist out in Afghan who said she'd buy me a drink if I was ever in Manhattan. So here I am."

I blinked rapidly.

"Oh, okay! Sure!" My laugh was a little nervous. "I definitely owe you a drink. After all, you did give me valuable sartorial advice about my footwear and, you know, saved my life."

He grinned for the first time since I'd met him.

"Sartorial advice on footwear? Did you swallow a dictionary, Ms. Journalist?"

"Did you graduate from charm school, Mr. Marine?"

He laughed loudly and several people turned to look at us, although it was possible all the females still in the building were already looking.

"So, how about that drink?" he asked again, his eyes flicking up and down me quickly, but not so quickly that I didn't catch him doing it.

"Do you usually take drinks from stupid bitches?" I asked, my voice bland.

He winced and looked uncomfortable for a second.

"I'd like to apologize for saying that…"

I interrupted him quickly.

"Well, I *was* stupid. I made a very bad error of judgment, and if it hadn't been for you and your men…"

My voice trailed off and a shudder ran through me as the memories made my stomach lurch.

"I'm still sorry," he said softly, then touched my arm, a light, fleeting touch.

His eyebrows lifted as we both felt the shock of something like electricity, a connection arc between us. I licked my lips and risked looking into his eyes. His gaze was so intense, I had to turn away quickly.

"But I'm only a bitch to ex-boyfriends," I said, trying to lighten the mood.

He grinned again, his eyes crinkling at the corners of his deeply tanned face.

"Noted. I think I'll take the risk."

I smiled as he held out his hand to me.

We might have had a very bad start, but now it looked like a very promising beginning.

Oo-rah.

Chapter Two

A ROCKY ROAD

"So, where do you want to go?" I asked.

Jackson smiled and shook his head.

"I'm just a lil ole country boy let loose in the big city. I might get taken advantage of. I'm countin' on you to keep me safe, Ms. Journalist."

"Hmm, I can see that. An innocent in the big, bad city."

"Waal now, I wouldn't say *innocent* exactly," he drawled, his eyes glinting.

No, there was nothing innocent about Jackson Connor.

"Don't worry," I said, patting his arm. "I'll protect you. You're on my turf now."

His eyes twinkled with amusement and I could see him holding back a smile. He was so different from the angry, intense Marine that I'd met in Afghanistan.

He walked with an easy grace, a long-legged stride, confident in his body, owning the space around him. I'd seen his calm competence in an emergency first hand. This was a restrained version of it—a certainty that he could face anything.

But as we walked along the street, I picked up on several nonverbal cues that he'd probably prefer I didn't notice. I'd spent enough time with military personnel that I recognized the signs.

His eyes roved constantly, even as he maintained a light-hearted conversation. I saw him swiftly assessing everyone who passed us, automatically estimating the potential level of threat. No one was excluded: shoppers, office workers, mothers with strollers, even an elderly lady with a cane was analyzed before being dismissed from his automatic threat triage. He glanced upwards frequently, checking the skyline for snipers, I guessed. A street vendor made him frown, and his right hand twitched, as if seeking an absent weapon.

He was friendly but he was alert, not truly relaxing until we entered *Walter's Bar*, a small, low-key hangout that I liked to go to. It had a dart board where I played with colleagues from work sometimes, and ESPN blared from the flatscreens around the room.

It was early evening and the bar was busy with the after-work crowd, so I led the way to my favorite booth opposite the horseshoe-shaped bar and plopped onto the cracked leather seat. It offered a little more privacy than one of the tables in the center.

Jackson took a position where he could see everyone who entered the bar, then, apparently satisfied with our seats, picked up the menu.

"What's good?"

"Pepperoni pizza or wings," I answered immediately.

Walter's had a small menu that served basic bar food, but I liked it because it was friendly and unpretentious, not because the food was great.

Jackson licked his lips and a small shiver of anticipation ran through him.

"Man, I can't tell you the number of times I dreamed of buffalo chicken wings while I was in the sandbox," he murmured.

"My treat," I reminded him.

"That wasn't part of the deal."

"I can buy you an $8 pizza," I smiled. "Not exactly the going rate for saving someone's life, but it's a start."

"Is that so?"

"Hell, I'll even let you get a side of fries, if you like," I winked at him.

He nodded eagerly.

"And a cold draft beer?" I suggested, knowing how much the guys deployed to Afghanistan longed for an ice cold, crystal clear beer on each and every one of those hot, dusty, draining days.

He groaned, an expression of yearning washing over his face which I took as a 'yes'.

I placed our order with the server and sat back in the booth.

Jackson fiddled with a paper napkin, absently shredding it, a small frown on his face as his eyes checked out the entrance for the third time in five minutes.

"Relax, Sergeant," I said, smiling to soften my words. "No insurgents here."

His chin jerked up as his eyes narrowed with irritation, but then he blew out a long breath and I saw the set of his shoulders loosen.

"Occupational hazard," he nodded with a wry smile. "I've only been stateside four weeks and away from the base for two days—not long enough to switch it all off." And then he murmured softly, "If it ever switches off..."

I smiled reassuringly. I knew that he couldn't turn it off any more than he could stop being a Marine, but maybe I could help him relax a little more. I understood how he felt. Once you've experienced something life-threatening, you're more aware, you can't help it. You'll always be watching, even if it's unconsciously.

"I get that. I felt like I was on the biggest rollercoaster for the first two weeks I was back home. Every time I heard a loud noise, I jumped. I'm better now. Although sometimes..." and I shrugged.

He nodded with understanding and maybe a little relief.

"But if you're interested, there's another exit out the back, although Walter is a little picky about who he lets walk through his kitchen."

Jackson grinned.

"Sounds like you've done a few covert ops in here."

"Something like that," I smiled, happy to see him begin to relax. "Dart competitions can get pretty intense."

He chuckled quietly, but then he went back to shredding his

napkin and an uncomfortable silence started to settle. Just as it was verging on awkward, he looked up.

"Did you find that girl? The one you were interviewing?"

"Anoosheh," I sighed. "No, I didn't. I heard a vague rumor that her family had made it to Pakistan, but ... it's just a rumor. I'm still hopeful ... or maybe I should say I'm still hoping..."

He nodded, his expression closed off.

I let my journalism training kick in—I was used to getting people talking, it was part of the job.

"So," I began, "what part of the south does this country boy come from?"

"Gulfport, Mississippi."

"Oh, my gosh! Don't tell me your parents named you after Jackson, Mississippi!"

He gave a low chuckle.

"No, ma'am. My grandpappy on my mother's side. But I can't say for sure where his name came from. What about you? Where do you hail from?"

"I'm a Philly girl."

"Good football team."

"You follow the Eagles?"

His expression hardened as he swallowed and looked down.

"My buddy did."

It didn't escape my notice that he'd used the past tense.

Luckily, the food arrived and Jackson inhaled his meal with barely a glance in my direction, although his moans and groans as he ate his chicken wings bordered on pornographic—certainly to my mind.

"Hungry?" I asked, lifting an eyebrow as I idly chewed on a French fry.

His tanned cheeks reddened with a faint blush and he looked up sheepishly.

"I'm just teasing you, Jack. But I promise, no one is going to try and take those wings away from you."

He muttered something under his breath and I watched with fascination as the tips of his ears turned pink. But then he leaned back in his seat and fixed me with an amused stare.

"So, havin' saved your life an' all, does that mean I get dessert, too?"

"Wow, you're pushing your luck now, Sergeant. Hmm, let me think about that. Yes, saving-of-life would definitely merit a portion of ice cream."

"Huh, is that right? I was thinking more of waffles with banana, brownies, hot fudge sauce and chocolate ice cream."

"Well, you're out of luck because *Walter's* has vanilla, chocolate or strawberry ice cream."

"Damn! I was really craving hot fudge."

"Why, Jack Connor! I'm sensing that someone has a sweet tooth!"

"I sure do like my sugar," he smiled right back at me.

And then he licked his lips. Those full, pink, sensuous lips.

The man was a darned tease.

And a flirt.

But he was only in town for a short visit, and hot as he was, I didn't do one-night stands. Not for a couple of years now. I wasn't cut out for it. No matter if I only slept with a guy once, my heart always seemed to get involved. Although something told me that making an exception for Jackson would be a memory worth having. But still...

"What are your plans while you're in town?" I asked, changing the subject.

He finished up the last of his wings, wiping his mouth on the napkin while he chewed thoughtfully.

"I've got a buddy up in Scranton that I'm gonna go see. But other than that..." He shrugged casually. "Guess I'll take a look at the Big Apple, see what all the fuss is about."

"You've never been here before?"

"Nope," he said, popping the 'p'. "Like I said, I'm a country boy at heart."

"Well, I'm sure your friend will really appreciate the visit."

His expression was hard to read as he nodded.

Instead of trying to figure out what it meant, I watched as the server brought his chocolate ice cream, smiling with fascination as four scoops disappeared in double-quick time. I could feel the pounds piling on my thighs just by looking at him. I swear that some calories are carried by air, like a virus.

When his dish was clean, we ordered coffee. I took mine with sugar; Jackson didn't bother with it. Honestly, he'd already had so much sugar, I was relieved that he hadn't fallen into a diabetic coma. Even though he hadn't been living on MREs the whole time he was overseas, the man had obviously missed pub grub.

Chatting with Jackson was easy once he'd relaxed, but I started to realize that we had almost nothing in common. He liked Country music and I liked anything with a Latin beat; he loved action movies and I liked weird and emotional European films; I'd gotten my Masters in Journalism and he'd graduated high school at 18 then joined the Marines; I'd lived in New York my whole life and this was his first visit, but he wasn't thrilled so far.

And yet ... and yet ... there was a pull, a draw, a something in his eyes that said he found our differences intriguing, maybe an invitation or a challenge. I wasn't foolish enough to think that his visit was simply to take me up on my offer to buy him a drink ... and yet...

I couldn't put my finger on it.

He was attractive—no one with eyeballs could deny that. But there was a self-sufficiency, a commanding quietness that drew me in. He moved effortlessly through his space, a man at ease with himself, a man who knew that he'd accomplished things beyond the understanding of most people. It wasn't arrogance, but simply confidence in his abilities and his place in the world.

And he made me laugh.

Who would have thought that the intense, aggressive Marine that I'd met under such trying circumstances could tell jokes and tease and flirt?

It was the most fun dinner I'd had in forever.

We'd had something of a tussle for the check before it came, and I'd cheated by paying when I went to the bathroom. Jackson hadn't taken it well and brooded for at least 30 seconds.

"Well, I suppose I'd better get going. One of us has to get up for work tomorrow," I said at last. "Thank you for a very entertaining evening. I'm glad you came by."

"So am I—best chicken wings I've had in nine months. And the company wasn't bad," he teased.

17

"Why, Sergeant Connor! You're in danger of paying me a compliment."

He laughed lightly.

"Is that a fact? Waal, my grandpappy always told me to treat a pretty girl like a lady. And he'd damn well kick my ass for letting you pay. But I can't say as I've gotten a lot of chances to mind my manners lately with any sort of female."

"*Any sort of female?*" I raised my eyebrows. "And now you're in danger of sweeping me off my feet with all that sweet-talk."

"Aw, you're not just any sort of female," he grinned at me. Then he leaned in closer. "In fact, I'd say you're mighty easy on the eyes."

"Thank you very much," I laughed. "Let me know when you've taken off your rose-tinted desert glasses."

"Why, MJ! Are you fishin' for compliments, girl?"

I rolled my eyes.

"If I was, it would be a very short fishing trip."

He laughed happily.

"I don't suppose there's any time in that busy city-girl schedule to escort this lil ole country boy for lunch tomorrow?"

"Good grief, Jack! You're laying it on pretty thick! Have you turned into Garth Brooks over a plate of chicken wings?"

"Is that a yes?" he asked, his eyes crinkling again as he smiled hopefully.

Oh yeah, that was definitely a yes. Even as my heart whispered warnings, I knew there was no way I'd turn down another meal with Jackson Connor and the chance to spend more time with him.

"I thought you were going up to see your friend in Scranton."

"He'll still be there."

"Fine, I'll sacrifice another few hours to keeping you safe in the big, bad city," I pretended to sigh.

"Why, thank you, ma'am!"

He nodded and stood up, holding out his hand to me as I slid awkwardly from the booth's bench-seat.

"I have to work for a few hours tomorrow morning," I warned him. "I'm interviewing someone in Australia and it's the only time that works for them. That's oh-nine-hundred hours to you, and then I want to write it up while it's fresh in my mind—it'll take a couple of hours. Sorry I'll be so late on a Saturday morning."

"No worries," he said, shrugging easily. "It'll give me a chance to do some tourist stuff first. What would you recommend? All I've got on my list right now is: collect free lunch—which I've done—" and he winked at me, "and the World Trade Center Memorial."

We shared a moment as we looked at each other.

I was 15 when it happened. We were in the middle of Algebra. One of the teachers interrupted our lesson to share the news. It didn't seem real, didn't seem possible. The school went on lockdown once the first tower was hit. And even though we were ninety miles away, I swear we could see clouds of dark smoke hanging in the sky over the city.

It was the reason I'd become a journalist—to always ask the question *why*, to report, to search, to seek to understand.

Jackson had also told me that 9/11 was why he'd joined the Marines. I'd heard a lot of men and women say that about the military.

I nodded, offering a solemn smile.

"Well, the 9/11 Memorial takes a few hours to go through and they recommend reservations, but for tomorrow morning, you might want to take a trip out to the Ellis Island Museum. The Holocaust Museum —that's really interesting, as well. And who doesn't want to see the Statue of Liberty? Then there's always loads to see in Central Park if you just want to hang out. I don't see you as a Barneys or Saks kind of guy."

"You call yourself a reporter and you go and make assumptions like that?" he laughed. "Would you be surprised if I told you that Bergdorf Goodman is on my to-do list?"

"Hmm, and that wouldn't have anything to do with a sister who's studying textile design, would it?"

He'd already told me during dinner that his younger sister was in school at Ole Miss.

He held up his hands in surrender.

"It might," he admitted. "Sheesh, you remember everything a guy tells you?"

I tapped the side of my head and winked at him.

"Locked and loaded."

He laughed out loud.

"Noted, Ms. Journalist. I guess I'd better watch my mouth doesn't run away with itself."

Oh God, I'd love his mouth to do that and a lot more.

I shook the thought away.

"I'll see you at 11 o'clock, Jack."

"You surely will, MJ," he smiled.

We were just about to leave the pub when the news came on. Jackson turned to watch, his mouth flattening as the newscaster described a scene of carnage. In Afghanistan.

"Last week, the relief organization Médecins Sans Frontières, known here as Doctors Without Borders, reported that 16 people, including nine of its volunteer staff, were killed in an overnight bombing raid in the embattled city of Kunduz in northern Afghanistan.

"Three children were among the fatalities and today General John Campbell, head of the US-led forces has apologized, admitting that, 'The strike may have resulted in collateral damage to a nearby medical facility as we launched an airstrike against individuals threatening the coalition force'."

Jackson swore under his breath, anger and frustration on his face.

There's nothing pretty about war. We both knew that mistakes happened, and it was grim and chaotic. One of the ugliest phrases was 'collateral damage', because it was a sanitized way of saying that someone had died for no reason. People died because they were in the wrong place at the wrong time: civilian, military, old and young. Journalists weren't immune to the danger either—as I knew all too well.

Jackson had already turned to leave when a guy standing next to me shook his head at the TV and said loudly, "Fucking meathead military. They should get some guys with brains over there, not mindless grunts who are so trigger-happy they don't know what the fuck they're doing. Waste of taxpayers' dollars."

Jackson froze. I tried to get him to keep moving even though I felt like punching the man who'd spoken, but it was as useful as trying to move a mountain.

Jack's eyes hardened as he turned to stare at the guy.

"What did you say?"

The man swung around, surprised. He took in Jackson's stance and furious eyes, and stepped back, more guarded now.

"You heard," he said, his voice wary. "They killed doctors, for God's sake."

"Jack, let's go," I said quietly, tugging on his arm again.

I saw the rage rush through him, and I saw his struggle to keep it under control.

"Time to go," I urged again.

He took a deep breath, turning to look at me, hearing me, listening to me.

"Come on," I said, taking his hand in mine.

He followed slowly, as if his shoes were filled with lead.

Outside, he put his hands on his hips, staring upwards, trying to catch a glimpse of the night sky among all the towering buildings. He breathed deeply, taking calming breaths before he spoke again.

"That guy ... these people have no fucking clue what it's like out there. Do they really think we don't care? That those guys who ordered the strike ... the ones who flew the goddam planes ... that they won't be haunted by that for the rest of their lives? Doctors and children..."

I nodded, watching him carefully.

"I know. I get it. That's why I do what I do—I report on the places no one wants to care about. And sometimes I get my ass in a sling and have to be rescued by the cavalry. Did I say thank you for that, by the way?"

His expression softened and he smiled ruefully.

"God, MJ, I'm sorry about that back there," and he jerked his thumb at the pub behind us. "It's hard to hear shit like that sometimes, when guys are still out there and friends of mine..." He paused. "It's not the greatest end to a date, is it?"

I blinked several times. He thought this was a date?

His casual words sent a rocket through all my plans to stay detached, to refuse to have my head turned by an attractive man whose ass looked great in camo.

If Jackson Connor, the man who'd saved my life, who'd sought me out in New York—even though he hated cities—if a man like that wanted to call this a date, how the hell could I protect myself against the assault on my good sense?

I tried to gather my scattered wits.

"Oh, I don't know," I said as casually as I could manage. "A bit of action, a potentially life-threatening situation—that's par for the course for us, don't you think? All of our encounters have a little drama."

"You're calling this an encounter?"

"A date implies that there'll be kissing involved."

"Kissing?"

"It's in the small print."

"I guess I must have missed that memo."

"Your loss."

"I'm a fast learner."

His eyes darkened as we stared across the empty space at each other, trying to read what this would mean.

He leaned toward me, his lips soft and tentative at first. But when I didn't back away, when my hands slipped around his neck and my body pressed against his hard chest, Jackson's kiss became more urgent, more desperate.

My fingers tangled in the thin chain around his neck and I realized that he was wearing his dog tags under his t-shirt.

My mind skittered back, remembering vividly the way his bare chest had glowed under the dim lighting of a dusty tent in a war-torn country.

What the hell was I doing?

If I fell for Jackson Connor, it would be as stupid and foolish as hitching my heart to a sailing ship.

What the hell was I doing?

Chapter Three

A NEW ROAD

I pulled back from Jackson, breathless and dizzy, only vaguely aware that we were still standing on a crowded Manhattan street.

My thoughts were fuzzy and indistinct, and those damn warning bells sounded far away. Instead, there was only one truly clear thought running through my brain: *Now that was a kiss.*

I brushed my hair out of my eyes as Jackson watched me closely, his own breathing faster now.

"Do you want to take this forward, MJ?" he asked, his eyes trained on mine, those strong muscled arms still circling my waist.

I wanted to smile. I shouldn't have expected anything other than a direct approach from Jackson. He didn't play games and he said what he wanted. It was refreshing. Except I knew that what he was offering was sex, not a relationship. During our four hours of talking, he'd made it clear that he wasn't a man who did relationships. From the sound of it, the tally of anything he'd call serious stood at one.

I took a step back and he released me slowly, as if reluctant to let me go. I reminded myself again that I didn't do one-night stands because I got involved too easily. My stupid brain couldn't help equating sex with love, even though I knew better.

But when was the last time the touch of a man had made my body sing and surge, as if electrical charges were zapping through the air, heating my blood, making the hairs on my arms tingle? Only once since high school, and that had been a short-lived, adrenaline-filled fuck-buddy relationship with another journalist when I was covering a humanitarian crisis in Ethiopia.

All these confusing, contradicting thoughts rushed through my brain in a split second. Although I could analyze and second-guess forever, my gut was telling me to take a chance. Because men like Jackson didn't come along every day.

How many times had I turned down a second date with a New Yorker because he spent more on manicures, haircuts, threading and waxing than I did? How many times had I wanted to meet a man who was raw and masculine without being arrogant?

Jack and I might not have had the smoothest start and it seemed certain that the road ahead would be bumpy, but...

"Yes," I said, with more assurance than I felt. "Let's see where this goes."

His face relaxed into a lazy, sexy grin.

"Can I come back to your place?"

Oh boy, he didn't waste time.

I knew the drill. I'd heard it often enough when I'd been embedded with military teams on an assignment: the old adage that you never felt more alive than when you were close to death. Men like that lived their lives now. Waiting until tomorrow wasn't an option when there might not be a tomorrow.

Even so, I shook my head. No. Coming back to my place wasn't going to work for me; that was too personal, sharing my space. And besides, I preferred to finish a date ... or whatever this had become ... when I was ready, on my terms.

"Let's go to your hotel."

I saw a flicker of disappointment, but he didn't argue. Instead, he offered me his arm. Just an old fashioned Southern gentleman ... having a very modern hookup.

We strolled through the streets, the crowds of commuters relaxing into people out to enjoy the warm evening of late summer.

There was no sense of urgency in his footsteps, but I still felt the tug of anticipation low in my belly, and I couldn't help sneaking glances at his profile. His straight nose and strong chin, those full lips and sharp cheekbones, the strength of his arms and body displayed to perfection in his simple, unpretentious clothes: unbranded jeans and a plain t-shirt.

He caught me looking, and winked, his fingers stroking over my hand as he pulled me closer so he could throw a possessive arm around my shoulders.

And I giggled.

Holy shit! I never giggled. A woman of 31 shouldn't giggle! I was mortified. In four hours, the man had reduced me to a giddy high-schooler.

I braced my shoulders and took a deep breath, stopping to read the menu in a new restaurant that had recently opened.

"You like Nepalese?"

"Sure," I said. "I'll eat pretty much anything. I think I've had to, at one time or another. Even MREs, although I'm not sure you could class those as food."

He laughed.

"Ain't that the truth! Man, some of that food, you can't even tell what it is. And whoever has a bottle of hot sauce is mighty popular."

Jackson was so easy to talk to. He didn't try to impress me with tales of valor. Instead, he shared ordinary stories about being deployed: the bad meals, sandflies, porta-potties. The heat and dust, the boredom. Boredom that we both knew could turn to gut-clenching fear in a matter of seconds.

But he kept things light, making me laugh again and again.

Until we reached his hotel. Then his tone turned serious.

"You can still change your mind, MJ," he said, staring down into my eyes.

"I know. But I don't want to."

He smiled with relief, squeezing my fingers lightly.

"I was kinda hoping you'd say that."

Ignoring the revolving door at the front of the hotel, instead he opted to use a smaller door, standing to one side as I walked in, his hand at the small of my back when he followed.

Then he wove our fingers together as we headed for the elevator.

The doors slid closed behind us and he grinned down at me.

"An empty elevator with a beautiful woman, it makes me want to do bad things."

"Such as?"

"A gentleman would never tell."

"Never?"

He pressed a quick kiss to my neck, his tongue flicking out briefly.

"No, but I sure want to show you as soon as we get to my room. Dammit, can this elevator move any slower?"

"I think it's going backwards."

But then there was a soft ding and we were on the seventh floor.

I took a deep breath as we stepped out, our footsteps silent on the thick carpet. Jackson squeezed my hand again, a small frown on his face.

"You doin' okay over there?"

"I'm fine. I haven't changed my mind. It's just ... I don't usually..." and I gestured toward his door as he pulled out his keycard.

The door swung open and Jackson gave me a level look.

"I haven't had sex in over a year, MJ. And I was only deployed for nine of those 12 months."

I was taken aback, in a good way. It wasn't that I'd pegged him for a player—he was too straightforward for that—I'd just assumed that hookups were not unusual for him.

"You know what I thought when I saw you in the sandbox?" he asked.

I tilted my head to one side as I answered.

"Something like: what the hell is that stupid woman doing getting herself caught up in a riot?"

He gave a small smile.

"Even when I was worried about getting you out in one piece, I thought you were hot. But when you tore a strip off of me in the cafeteria and showed me how much it meant to you—reporting, the Afghan civilians, that girl you interviewed—you were passionate and committed. It's easy to get jaded out there after all the shit you see.

But you still had ideals." He gave me a sideways look. "Even if I didn't agree with them."

I couldn't help a surprised laugh bubbling out of me.

"And then you came to our tent and heard me mouthing off about you ... I'm sorry for calling you a bitch."

"You've already apologized for that, Jack. I'm not going to hold it against you."

"I know. That's what I mean. I could have been on punishment duty for a month for saying that about you in front of my CO, but you pretended that you hadn't heard. It was really cool of you."

I shook my head.

"Well, I'm happy to take the credit for that, but I wanted to thank you. You and your men saved my life. It was the least I could do."

He smiled.

"And you bought me dinner."

"We're still not quite even for you saving my life, but it's a start. And anyway, as well as calling me a bitch, you said I was smoking hot," I reminded him.

His smile faded.

"Damn straight. You blow my mind, MJ."

He reached out to cup my face with both hands, bringing his lips down softly on mine, angling my head to suit the slant of his mouth while he kicked the door closed behind him.

My hands looped themselves around his waist and he moved into my space like it was his to own. But it gave me access to the smooth silk of his broad back, and my eager hands moved upward under his t-shirt, feeling his muscles twitch and his skin pebble with excitement. It made me feel powerful and in control, which was a complete illusion because the man could snap me like a twig.

Instead, his hands were strong but gentle, one sliding to my neck while the other pulled me firmly against him.

I sighed with pleasure as I felt his erection pressed against me for the first time.

His fingers tangled in my hair, then he wrapped the ends around his fist and pulled back gently, kissing down my neck, sucking softly on the sensitized skin.

His other hand moved up to cup my breast, his thumb pressing through two layers of fabric, but still able to find my hard nipple.

My short nails scratched down his back and he arched into me, a soft groan of desire, a low masculine moan rolling up from his throat.

He opened his eyes and stared down at me, his intense gaze making me feel hungry for attention and suddenly filled.

I reached up to his shoulders again, dragging my nails down his back, and once again he arched like a cat, almost purring.

Then he reached behind and yanked his t-shirt over his head, gripping the neck of the material in that way that men and boys seem to do naturally, the shirt all but ripping from its rough use.

His dog tags gave a soft *chink* as they landed back on his chest. I stepped away, taking a moment to appreciate the artistry of his body, honed by work, chiseled by the boredom of deployment with nothing to do but hours spent burning energy in a dusty gym.

His eyes urged me to touch him and I was more than happy to accept, permission to slide my fingers over all that golden skin.

Then I held his dog tags in my hand, using them to pull him toward me. He grinned, pleased with my command.

This kiss was more urgent, sexual, insistent, his probing tongue a prelude to the madness to come. His hands tightened authoritatively around my waist, then rose upward, taking my shirt with them.

Another soft groan escaped when he lowered his lips to kiss my breasts, wetting the fabric of my bra.

I started to reach behind me to undo it, but he stopped me.

"No, let me. I've been fantasizing about this," he admitted.

"Really? For how long?"

"About five minutes after I met you," he chuckled.

"Ah, I see. Immediately after rescuing me from a murderous mob. Good to know your mind was on your work, Sarge."

He shrugged, smiling slyly.

"I can multitask."

I pressed my lips against his chest, feeling the strong even beat of his heart.

As I leaned forward, his deft fingers found the catch on my bra and popped it open. I shimmied out of it, and he caught my breasts in his hands, his head moving between them, circling my nipples with his warm tongue, bringing pleasure to every part of me.

His callused fingers took over where his tongue left off, and then he kissed me thoroughly, possessively, our tongues fighting for dominance —a fight that I'd ultimately lose without giving a damn.

I'd never been with a man like Jackson before. He was so confidently male, so unashamedly strong without being brutal, although maybe just a little rough, which I hadn't known I'd like.

He handled my body as assuredly as he handled his MK-16, almost like an extension of himself.

And that powerful, beautiful body was my playground. My hands touched everywhere; my tongue tasted all that I could reach while we were still partially clothed.

I could feel his hands exploring my waistband, tugging at the zipper.

"I have to take my shoes off," I muttered against his neck, my new favorite place.

He laughed softly as he kicked off his own sneakers and dropped his jeans in a second.

And I couldn't answer the eternal question of boxers or briefs, because he wasn't wearing either.

My eyes snagged on his cock, my hands pausing with my pants half down, but then something else caught my attention and held it hostage.

White scars, like slashes of rain marred the smoothness of his left hip and thigh.

"Shrapnel," he said, answering my unspoken question as I traced my fingers across the ridges of shiny scar tissue. "At least I didn't get my dick shot off."

I let out a puff of air that would have been a snort of amusement in other circumstances—but it just didn't seem appropriate in the presence of nine inches of engorged flesh pointing in my direction.

I let my slacks drop to the floor, clad only in boring white panties, mesmerized by his body with all its beauty and all its flaws.

From the rain burst of scars, my hand dropped lower, running my palm across the length of his shaft, smoothing my thumb over the broad crown, watching his stomach muscles tremble as I touched and teased and stroked.

I glanced up as he sucked in a breath, the thick ridges of his abs quivering. I had intended to lick each and every part of that amazing body, losing myself in all the dips and crannies.

The dark blue of his eyes had become stormy, and I sensed that only his iron willpower was holding him back at this moment. I shivered, wondering what Jackson Connor unleashed would be like. My body welcomed the moment, but my timid heart knew he had the power to slay me.

He shocked me by falling to his knees, his nose pressing against my pubic bone as he inhaled deeply, then pressed a soft kiss to my damp panties.

I ran my hands over his closely-cropped hair, his bowed head making him seem vulnerable.

But then he hooked his fingers in my panties and slowly slid them down my legs. His eyes flared with heat and something primitive, and then he cupped my ass to pull me closer so I was almost astride his head.

I hissed and squirmed as his tongue sank into me, but he held me firmly even as I lost my grip on his too-short hair.

His tongue continued to stroke and press and explore until my thighs quivered and I cried out softly.

Even as my eyelids drooped, I saw him smile with satisfaction. Then he carried me to the bed, positioning my body, altering the cant of my hips to suit himself.

A condom was in his hand, expertly sheathing himself, a slight tightness to his lips giving away the fact that he was affected by this.

As he pushed inside, he muttered something under his breath, but I was too entranced to make him repeat it, and I wasn't sure it was for my ears anyway.

I cried again softly as he filled my body, my knees automatically lifting, my ankles wrapping behind his back, digging in with my heels as I urged him deeper.

"Goddam, MJ," he said roughly.

And then he lost control.

He pounded furiously, shaking loose the confines of my ankles so my feet bounced helplessly against his back, my breasts quivering with every thrust. My hands were pinned by my sides in his iron grip, and the ferocity in his gaze dried my throat. The intensity was almost scary, but then he came suddenly and unexpectedly, hissing out his release as his heavy body covered mine.

He swore softly and rolled off, disengaging his still impressive dick.

"Goddam, MJ," he said again, more softly. "I was going to make that last, but you're too much for me, woman."

I laughed breathlessly.

"That was fine for me. Damn fine, I'd say."

He gave me a lopsided smile.

"It'll be better next time."

Next time.

He pulled off the condom, tied a knot in the end and lazily dropped it on the floor, grinning at the disapproval that was written all over my face.

"I'll pick it up later," he said, reaching out to cup my breast. "Promise."

"You'd better. It must be hard enough being the hotel maid without … you know what, never mind. I'm just going to lie here in a happy state of post-coital bliss."

He squeezed my breast again.

"You look beautiful, all pink and warm. Shit, seeing you come all over my tongue was somethin' else."

I hoped he couldn't see my cheeks growing redder from his words, even though I liked them a lot.

We lay in silence, but it wasn't uncomfortable. My fingers played with the smattering of hair on his chest, tugging gently.

After a while, my words unglued themselves from their lazy state. I had questions.

"Jack, you said you didn't have sex last time you were on leave."

His blue eyes settled on mine confidently.

"That's right."

"Why?"

He puffed out his cheeks.

"I'm not naïve enough to think that you couldn't have, if you'd wanted to," I added.

He smiled slightly.

"If I was twenty, yeah, I won't lie to you. I'd have been at the beach coaxing co-eds out of their bikinis."

I laughed ruefully at the all too probable image.

"But I'm not twenty," he went on. "And being with a girl just so she can say she got laid by a Marine, it gets old. Well, it has for me. I just didn't meet anyone special last time I was home." And he leveled those honest eyes at me. "I had to wait until I was back in the sandbox to meet a woman who caught my interest."

I smiled with the pleasure of warm satisfaction.

"What about you, MJ? You're in a city with eight million folks, half of them men. How come you don't have a guy?" He paused. "Or maybe you do."

I raised one eyebrow.

"I've dated, but no one special caught my eye. I had to wait until I was on a hot and sweaty embedment in Afghanistan before I met someone I could be interested in."

He grinned at me.

"Could be interested?"

"Jack Connor, are you fishing for compliments?"

"Would I catch anything if I tried?"

"Well, I could say that you have a beautiful dick."

He choked on a laugh.

"Thank you, ma'am. Not a compliment I'll be sharing anytime soon."

He rolled out of the bed, stretching languidly, that perfectly chiseled body on display, not a shred of embarrassment as he walked naked to the bathroom.

I turned onto my side to watch my own private floorshow. God, his butt! Two perfect globes of muscle. It made me want to sink my teeth into them.

But it was cute—his ass was paler than the rest of him.

"Not much naked sunbathing when you were in Afghan, Sarge?" I called after him.

He turned and grinned, leaning one hip against the bathroom door.

"Usually, yes. But we had some gals from the motor pool in the hardback next door—the framed tent where we sleep. Their CO complained that she kept gettin' flashed, so we were told to cover up."

"I bet her team hated her for that," I teased.

"Yeah," he agreed. "Tears at bedtime."

"Not binoculars?"

His eyes widened as he pretended to look shocked.

"MJ! You tellin' me you like to perv on naked guys?"

I shrugged.

"It's working out pretty well for me right now."

He laughed and disappeared into the bathroom.

I heard the sound of running water and a moment later he reappeared.

"What does MJ stand for?" he asked out of the blue.

I shook my head, pretending to be shocked.

"Sarge! Are you telling me that you're the kind of man who sleeps with a woman before you know her name?"

He raised one eyebrow.

"Fine, don't answer that. It stands for Margaret Jean, but I prefer MJ."

He grinned.

"Suits you, Maggie."

I winced.

"I think you have earwax. I'm pretty sure I just said that I prefer being called MJ."

"Yeah, but I like having a name for you that no one else uses—I like Maggie."

My smile faded and Jackson frowned.

"What's wrong, sugar?"

"Nothing. It's nothing."

"No, I said somethin' that upset you. If you don't want me to call you Maggie then I won't."

He sat on the bed and reached forward, pushing my hair over one ear and rubbing his thumb gently across my cheek.

"My dad used to call me Maggie. No one else has since he died. But it's kind of nice to hear it again," I admitted.

He smiled softly and kissed me gently.

"Thank you for sharing that."

I lifted a shoulder, unwilling to confess how much it affected me.

I laid back on the bed and stared up at the ceiling, feeling the mattress dip as Jackson stretched out beside me.

Then he rolled onto his side and pulled at my hip until we were facing each other. And somehow that gesture was more intimate than when he'd been moving inside me ten minutes earlier.

He didn't speak for a while and I wondered if he was drifting asleep. But then his eyes opened again.

"I've had a really great night," he said, stroking one finger along my shoulder and arm, slowly trailing down across my waist, until his warm hand was resting on my exposed thigh.

I tensed slightly, waiting for the whole, take your time showering before you leave speech, or some version of it.

"Come to Scranton with me tomorrow. Meet my buddy, Gray. You'll like him."

I blinked, surprised.

Wait, what?

That's not how the script was supposed to go.

I studied him closely, wondering if he was simply feeling obliged to let me down in a more gentlemanly way than usual, being southern and all. But as I looked into dark blue eyes, I saw nothing but sincerity, as well as something deeper—a longing, maybe even hope that we'd made a connection.

I smiled cautiously, prepared to give him an out.

"He's expecting to see you, not some random woman you picked up."

Jackson frowned.

"You're not random, Maggie."

Hearing him use that name slayed me. It woke too many feelings, but it warmed me through all the same.

"Then I'd love to," I said at last. "I've never been to Scranton."

He grinned and planted a sweet kiss on my forehead.

"Me either."

I was tempted to snuggle into that amazing chest, breathing in his warm, spicy scent as I drifted asleep. But I'd planned on going home. Especially if we were going to visit his friend tomorrow, I needed clean clothes.

"I should go," I sighed, pulling away and sitting up, enjoying the way his eyes dropped to my chest before returning to my face.

"Stay," he said, sitting up and cupping my cheek with his hand.

"I really should get going..."

"Please," he said softly.

Damn, those southern manners were going to be the death of me.

"We'll get a cab to your place in the morning, so you can change your clothes and get your female do-dads. We'll leave after you've done your work."

I burst out laughing.

"Female do-dads? Really?"

He laughed with me.

"Isn't that the technical term? Dang! I must have missed the memo."

"Never mind, Sarge. I'll get you caught up with all the new-fangled words like cell phone and automobile."

"Oh, you think you're pretty funny!"

His eyes flashed wickedly, and then he pounced, tickling the hell out of me until I was screaming for him to stop.

He pinned my hands to the bed, both of us breathless. I felt his hardness against my belly and then his mouth was on mine, his tongue hot and determined as he kissed the hell out of me.

I decided there and then to reschedule my early morning call. Very unprofessional. Very unlike me. And definitely the right decision.

Round two.

Chapter Four

AN OLD FRIEND

The bed was too hot, and I felt sweaty and uncomfortable as I tossed the duvet away and sat up, my eyes snapping open when I heard a muffled yelp.

Memories of last night came racing back, and I couldn't help an apologetic chuckle as Jackson pushed the duvet from his face, rubbing his chest where I'd accidentally elbowed him.

"You always this rough on your men, Maggie?"

I laughed at him over my shoulder.

"Stop pretending I hurt you! Surely the big, tough Marine isn't afraid of little old me?"

Jackson gave me a wry smile.

"That's where you're wrong, sugar. As far as I'm concerned, females are weapons of mass destruction, created with the sole intention of bringing a man to his knees. And besides, women are from Mars and men are from Venus."

"I think you mean *men* are from Mars."

"Uh-uh! Women are way more bloodthirsty."

"Is that a fact?"

"More like a life lesson."

He grinned up at me, his short hair flattened slightly on one side, his face softened by sleep and now covered in light brown stubble.

My eyes wandered down to his bare chest, frowning slightly at his dog tags, a reminder of his dangerous occupation that would take him away from me as soon as his next deployment was ordered.

I shook my head. He wasn't mine, and there wasn't much future with a man who was married to his job. But we had here and now, and that would have to be enough.

"What's going on in that busy brain of yours?" he asked gently, reaching out to stroke a finger along my jawline. "I can see the gears turning."

"Just planning on living in the here and now," I said honestly, although somewhat economical with the truth.

His smile widened.

"That so? Waal, how about you come over *here* and I'll show you some lovin' right *now*?"

"Let me guess, you have some morning wood that would just be a criminal waste not to use?"

He laughed, his eyes creasing with happiness.

"Woman! The things you say!"

"You don't have morning wood?"

"Sugar, I could have a whole logging company down here, but you'll never find out standing all the way over there."

"I am an awfully long way away," I agreed, standing up and inching my way toward the bathroom, "but I really have to pee. Hold that thought."

As I closed the bathroom door behind me, I heard him mutter, "I'll hold somethin'."

His words brought a smile to my lips.

After I'd washed my hands, I stared at myself in the mirror. My skin was flushed, and I had a small bite-shaped bruise beneath my left breast, a reminder of Jackson's out-of-control passion the previous night. But it was the brightness of my eyes that caught my attention. Despite getting only a few hours' sleep, I looked alert and energized. I looked … happy.

I sighed, my smile slipping. I knew myself too well. I was falling for a man whose ass looked great in cammies or jeans, whose smile could stop traffic; a kind man, an honorable man. A man who made me laugh and knew how to make a woman cry out his name. But despite all that, Jackson Connor would be a dangerous man to love—and my heart was right in the firing line.

A low growl of frustration ended with a sharp huff as I scowled at my reflection. *I'm so bad at this!* So bad at having casual sex. It always ended up meaning something to me when I knew it shouldn't.

There was a soft knock at the door.

"You alright in there, Maggie?"

I grabbed a towel, wrapping it around myself firmly, nakedness just adding to the vulnerability I felt. I opened the door, forcing a smile when I saw Jackson's worried expression.

"Just contemplating the meaning of life," I answered lightly.

"Find any answers?"

I laughed quietly.

"As many as the next person."

He leaned against the door jamb, wearing only a smile, at home in his skin.

"Come here," he said, gently pulling me toward him.

I wrapped my arms around his neck, feeling his strong hands at my waist, his head burying itself in my neck as he kissed me sweetly.

"It's a new day," he murmured against my flushed skin. "Let's just see where it takes us."

"I like your plan," I said, my head thudding backward against the bathroom door as his talented tongue licked the salt from my neck, and his soft lips kissed along my pulse point.

He drew me towards the large bed, tugging my towel free, and in the morning light, with all my imperfections and flaws displayed, Jack Connor made soft, sweet love to me, his body urging me to enjoy life with all its fleeting moments of pleasure. Because that's what life is— many moments of joy and sorrow, connections with other people, small and great, making memories.

And I understood that whether I knew him for a few more minutes or days, weeks or months, I would never forget this man or this moment.

. . .

Manhattan had woken with a rumble of passing traffic and the inevitable, swirling, colorful mass of humanity. It never truly slept, but now the city roared into life, cars and buses and taxis crawling along the grid-pattern of streets, commuters making their way to work, the hum and noise that even a Saturday morning couldn't slow.

My stomach grumbled quietly, and Jackson smiled.

"Do I need to feed you?"

I raised an eyebrow.

"That makes it sound like I'm expecting you to go hunter-gathering. But don't worry, I won't let us starve. You're in *my* neighborhood now and I know some great places for breakfast. I even know somewhere that specializes in Southern cooking: grits, biscuits, sweet tea, all of that."

His eyes lit up.

"Really? Because if you're teasing, you might just see a grown man cry."

"I wouldn't do that to you, Sarge. I know how serious you are about your food."

He grinned.

"If you'd lived off of MREs for most of your adult life, you'd be serious about food, too."

We were laying in bed, face to face, knees touching. My hands were curled in front of me while Jackson rested his head on his right hand, his left idly stroking my hip.

"There is one flaw in our plan ... it requires moving."

"Hmm, that is a problem." He sighed. "Then I guess I'd better get my ass out of this bed."

"And you want to see your friend today," I reminded him.

His smile faltered, and if I hadn't been staring at his beautiful face, I'd have missed the fleeting expression of concern that clouded his eyes, but it was gone so quickly, I wondered if I'd imagined it.

"Yeah, I do." He leaned forward, pressing a soft kiss against my willing lips. "Gotta hit the head."

"Such sweet nothings you whisper," I laughed.

"Sorry, sugar. I'm out of practice being around civvies."

"You did fine last night and earlier this morning," I reassured him.

He gave me a very wicked grin.

"That right? I was sure I could use some more practice."

"Oh definitely," I nodded sagely. "Lots and lots of practice."

He winked at me and disappeared into the bathroom.

I stretched out in the bed, feeling the pull of well used muscles. Jackson was a man in his prime—his love-making was on the athletic side. *God, was it ever!* And if I thought he'd be around for any length of time, I'd cancel my gym membership. I smiled at the thought.

A moment later, Jack stuck his head around the bathroom door.

"Shower with me, Maggie?"

An offer I had no intention of refusing.

The steam drifted around us as he washed my hair with firm, gentle hands, soaped my body and rinsed the suds away.

And when I got on my knees to show him how much I appreciated the way he took care of me, his groans of pleasure were another special memory filed away for future use.

Pink, shiny and satisfied, I wandered into the bedroom while Jackson shaved.

It was a pain having to put on dirty clothes, but I was used to it. In fact, on one embedment when I was in South Sudan reporting on the Civil War and refugee camps, I didn't wash or change my clothes for nearly two weeks.

I'm happy to say that back in New York, my standards were usually a little higher.

I frowned as I pulled on my underwear and shirt, sniffing discreetly and not finding anything too objectionable. Still, I was looking forward to clean clothes back at my apartment. I would have borrowed a pair of underwear from Jack, except he didn't seem to wear them.

He caught the direction of my gaze as he buttoned his jeans.

"The uniform is skivvies, so when I don't have to wear them..."

"...you let it all hang out."

He laughed.

"You do have a way with words, Ms. Buckman."

"Journalistic training," I agreed with a smile. "I get paid by the word."

"That why you use so many big ones?"

"Are you saying I talk too much?"

"Waal, you *are* a woman."

"Glad you noticed—but I'm not so keen on the stereotype."

He pulled me into his arms and buried his face in my hair.

"I like that you won't take any shit from me," he breathed against my neck. "It's refreshin'."

I nipped his earlobe gently.

"I'll bear that in mind. Consider yourself warned."

It took Jackson all of thirty seconds to pack his bag, ready to check out of the hotel.

As we rode the elevator to the lobby, smiling at each other stupidly, he held my hand.

"Never thought I'd take to a big city," said Jackson.

"Oh? How much of it have you seen so far?"

"Your office building, the pub last night and my hotel room."

I laughed.

"I can see why the Big Apple is sweeping you off your feet."

"Yes, ma'am. Best view since my bedroom is in this elevator."

The doors opened and the silly grin that I'd worn almost since the second I'd woken didn't leave my face.

His car was parked in the hotel's underground parking lot.

"A sedan? I figured you for a Jeep, Sarge."

"We have a saying in the Marines, 'Any fool can be uncomfortable'."

"I like it."

"Catchy, isn't it?"

He opened the passenger door for me, helping me inside, then tossed his heavy bag in the trunk.

I watched him from the corner of my eye as he handled the large car, easily navigating the unfamiliar streets, until we had a minor miracle of finding a parking spot and pulled up just around the corner from a cheap breakfast/brunch place famous for its chicken and waffles.

"Glazed Virginia Ham! Corn Beef Hash! Oh man! Catfish! Waffles!

They do fried or smothered?" Jackson asked as he peered through the window, his eyes wide with hope and expectation.

"Both," I answered with a wink.

"Damn, I think I died and went to heaven," he said, pushing the door open and ushering me inside.

"I think you got a little drool, just there," I laughed, touching the side of his lips.

His tongue flicked out and licked my finger, sucking it gently into his mouth.

"You taste better than anything on this menu," he whispered.

"Oh, if you're not hungry, we can leave..." I teased him.

His face fell.

"Maggie..."

"Come on in before you pass out from hunger or die from disappointment."

He smacked my butt on the way through the door. I'd get him back.

Jackson looked like he was positively in pain when he had a menu in his hand, a coffee in the other, and our waitress was running through the specials. I wouldn't have been surprised if he'd said he'd take one of everything.

I watched him eat waffles with pork sausage, bacon, fried eggs and grits on the side, while I settled for French toast and as much caffeine as I could ingest without bursting. I hadn't gotten much sleep last night.

Finally sated, if only temporarily, Jackson rubbed his stomach and grinned at me.

"You coming up for air at last?"

"That was a fu— freakin' great meal. You sure know the way to a man's heart, Maggie."

I smiled politely, because I knew he didn't mean it.

With a couple of coffees to-go, we climbed back into Jack's sedan and made a quick stop at my apartment. I packed a bag and emailed my Australian contact with apologies, promising that I'd be in touch on Monday. And yes, I did feel guilty—I'd never blown off work for a man before. It left me with an uneasy feeling.

While Jack found somewhere to fill up with gas, I threw on a clean shirt and jeans, and tossed some toiletries and underwear into my weekend bag.

When he rang my cell, I ran down the steps and jumped into the car. Then we joined the line of cars creeping toward the Holland Tunnel.

"So, tell me about this friend of yours we're going to see," I said, when silence had settled in the car and the traffic was moving freely.

I was surprised when Jack's hands tightened on the wheel until his knuckles turned white. It had seemed like an innocuous question, but clearly there was a back story.

I remained silent. If Jackson wanted to tell me, he would. If not, I'd find out for myself in a couple of hours.

After several long minutes, Jackson spoke.

"He was a guy on my team."

I glanced across at him, waiting for more. But his lips were pressed together and he had a strangled expression on his face.

"What's his name?" I asked gently.

"Grayson. Gray, to his friends." Jack cut me a look. "He also answers to Shitneck," and he gave a small smile.

"Well, darn me, you Marines sure have catchy nicknames. What do they call you?"

"Sarge," he deadpanned, and I couldn't help laughing.

"Well, you certainly lucked out more than Shitneck. I don't think I dare ask how he came across that name."

Jackson cracked a smile.

"I'll tell you sometime—just not right after we've eaten."

I rolled my eyes. Military guys had the same humor level as ten year-old boys. My smile faltered when I thought that a lot of the young guys I met when I was on an embedment were barely out of their teens. But by the end of their first deployment, they had the eyes of old men.

"I think I'll stick to Grayson," I said mildly.

As we headed through Parsippany, Jack tuned the radio to a soft rock station, humming along with the music. I wondered why he'd asked me to come with him on this trip when he didn't want to talk, or even seem to want company that much. But I didn't push him. It was obvious that today's visit was going to be difficult for some reason. I had a few theories about that.

As we approached Scranton, Jack's mood took another dive.

Despite being from Philly, I'd never been to this part of Scranton and it was prettier than I'd expected, with the river winding its way through the low hills.

Heading north along the Lackawanna River, we stopped in the older suburb of Dickson City and a quiet street where most of the houses were painted white with small wooden decks at the front.

Jackson pulled up outside a neat two-story house with a large attached garage.

He took a deep breath, his hands still gripping the steering wheel.

I didn't say anything, but I touched his knee gently, letting him know I was here and supporting him, whatever it was.

He gave me a stiff smile and climbed out of the car, holding my hand tightly. I squeezed his fingers as we walked toward the house.

The door swung open and a woman with curly brown hair and pleasant face stood in front of us. Her smile grew as she stared at us—well, at Jackson.

"Oh my God! Jack! You came!" she said joyfully, throwing her arms around his neck.

I stood awkwardly to one side while he hugged her warmly.

"Hey, Jules! I told you I'd be visiting."

"You did, but I didn't believe you," she laughed, then turned to me, smiling. "Where are your manners, Jackson Connor? Introduce me to your friend."

"Hi, I'm MJ," I smiled, at the same time Jack said "Maggie."

I grinned at him and he gave a wry shake of his head.

I held out my hand to Jules, but she ignored it, instead pulling me into a hug.

"Any friend of Jack's is welcome, MJ Maggie," she smiled, the warmth in her eyes telling me she was sincere. "Have you traveled far?"

"Just up from the Big Apple," Jackson answered for us.

She turned to stare.

"Seriously? You were in the city? I can't imagine that, a good ole

44

country boy like you!" Then she threw me a sly look. "Although maybe I can. Come on in. Gray is in his studio."

We followed her through a living room cluttered with children's toys into a kitchen that smelled of laundry and baking bread.

"Please excuse the mess," she said, "we weren't expecting company. Honestly, Jackson Connor! You couldn't give me a heads up? I would have made your favorite peach cobbler!"

Jackson mumbled something unintelligible and shoved his hands in his pockets. Jules shook her head, still smiling, and opened a door off the kitchen.

"Gray, we have company!"

We heard a muffled curse and Jules laughed quietly.

"He gets grumpy when he's interrupted, but ignore him. He'll be happy to see you. Go on through."

Jackson tentatively walked into the room and I followed a few paces behind, unsure if I should stay with Jules or follow Jack.

The space that must have once been a three-car garage had been turned into a pottery studio. Glazed and unglazed ceramics stood in varying stages of completion on wooden shelves, and the man seated at a workbench was shaping a pot on a turntable.

He was about the same age as Jackson, but his hair was prematurely salt and pepper, and lines of worry creased his forehead. But when he saw Jack, his smile was immediate.

"Fuck me, Jack Connor!"

"You're not my type," Jackson laughed, leaning down to hug his friend and slap him on the back. "Good to see you, man."

"I'm seeing it, but I don't believe it! How long has it been?"

Jackson's shoulder twitched uncomfortably and he scratched the side of his face with his thumb.

"A year or so."

"Try two-and-a-half years, asshole!"

"Yeah, sorry. Been busy."

"So I see," smiled Gray, raising one eyebrow. "You going to introduce me?"

"Uh, this is Maggie, my ... friend."

"He's lying," I said cheerfully, shaking Gray's hand. "We hooked up last night and he invited me on a road trip to meet you."

Gray laughed loudly and grinned at Jackson who was uncharacteristically flushed.

"I like her. She's got you on the run already, buddy. Good to meet you, Maggie."

"It's not like that," Jackson muttered, shooting me an irritated look. "We met three months ago. In Helmand."

Gray threw me a surprised look.

"Truth?"

"Yes, I'm a reporter for the *New York Times*," I said. "But don't let that put you off. I was working on a few stories out there and Jack just happened to save my life."

Gray nodded slowly.

"Yeah, he does that."

Then he stood up and walked around his workbench. It was a warm day and he was wearing shorts, so I couldn't help but notice that two carbon fiber prosthetics replaced his legs.

He saw my gaze and answered the unspoken question.

"IED, three years ago. Our APC cargo carrier drove over a landmine. The rest of the team were killed—Jack dragged me out." He laughed bleakly. "I was 6'1" and weighed 190 pounds. Now I'm 4'2" and weigh 130 pounds. But I'm alive—thanks to this guy."

Jackson was rigid, his face frozen, but when Gray walked toward him and hugged him, his stance relaxed. I looked away while Gray whispered something to him as Jackson shook his head.

I left them to their reunion, retracing my steps to the kitchen.

Jules was standing at the sink, gazing out into the yard.

"How's he doing?" she asked.

"They're having a moment," I said quietly.

"I meant Jack. How's he doing?"

"Uh..."

I wasn't sure how to answer that, and I stared at her questioningly.

"He blames himself," she said. "Jack was the driver that day. He shouldn't have been, but the regular driver was sick. So ... he pulled Gray out of the burning APC even though he was injured himself. Got a medal and everything," she said with a small sigh. "This is only the second time he's seen Gray since it happened. The first time was in hospital. They were best friends. But you probably know that."

"No, I didn't," I admitted. "Jack and I ... it's new. Whatever it is."

She turned to smile at me.

"Well, whatever you want to call it ... or not call it ... if Jack brought you here, you're someone special to him. I'm not sure he'd have come otherwise. Thank you for that."

I shook my head.

"It's nothing to do with me. Jack was already planning to come here —he just asked me along for the ride."

"Well ... thank you for coming. It means a lot to both of us." Her gaze returned to the window. "He kept saying he'd visit, but then there was always another deployment, another job. Gray was hurt at first, but he gets it now—you know, Jack's survivor's guilt."

That explained so much, and my heart hurt for Jackson. I'd seen enough of war and the cruel things that human beings did to other humans to understand that it was random: fate or luck, kismet or karma—whatever you wanted to call it. And it rarely made sense. But those same human beings, those same people, we were left to pick up the shattered pieces.

"Jack and Gray grew up together, enlisted together, and fought together," she said.

"I thought I detected some southern in Gray's accent."

Jules smiled.

"You wait until they've had a couple of beers together—we'll need a dictionary!"

"I've learned a few things," I chuckled. "One of which is never to keep Jackson from his waffles."

"Oh my God, I know!" she laughed. "I've had to learn to fry pretty much everything. Although I have to say, when Gray has been fishing and he brings back trout, it makes for some pretty great frying. I think I have some in the freezer ... if you're staying for dinner? It would be great if you could meet the kids—Josh especially used to be really close to his Uncle Jack. They're both at soccer practice till five; it was our neighbors' turn to take the kids today.

Josh is eight and Becca is six. I'm not sure she'd remember Jack," she sighed.

"I don't really know what our plans are. Jack didn't tell me much on the way over."

She nodded sadly.

"Guess we'll play it by ear."

There was an awkward pause, then she turned to smile at me, crossing her arms over her chest.

"So, how did you two meet?"

After I'd explained about my work and how Jackson saved my life in Afghanistan, her eyes were round with surprise.

"Wow! That's quite a story! Obviously there was some serious chemistry going on even then."

"It certainly seems that way," I smiled. "Where we go from here, I have no clue."

"Early days, Maggie," she said. "Marines are complicated men. They compartmentalize their lives—there's a lot Gray won't or can't tell me. It must be strange for Jack, having met you the way he did."

I shrugged because I had no answers for her. Or for myself.

Jules sighed.

"I'm glad you came—both of you. Gray's doing really well, but I know he gets frustrated not being able to talk about all that military stuff. He says I won't understand, and really, how can I? I do my best, but..."

"He seems ... well," I offered gently. "And pretty mobile."

"Yeah, he's doing great now. It was hard at first—really hard. Especially on the kids. I didn't know if he'd make it ... if we'd make it. But he had OT when he was in Walter Reed, and he discovered he had this gift for clay—shaping and molding things. He's selling his work online now and doing really well."

"His ceramics are pretty amazing. I'd like to write a feature about him for the paper if he wouldn't mind."

"Oh my God, really? That would be amazing! Thank you, Maggie."

And I meant it. Men like Gray deserved to have their stories told—not just about the terrible, awful things they'd been through, but the way they'd taken hold of their lives and done something positive to channel all that energy. I knew as well as anyone that a man was a Marine for life, even when he was no longer a combat warrior. Men like him needed something to get them out of bed in the morning. Something that drove them.

And I'd also seen another layer of Jack Connor—the man whose scars weren't all on the surface.

I looked up to find him watching me, desire mixed with wariness, questions in his expressive blue eyes.

Twenty-four hours shouldn't have been long enough for me to feel every chaotic emotion that rampaged through me in that moment. *It shouldn't be long enough.*

I was in trouble.

Chapter Five

A LONG WAY FROM HOME

I really liked Jackson's friends. They were easy to talk to, fun, and teased the hell out of Jack, which made me laugh. I got the impression that they hadn't met many of his girlfriends before. I wasn't sure if I fell into that category—it was too early to say.

I also spent an hour interviewing Gray about his time in the Marines, what it was like being a civilian now, and how he'd built up his ceramics and pottery business. We touched on the issues surrounding his double-amputation after the IED attack, too, but the focus of the article was going to be on his life since then.

And talking with Jules, she gave me an insight into being the wife of a Marine. She'd felt as much a part of the service as he did, so when Gray had left, they both felt like they'd lost their family, to some extent.

"It was hard, at first," Jules said thoughtfully. "Well, none of it's easy, because you're not just marrying your husband, you're marrying the whole team. Sometimes it feels like I married the whole darn Marine Corps."

"So long as I'm the only one keeping your bed warm at night," Gray laughed.

Jules winked at him. I could see the love they shared, and I felt a small frisson of jealousy, even though I was not the marrying kind.

"But seeing as you're here with our boy Jack," Jules said to me, "you'd best have Julia's Crash Course in Dating a Uniform."

Gray and Jackson both groaned.

Dating? Is that what we were doing? I shot Jackson a look, but he just smiled at me.

"Counting down to the next deployment is part of the deal—they're always around the next corner. So if you can't cope with that, your life will be hell," she said. "Simple as that. A lot of military wives get swept away with the whole romance of the uniform, but there's nothing romantic about being a single woman with a ring on your finger for six months, or nine months, or a year—however long the deployment is. And you've got to be prepared to move around with a few weeks' notice, or even a few days' notice. Add kids into the mix ... well, you get the picture."

I nodded, understanding what she said.

"And they can be hard to live with when they're home."

I could hazard a guess that it wasn't easy.

"I get it. I've interviewed a lot of men and women in the armed services. It's a strange dichotomy: when they're away from home, they can't wait to come back, but when they're home..."

"We're always waiting for the next mission," Gray finished with a nod. "At least you understand that, Maggie. Most stay-at-homers don't."

"Because I'm the same. When I'm away, I'm focused and professional, but also longing for home. When I'm home, life seems to move in slow motion, and I'm waiting for the next assignment. Hell, I go searching for the next assignment."

Jackson nodded his agreement.

"It's addicting."

"Yes, it is."

He met my gaze unblinkingly.

"It's a good life for a single person ... the military."

I wondered if he was sending me a message; it certainly wasn't a subtle one.

"It's tough for the ones left behind," Jules added. "You've got to be resourceful. There's no use whining on to him about a clogged gutter or ants in your kitchen when he's 5,000 miles away. So it's tough—like make or break tough. Deployments are mostly planned well ahead, but shit happens, you know? So you're never sure if the next one will be in six months or sixty minutes."

"In some ways you're describing my life, Jules," I explained. "I never know where the next story is going to break. I need to be able to throw some clothes in a bag and get on a plane within a few hours. My body armor is under my bed and I pack portable solar power cells so I can keep my phone and laptop charged. I could be away a few days, or maybe a couple of months. I might even get offered the job of foreign correspondent for the Middle East, which would mean I'd have to go live over there."

"Is that likely?" Jackson asked, looking serious.

I shrugged.

"It's possible. It would be great for my career."

I didn't tell him I'd been lobbying for that job for more than two years now. I was in line when the current incumbent retired, but there were two or three equally qualified journalists.

His lips pressed together, but he seemed thoughtful rather than irritated, which was my usual experience of how most men viewed my job. The guys I'd dated before had liked the idea of being with a journalist, but when it came to working late on a breaking story or missing a date at the last moment because I was booked on a flight, they didn't like it so much.

I gazed at Jackson.

"That's my life, my job, and I love my job. So I guess it has similarities since not everyone can deal with my lifestyle and career choices."

Somehow the conversation had turned serious, and I saw Jules glancing at Gray apprehensively.

I didn't know what *this* was with Jackson. He intrigued me and I'd begun to imagine that a relationship might be possible, but I needed to lay out the realities of my work. But perhaps now wasn't the right time.

"Anyhow," I said, trying to lighten the tone, "I try and make the most of my time when I'm home—make memories, you know? So I'd like to propose a toast: to new friends and good times."

They all raised their beer bottles and saluted the toast. As we clinked our bottles together, I almost missed Jackson's softly spoken words.

"I can deal."

Jackson was pensive during the rest of the afternoon, quieter than usual. I felt his eyes on me frequently. He didn't look away when I caught him watching me, but his smile seemed tinged with sadness. I didn't know why.

Shortly after 5PM, we heard a car pull up outside and the sound of children's voices. The front door flung open and two children ran inside.

The boy was the spit of Jules, but the girl looked more like Gray. They went from talking at a hundred miles an hour to nearly mute when they saw me.

I waved as Jules introduced me, then Jack came and stood beside me.

"Wow, you got so big!" he grinned, reaching out to shake hands with a suddenly shy Josh, ruffling his hair kindly. "And look at you, little lady. That sure is a pretty bow you've got in your hair."

Becca obviously didn't remember him, but nodded seriously and shot an angry look at her brother.

"Josh said it was stupid and that soccer players don't wear bows in their hair."

"If it helps you see out from all of those curls, I guess it makes sense."

Jack picked up a soccer ball and bounced it.

"Anyone want to play?"

"You're not allowed to play soccer in the house," Becca chastised him, and Jules agreed.

"Yeah? Waal, maybe we can play in the backyard."

Jackson led the children outside, all shyness gone in the face of his warmth and enthusiasm.

I watched him playing with them, and Jules came to stand next to me.

"He's great with them," she said quietly.

"Yes, he is," I agreed.

I was roped into helping later, when bath time turned into story time, and Becca asked me to read to her.

Jack, of course, was having 'man talk' with Josh.

Jules was right—he was really great with children; certainly these children.

I'd never been particularly maternal. I don't know if that was because my own mother had died when I was young. I'd been close to my father, but having a family of my own? Only one of my close friends had children and she was so busy, we rarely had time to hang out.

Besides, work had always been more important to me. I couldn't imagine being tied down by having children. Although that didn't mean I couldn't see the happiness and pride that shined in Jules' eyes as she watched her husband with their children.

"Waal," Jack said, interrupting my musings as the sun began to set, "we should be getting going now and..."

"Jackson Connor!" snapped Jules, her eyes flashing with annoyance. "Do *not* tell me that you drove all this way just to be heading back so soon!"

He shifted uncomfortably in his chair as I watched the exchange with amusement. I wondered if Jules was the only woman who bossed him around.

"Maggie needs to get back to the city..."

I smiled beatifically.

"Nope, I'm not working tomorrow, Sarge. I'm good."

He gave me a look that said he didn't appreciate being thrown under a bus.

"Then that's settled," Jules said decisively. "I've made up the bed in the guest room already."

Jackson grinned ruefully, looking at both of us.

"Guess you weren't planning on taking no for an answer, huh?"

Jules threw him a stern look.

"It's taken you two-and-a-half years to get your ass to Scranton. You're not getting away that easily. Besides," she said, her smile softening the words, "the kids would be so disappointed if you weren't here in the morning ... and I'm making buttermilk biscuits with gravy, sausage, eggs and fried potatoes for breakfast ... if you're interested."

Jackson's eyes lit up.

"Why didn't you say that to begin with?"

"An army marches on its stomach," I said drily, quoting Napoleon (or Frederick the Great, depending on which source you're using).

"Ain't that the truth," laughed Gray.

"I'm just saying one thing," Jackson said grumpily. "MREs."

Gray nodded seriously.

"Three lies for the price of one: it's not a Meal, it's not Ready, and you can't Eat it."

"Truth," nodded Jackson. "Meals Requiring Enemas."

"Meals Refusing to Exit," sniggered Gray.

"Meals Refusing to Excrete," Jackson added with a grin.

"Massive Rectal Exp..."

"Enough!" Jules bellowed, her face turning red while I put a hand over my mouth, holding in the laughter. "It's like having a couple of sixth-graders!"

She was yelling, but I could tell she was pleased to see Gray so light-hearted. Disgusted, too, but I was used to grunt humor and I didn't mind. Seeing Jackson laugh was good enough for me.

"You kiss your momma with that mouth?" she asked furiously.

"Sure do," Jackson grinned, planting a kiss on Jules' cheek as she smacked him on the shoulder.

We sat late into the night chatting easily as I listened to stories of Jackson and Gray at boot camp and all the trouble they'd gotten into. But when Jules started yawning, we all agreed it was time to throw in the towel.

As we climbed the narrow stairs, I felt Jackson's eyes on me.

"Are you staring at my ass?"

"Yeah, it's kind of mesmerizing. Like two juicy watermelons."

"You did *not* just say that!" I huffed over my shoulder.

I was slightly self-conscious about my ass. I had a decent rack and trim waist, but my ass and hips were on the generous side.

"Aw, sugar! Don't be sore!" And he lowered his voice so it wouldn't carry. "You know I love holding your beautiful butt in my hands when I'm pounding into you."

My face flamed and I felt the first tingle of arousal. God, the man turned me on with just a few, well-chosen if crude words.

"Why, Maggie Buckman! Don't you have a single word to say, darlin'?"

"Yes, actually I do. You're wearing too many clothes."

He laughed quietly.

"Waal, maybe if you take yours off, I'll make it worth your while."

"How long is a 'while' exactly?"

"Long enough," he said, his voice low and rough.

He locked the door to the guest room behind him and made good on his promise. For several hours.

After a magnificent breakfast that probably added ten pounds to my waistline and 'juicy' butt, we said goodbye to Jules, Gray and the kids, promising to visit again. I didn't know if it was a promise I'd keep, but I hoped so.

Jackson hadn't said anything to me about another date or even staying in touch, and I vowed that if he hadn't brought it up by the time we were back in the city, then I would. My heart beat a little faster at the thought. Being rejected in person was never fun. Being rejected when I had a strong suspicion that I was falling for Jackson was an even less pleasant thought. But either way, I wanted to know where I stood. For my own sanity.

My phone rang when we were just over halfway home, and I frowned. It was my editor's number, which meant something had happened: a story, somewhere in the world.

"Ben? What's up?"

"Where are you, MJ?"

"About 90 minutes from home."

"Good, I need you on a flight to Amman leaving at 9AM. We've got permission for you to join an MSF contingent traveling to Zaatari.

Swing by the office first—Allison will have your visa. Please tell me all your shots are up to date?"

"Yep, fully medicated," I said, and Jackson gave me a quizzical look.

"This is going to be a big one, MJ."

"I know. Thanks, Ben."

I hung up, watching Jackson's face.

"That was work?"

"Yes. I'm on a flight to Jordan first thing in the morning. There's a group of Médecins Sans Frontières doctors going to one of the biggest refugee camps on the Syrian border. Ninety-three thousand people, Jack. That's like a city the size of Albany. Living in tents, hardly enough food or clean water."

Jackson was silent.

Was I asking for his approval or just hoping that he'd understand?

He sighed and his shoulders hunched with tension. I waited for him to speak.

"Damn," he said quietly. "I thought we'd have more time."

I bit back the words *I'm sorry*. This was my job, and I wasn't going to apologize for it.

"How long will you be away?"

"A couple of weeks. Maybe a month..."

"What time's your flight?"

"Nine. I have to go to the office first to pick up my documents."

He nodded.

"I'll drive you."

"You don't have to."

"I'll drive you."

I gave him a small smile.

"Hmm, does that mean you want to spend the night in my apartment?"

He gave me a serious look.

"I want to spend every goddamn second with you, Maggie."

I swallowed and looked away.

"I'd like that."

.   .   .

57

It was strange having Jackson in my apartment. His large body dwarfed the place, filling it in a completely masculine way. My homey space seemed diminished with him there, and yet it seemed right.

Part of me felt like I'd known him forever, but I had to be realistic. I didn't know him and he didn't know me. What I *did* know, I liked a lot, but I'd noticed that there were subjects he deliberately avoided. That didn't make me nervous exactly, just ... aware.

He stood in the middle of my small living room, examining the photographs on my walls. Most of them were from assignments, but there were a few family ones, too.

"Is that your dad?"

"Yes, that's him. Mike."

"You look like him. You have his eyes."

"Thank you."

"Just sayin' what I see," he said, his own eyes warm with compassion.

"So, what are you going to do tomorrow? You're welcome to stay in my apartment, if you like?"

I felt as though I should offer, but it would be strange having Jackson living here without me. He smiled briefly.

"Thanks for the offer, sugar, but I'm going to see my family. Mama has been asking when I'll come visit. Maybe we can hook up when you're back?"

Hook up? Although at least it sounded like he wanted to stay in touch. Sort of. Did he just mean a booty call?

"Sure," I said, and I knew by his raised eyebrows that my lack of enthusiasm surprised him.

It wasn't lack of enthusiasm for him—of course it wasn't. But a hookup wasn't dating—it was simply an offer of more sex. Wonderful, life-changing, heady, earth-shattering sex. But nothing emotional. I wasn't sure I could do that—in fact I knew I couldn't. But I wasn't ready to end it with him either.

He cocked his head to one side.

"I'd better go and pack," I said. "Can you order a pizza or something? There's a bunch of menus in the kitchen drawer and there's beer in the fridge."

"Damn if you aren't the perfect woman, Maggie," he said with a grin.

I couldn't help smiling. He certainly made me feel that way. That was new and unexpected, but very wonderful.

I pulled together everything I needed for my trip, pushing it into a large duffel bag that I'd kept after an embedment with USAF a couple of years back. The body armor went in last, because although it was the heaviest, I always ended up having to take it out at airports during security checks.

I piled the clothes I'd need onto the bed—all things that could be rinsed and dried easily. Plenty of underwear, tampons and unlubricated condoms. Not that I was planning on having sex, but they had a range of off-list uses, including storing water. They were also surprisingly useful to put over the lids of difficult to open jars—added traction. Who knew? (And when you were eating MREs every day, spicy sauce could make a hell of a difference.) Condoms also made very useful waterproof cases for cell phones and microphones, or even bandages.

The front door buzzer rang while I was finishing my packing, and immediately the smell of Thai curry filled the room.

"Wow, I'm impressed!" I smiled, walking into the living room. "You ordered my favorite! How did you know?"

Jackson grinned and tapped his forehead.

"Need to know, Maggie. Need to know."

"Let me guess, you picked the menu that looked the most used."

"Aw, you're spoilin' the surprise!"

I kissed him on the lips quickly.

"Thank you. It's a lovely surprise."

His blue eyes darkened with desire, but then he pulled back and waved a hand at the boxes of food spread across my living room coffee table.

I tossed a bunch of throw cushions on the floor, and we sat cross-legged to eat our food.

I felt more comfortable now I was getting used to seeing him in my space. He was easy company, liking having an old friend over that you haven't seen in a while. An old friend that I badly wanted to have in my bed.

Eventually, we pushed the plates away and I finished packing while Jackson took out the trash and cleaned up in the kitchen.

When my bags were ready and waiting by the front door, I walked into the kitchen and put my arms around Jackson's waist while he stood at the sink, pressing my cheek against his broad back.

"You've got an early start, Maggie," he said softly. "I guess we should turn in soon. To sleep."

"Are you sure about that, Jack? Your lips say no, but your body says yes," and I rubbed the front of his jeans, feeling his hardness grow under my fingers.

He groaned and turned around to face me, his wet hands landing on my hips.

"I can't help that," he said, gesturing to the bulge behind his zipper. "It's like feeding a stray dog—he keeps coming back for more even though you've told him to go home."

I laughed lightly and pushed my hand into the front of his jeans, feeling his dick hot and hard and straining against my clutching fingers.

"I think we should go to bed now, Maggie," he hissed.

"Not up for some kitchen action?"

"Oh yeah, I'm always *up* for some kitchen action," he said, rocking into my hand, "but right now I'm craving a soft bed, so I can spread you out and take my time kissing every part of you. Slowly."

The man's mouth was wicked lethal.

I grabbed his hand and pulled him toward my room. But he stopped me so he could open the door, giving a little bow as he turned the handle.

"Thanks for getting the door open for me. Tricky things, doors."

"Learned it all from my grandpappy," he whispered huskily in my ear. "He said if I was going on dates where I planned on opening a condom wrapper, then the least I could do was open the door for a girl as well."

I choked on a laugh.

"Good to know you have standards, even if they're low ones."

"They're the best kind. Although I wouldn't call you 'low' exactly," he said with a wink.

I punched him in the arm, shaking out my fingers when I hit solid muscle.

"Ow," I said, unnecessarily.

"Want me to kiss your boo-boos better?"

"I want you to kiss something."

His eyes flared with excitement.

While he was busy undressing me with his eyes, I pushed him hard in the center of his chest so he fell backwards onto the bed.

"You don't always have to be the one in control, Jack. I might even say that watching you lose control is hot. Very hot. I think I'd like to see you lose control again."

His eyes burned with intensity and he licked his lips, a slow smile drawing his mouth into a sexy smirk.

"Is that right, sugar? Waal, there's a 100% possibility of you getting what you want."

What I wanted? Now there was a loaded statement. What did I want from Sergeant Jackson Connor?

His expression became serious, no doubt matching my own.

"I don't know what this is, Maggie, what's happening here, but it feels good. Real good. And I don't want it to stop. I have absolutely no fucking control when I'm making love to you. And that's what I want to do. Right now."

The sweet intensity of his words touched me. Everything he said made me want to hold him and never let him go. And that was a foolish thing when his first priority, his first love would always be the Marine Corps. I was also aware it made me a hypocrite—my career was everything to me. And I was leaving first thing in the morning.

"I'm on board with that idea," I whispered, pushing away my darkening thoughts as I concentrated on running my fingers down his broad chest, watching his muscles clench and release.

He yanked his t-shirt over his head, exposing all that deeply tanned smooth skin, looking as perfect as the day I met him. More perfect, because he was here in my bed, not just starring in my dreams.

I pulled down the zipper of his jeans, and he sighed with pleasure as his dick sprang free. I took him in my mouth and his sigh turned into a groan, as if I was pleasuring him to death.

"Maggie, you gotta slow down," he said, his voice strained. "Otherwise this is going to be over fast."

"We have all night," I reminded him.

And maybe his mind moved on a parallel road to mine, acknowledging that this would be our last night together in who knew how long. Maybe ever. A shadow passed over his eyes, clouding the sparkle, but then he forced a smile as I took him again.

He could have tossed me onto my back at any time, but he let me have control. Because I wanted to, because I'd shown him what I wanted, what I needed. And because he was enough of a man not to feel the lesser for it.

I took him to the brink and beyond, luxuriating in the moment when he gave me complete control as he lost his own, the moment his body tensed and his hands fisted the sheet beneath him. And then, when his breaths had evened out and his eyes told me it was time to return the favor, he undressed me slowly, kissing every part of me, showing me with his body if not with his words that this meant something.

He started with the tips of my fingers, kissing them softly and sweetly, then sucking them into his mouth and tickling my palms with the stubble on his chin.

Gentle fingertips grazed my arms, raising goosebumps wherever and whenever he touched me. I stretched out, naked and flushed with desire, exposed, willing and trusting.

How foolish to trust this man—not because he was bad, because he was so obviously good, his soul bright despite everything he'd seen and done. No, it was foolish because he already had the power to hurt me. I prayed the pain would be over quickly.

He kissed, stroked, touched and teased every part of me, and I let him. I gave back the control he'd willingly ceded to me, enjoying every touch, every taste, every stroke of his tongue or press of his soft lips.

His face was taut with strain when he finally kneeled up, his mouth pressed in a thin line as he rolled a condom down his shaft, then his dark eyes met mine, burning with need and intensity.

And when he sank into me, his eyelids fluttered, desire tightening his whole body.

"I've waited all day for this."

He started circling his hips, arms at full stretch as he gazed down at me, his spine curved. Hot, rough amusement shone in his eyes as I linked my ankles behind the globes of his ass, digging in with my heels.

He began to thrust harder, willingly losing control, his thrusts more savage, almost brutal, until he came with a feral intensity that shocked and gladdened me.

We slept, we woke, we made love, again and again, the whole night through.

The next morning came too soon. We shared a quick shower, a quicker breakfast, and then Jackson drove me to the office.

Allison, my PA was waiting for me at my desk.

"Morning, MJ. Here's your visa, letters of introduction, emergency plan, checklist, money for bribes, spare flash drives, plus all the usual things. Anything else you need?"

"No, that looks good. Thanks, Allison."

She stared at me impatiently.

"Well? How'd it go with Sergeant Hottie on Friday? You can thank me by telling me everything. I want details."

I smiled serenely.

"We had a very pleasant dinner. Thank you for asking."

Allison was a fantastic PA and someone I considered a good friend, but that woman liked to gossip more than the average twitterholic.

"Is that all you're giving me?"

"I had pepperoni pizza. He had chicken wings."

"Oh, come on! Really?"

"Yup."

"You know you want to tell me!"

"See you when I get back!"

"Tease!"

She threw a balled up piece of paper at me, then pulled me into a tight hug.

"Safe travels, boss."

. . .

The drive out to the airport was silent and full of tension. There was so much to say. A lifetime of things, maybe. And here I was, the wordsmith, living by my writing, unable to form a single sentence.

Jackson pulled into the drop-off area and hauled my duffel out of the trunk. Then he grabbed my shoulders and pulled me against him, burying his face in my neck as his large body curved over me.

"This feels so wrong, leaving you here like this."

"I'll be fine."

"You'd better. Just ... be careful, Maggie."

"I always am."

"Is that right? You forgettin' already how we met?" He hugged me tighter. "Do it smart and safe. Maybe you could call me sometime ... if you want to."

"I will, Jack. I promise."

His voice was uncertain, hesitant.

"I'll be waiting."

Chapter Six

COMMUNICATION FAILURE

I was in love with Facetime. No more waiting in an Army base comms unit for Skype via whatever crappy IP provider Uncle Sam was paying for. I had a boosted cell phone and solar powered charger, courtesy of the *New York Times*, and better still, they were picking up the bill.

I didn't get a chance to call Jackson as often as I'd have liked. Apart from anything else, Jordan was eight hours ahead of the East Coast, so the time difference made it difficult. It was definitely worth the wait.

My heart jolted with joy when he answered on the third ring.

"Hey, Maggie! It's so good to see you. You look..."

Jackson bit off whatever he was going to say, and I was thankful for that.

"I know, I look awful," I said, running a hand through my lank hair. "Rough day."

"No, you look great," he lied. "I just meant tired. You want to tell my why it was rough? Are you okay?"

"I'm fine," I shrugged. "It's hotter than hell and I didn't hydrate enough. Headache."

"That's not all, is it?"

I shrugged helplessly.

"You know what it's like out here ... the things you see. I'm used to seeing dead bodies ... well, not used to it, but it doesn't affect me like it did the first time, or the second..." I took a deep breath. "But when they're children..."

He swallowed and nodded. And I was so grateful that I didn't have to explain. Because Jack knew. He knew and he understood.

"Yeah. But you're doing great, Maggie. I read that article you wrote about the MSF. It was real good. Too good," he said with a grimace. "And those photographs..."

His words trailed off and he looked away.

"How are you doing?" I asked gently, knowing how hard this was for him, for both of us. "How's Gulfport treating you? Met any debutantes lately?"

I was hoping to make him smile, but it wasn't working.

"It's a double whammy. You're over there, up to your neck in shit, dodging bullets, and I'm over here. As useful as tits on a bull."

"Jackson," I said quietly, "you of all people know that..."

"Yeah, yeah," he said roughly. "Ignore me. I'm real happy to hear your voice."

And he gave his patented panty-dropping grin. He was trying. We were both trying. For what? Some sort of normalcy when that was just an illusion?

"So, what are you up to?"

"Sitting here drinking a cold beer."

"Oh, shut up!"

He laughed unapologetically.

"Glass is frosted, too."

"I hate you!"

"No, you don't. You love me really."

There was an uncomfortable pause as he sucked in his breath, trying to bite back the words we weren't ready to say.

"Nah, I only want you for your body," I teased. "Take your shirt off."

Jackson grinned.

"Only if you take yours off."

I shot him a wry look.

"Um, probably shouldn't do that right now," I said, letting my phone show the body armor that I was wearing, my helmet sitting on the cot next to me.

"Ah shit, Maggie," he said softly, screwing up his eyes with concern.

"I'm fine, Jack. Really. Just being careful—like you said. But it would cheer me up if you took your shirt off," and I gave him a flirty wink, reaching for the light-hearted tone I needed to hear from him.

He forced a weak smile, because he was supposed to, because I'd asked him to, but it soon faded.

"I probably shouldn't start undressing either. Mama has her friends over. I snuck away for some peace and quiet."

"A tactical withdrawal?"

"Something like that."

"Aw, poor baby! Can't you handle some cougar action?"

He pulled a face.

"Not from my mama's friends. They've known me since I was a twinkle in my Daddy's eye. That would just be so wrong."

I laughed at the expression on his face. But then I heard a woman's voice in the background.

"What are you doing out here all by your lonesome, Jack, honey?"

He must have put his hand over the phone because the picture went dark and his voice became muffled.

"Just talking to a friend, Emmy."

I didn't hear what came next but it was several seconds before Jack's apologetic face was back.

"Sorry about that."

"Emmy?"

His mouth tightened.

"An old ... friend."

"Okay..."

"There's nothing going on, Maggie, I promise. Her mama and mine are kissing cousins."

I gave him a reassuring smile.

"I'm not worried, Jack," I said honestly. "I'm jealous as hell that she's with you and I'm over here, that's all."

"Really?"

"Truly."

He rubbed his face and I couldn't help wishing that it was my fingers trailing over that lightly stubbled jaw.

"God, Maggie—you're amazing."

"Not so bad yourself."

He smiled and winked, his tight expression relaxing.

"Tell me something no one knows about you."

He gave me an amused smile.

"Feel free to ask the easy questions!"

"I'm serious. Things you don't tell anyone. It doesn't have to be big —just silly stuff."

"Like what?"

"I don't know. Anything!"

"Give me an example..."

"Like ... whenever I finish a bag of chips, I lick the salt off my fingers then tie the packet in a knot. I don't know why I do that, I just do. Silly, right?"

I could hear his deep laugh over the miles and miles of fathomless air.

"Uh, okay. I love to walk on the beach in the rain."

I couldn't help the sigh that fell from my lips.

"I know it sounds weird," he said defensively, "but the sea goes slate gray, and it's wild and rough, and I'm usually the only person there. It's ... cleansing, peaceful. I just really like it."

It told me so much about him. And that he was a romantic at heart.

"We should do that when I..."

Christine, have you got a prettier divider??

Suddenly, there was a massive explosion and all the lights in the camp went out. I dropped my phone, grabbed my helmet and flung myself under the cot as missiles sang overhead.

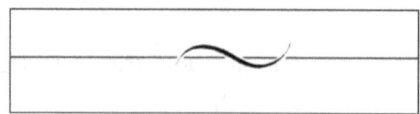

Six thousand miles away, Jackson reached for a weapon that wasn't there, his heart hammering in his chest. He stared at the blank screen of his phone.

"Oh, Christ! Maggie."

Chapter Seven

A ROAD DIVIDES

Jackson stared at his phone, his heart thundering as if he'd just sprinted a mile with his M16 and an eighty pound pack.

He'd recognized the sound he heard just before Maggie's call was dropped. He knew all too well the tell-tale whine of a rocket-propelled grenade flying through the air before exploding. And he'd seen the terror in her eyes before the screen went black.

Cold sweat covered his body, and only a decade and more of training stopped him from freaking out. His hands didn't shake as he redialed her number three times, but his mouth was dry and his muscles were tensed, trained and ready to spring into action.

He felt so fucking futile.

He forced his fear for Maggie's safety into a tiny space in the back of his mind and locked it away. Going crazy with worry was not an option, but he needed to do *something* or he might just find that small, dark space wasn't sealed as tight as he wanted it to be.

He rang her number two more times, but all he got was her voicemail:

You've reached MJ Buckman.
Please leave a message and a contact number.

Alternatively, you can leave a message with my office.
212 221 9595 extension 703.

Hearing her recorded voice tightened the vise around Jackson's chest.

"Goddammit, Maggie," he growled, standing suddenly, needing to do something with the adrenaline surging through his body.

He dialed her office number, but got another machine, this time MJ's assistant, Allison. He snapped out a short message, then hung up, slamming his phone onto the table. He swore again when he saw that he'd cracked the screen.

Cursing up a storm, he stomped toward his mother's house, dodging the bevy of her friends with unmarried daughters who had been circling him all day like vultures over roadkill. Not that his mama was immune from wishing him married—she'd been dangling 'suitable' girls at him since before he'd graduated from high school.

He was used to his mother's attempts to get him hitched, but he was also a US Marine, skilled in stealth and evasion, and he had no plans to marry some female who only thought about where her next manicure was coming from.

Okay, so that was a massive generalization. Even in his present state of heightened anxiety he knew that he was being unfair. But he was *not* in the mood for pleasantries. So he ducked around the side of the house and slipped in through the open kitchen door.

He ran upstairs, taking the steps two at a time, then skidded to a halt, wondering what to do next. His pent-up energy needed direction, needed a release. *Think, dammit! Think!*

He barely noticed his surroundings because the last look of fear that he'd seen on Maggie's face tortured him, playing relentlessly like a horror movie in his mind.

Slamming his bedroom door, he gripped his hair and swore for half a minute without stopping. When he opened his eyes, he didn't feel any better.

His bedroom hadn't changed much in the last decade. Football trophies and pennants still decorated the room, and his high school yearbooks lined the bookshelves alongside photographs of his graduation from Boot Camp.

He didn't feel much connection with the place he still called home.

When he was on leave, he usually found excuses not to go back, preferring to stay with friends. When possible, his mother and sister flew out to see him, wherever he was. He told himself that they liked making the trips, amazing him with their ability to shop, wherever they were. But something about spending time with Gray, listening to him talk about Jules and the kids, listening to Maggie talk about her father, it made him nostalgic. So he'd made the trip home.

He stared around his childhood bedroom.

He'd probably only slept there a half-a-dozen times in the last ten years. Not that he thought about it much—not when he'd slept in places that even rats avoided. And with the things he'd seen—and done—closing his eyes wasn't always restful. In fact, the best sleep he'd had in recent years was when he'd been tucked around MJ as she muttered softly and snuggled against his chest.

Christ, he'd never been a snuggler.

He wasn't sure it had been a good idea going home. For one thing, Mama hadn't been impressed that he was seeing a Yankee.

"And there are so many lovely Southern girls who'd suit you so much better, Jackson Connor."

His mother had no idea what kind of girl suited him, and up until recently, Jack hadn't known either.

But he knew now.

He'd finally found someone he could imagine a future with, and he'd let her go to Hell on Earth, where he couldn't protect her.

God dammit!

She could be hurt, she could be in some crappy medevac hospital injured, and there was nothing he could do.

And in all the years he'd been a Marine, he'd never felt more helpless.

He took a deep breath, then sank into the hard chair by his desk. Steadying his breathing, he flipped open the lid of his laptop and searched online until he found the number for the *New York Times* editorial offices, then he dialed from the house's landline.

It took a teeth-grinding 17 minutes to work his way through the ranks: from the woman answering the phone, to the foreign affairs desk, until he finally hit a brick wall. No one knew anything and if they did, they wouldn't tell him as he wasn't related to Ms. Buckman. That was a direct quote from some butt-shining asswipe.

He slammed down the phone with another curse.

"Think, dammit!" he fumed, pacing his room, his broken cell phone clamped in his hand.

Forcing himself to calm the fuck down, he sat at his desk again, his callused hands hovering over the keys.

He searched all the news sites he could find, scanning them for any scrap of information. And then he came across a 'breaking news' bulletin that nearly stopped his heart.

BOMB ATTACK ON REFUGEE CAMP AT SYRIAN BORDER— DOZENS KILLED

As the minutes ticked by, each one feeling like an hour, more details came in. ISIS or DAESH or whatever the evil fuckers called themselves, were claiming responsibility for the attack.

Jackson's stomach turned as the reports increased in detail. The majority of the dead and injured were women and children, most of the men having been recruited for one army or another. Since when was war made on the innocent?

Since always, thought Jackson, rubbing his forehead.

He hated feeling so fucking useless. Marines were trained to think, to fight smart, but now the enemy was thousands of miles away and Jackson was unarmed, unprepared, and out of the loop.

Why hadn't he gotten Maggie's emergency contact details before she left? Why hadn't they talked about this possibility? Even though everything had happened between them so quickly, they should have discussed it. For fuck's sake! He, of all people, knew how dangerous it was in the Middle East.

But he also knew the answer as he fumed silently: they hadn't wanted to spoil their final hours together. The irony spread a bitter smile on Jack's face.

He stood up and paced around his room again feeling caged and impotent, but forcing himself to think. *THINK!*

And then, at last, a fresh thought came to him. Someone was passing information of the attack to news teams, the story spinning out across the world's airwaves. Some unnamed journalist knew what was happening.

He returned to his online search, spitting out curses when the reports seemed to stall or peter out, anonymous reporting considered more important than putting a journalist's life at risk by giving their name or byline.

"Is it you, Maggie?" he whispered. "Please let it be you."

It occurred to him belatedly that what he was going through was the fate of every man, woman and child, every mother, father, wife, son, husband and daughter who had a member of the family, a loved one, in the military. They suffered this, day after day for months on end, years even.

He was aware of it, of course he was. His mama had reminded him enough times of what he put her through, and he'd acknowledged it, taken it as part of the cost of his service. But he'd never experienced it like this before. Never. And it sucked giant hairy monkey balls.

It was Saturday afternoon and he couldn't face the thought of waiting until Monday morning to phone the main offices at the *New York Times* to find out what was happening to the woman he...

Jackson paused, his eyes widening with shock.

Maggie had been in his life for just a few days, although she'd been in his thoughts a lot longer—from the very moment that they'd met.

He wasn't a stupid man, and even though he'd been a Marine for all his adult life, he wasn't totally alienated from his feelings. During the days he'd spent with Maggie, respect had turned to friendship, and lust had turned to love. Maybe. Possibly. Dammit, definitely! If love meant that the thought of her not being in his life was intolerable, then he fucking loved Maggie-MJ-busting-his-balls Buckman.

He remembered her dark eyes, wide and fearful the first time they'd met, then flashing with anger and righteous indignation as he'd stomped all over her idealism in his size 12 boots. But she'd come back swinging, not giving an inch, and forcing him to see how important her job was, however much he hated that.

She was a woman in a million.

He squeezed his eyes shut, treasuring the memory of her body soft and pliant beneath his large hands, her lips pink and her gaze fierce as her body heated with arousal. She'd given and taken and sent him over the edge.

Jackson's eyes shot open. While he'd been getting hot and bothered thinking about being in the sack with his woman, his subconscious had solved the problem. Maybe.

Michael R. Gordon, the NYT Chief Military Correspondent, and a man that Jack had once met.

He sat down at his laptop, newly focused, and typed in Gordon's name.

He already knew that Gordon had been the only reporter embedded with the allied command in Iraq back in 2001 when Jack was still in high school, and Gordon was the first to report on Saddam's alleged nuclear weapons program the following year.

The guy wasn't a vet, but he would help. Jackson was sure of it.

Finding Gordon's email wasn't too hard, but Jackson wasn't going to rely on that. He needed to speak to him—to find out what he knew and who he knew to get the inside info. But his internet searches brought up exactly jack shit.

Time for Plan B, which had been hatched about two seconds after Plan A bit the dust.

He dialed a number he knew by heart: Marine HQ press liaison.

His forehead creased slightly as he waited for the phone to be answered. He'd looked at this number enough times when he'd tried to stop Maggie from being embedded with his unit in Afghanistan. Well, he'd called once and his CO had found out, ripped him a new one, told him to obey orders and suck it up.

He gripped the cordless phone as he continued to pace the room. Surely the Marine Corps didn't close on weekends? Where the fuck was everyone?

Finally, the phone was answered, but the first person he spoke to was next to useless.

No, they couldn't confirm or deny that there'd been an RPG attack on the Zaatari refugee camp. No, they couldn't confirm that there had been deaths. No, they couldn't confirm that a US military escort had been with journalists who may or may not have been in the camp. And no, they definitely couldn't confirm that Jordan was a country in the Middle East or that the sun rose in the east and set in the west or a bear shits in the woods.

But when Jackson had politely insisted that the call go up the dickwad's chain of command, he'd finally gotten a result.

Well, it was polite for a seriously stressed out Sergeant Jackson Connor.

"Listen, you fucking desk jockey, my girlfriend is out there reporting on the refugee crisis and I know for a goddamn fact that there's been a fucking 'incident' in Zaatari, so stop jerking off to the Marine Corps Manual, put your pencil dick back in your pants and then go walk your sorry shitstain of a self over to someone who knows their ass from their elbow. Thank you."

The line went silent and Jackson held his breath.

"Yes, sir! Right away, sir!" came the worried reply.

Several minutes ticked by where Jackson felt sure he was growing gray hairs, until a new voice spoke.

"Sergeant Connor, this is Captain Walter Hicks, Office of the US Marine Corps Communication, Community Relations. Do you mind telling me why you've got my Corporal pissing his Alpha Charlies?"

Jackson explained for what felt like the millionth time that afternoon, trying to rub away a burgeoning headache.

Captain Hicks listened to the story, took Jackson's details and promised to call him back. He didn't promise to find the intel Jack needed, but it was something.

He paced his room, rubbing his fingers over his breastbone and intermittently massaging his temples. Waiting sucked. On deployment, he was known for his patience and stoicism, but Jackson knew this was different, and he felt frustrated and powerless.

Water and ibuprofen would help the headache, but nothing was going to ease the growing hollow ache in his chest until he knew that Maggie was safe.

And when he got her back stateside, he was going to goddamn tie her to his bed and never let her go again.

Sticking his head out of the bedroom door, he snuck downstairs into the kitchen and snagged some painkillers and a glass of iced water. He also liberated his mama's cell phone from her purse, and swapped SIM cards, leaving her an IOU note and a promise to upgrade her phone as soon as he could get to a store. Dirty tactics, but he wasn't going to apologize for them.

"Jack, honey, what are you doing in the kitchen? Hidin' out again?"

Emmy raised an eyebrow and smiled at him as she pulled a pitcher of iced tea from the refrigerator.

"Waiting for a call," he said shortly, pointing vaguely at his borrowed cell phone.

"Is it that girl you were talking to earlier?" she asked.

Jackson shook his head.

"Not exactly, but it's about her."

Emmy's mouth turned down and she looked away.

"Well, I hope she knows how lucky she is. I hope it works out for you, Jack."

He watched Emmy's retreating back, poised and elegant as ever. Beautiful, too, if you liked that sort of thing. And once Jackson had liked that sort of thing a lot. Enough to put a ring on her finger, but not enough to give up the Corps when she asked him to.

For the first time, he understood what it must have been like for her every time he was deployed. Each of his deployments since he joined the Corps had begun and ended with her tears. At the time, he'd been half irritated, but Fate was sure laughing at him now. It didn't feel good. Worse still, he felt like he owed Emmy an apology. But he didn't want to go down that rocky road right now.

So instead, he headed back to his room and started doing crunches to get rid of the build-up of adrenaline which was making him jittery.

He'd got to 93 when his phone finally rang.

"Connor, this is Hicks. I have some info, but it's not much. In addition to your friend, Ms. Buckman, there was a journalist from the

Washington Post, Murray Sanders. He's the one who's been posting online reports. Don't read anything into that…"

Too late. Jackson's heartrate had shot up.

"There are no reports of American casualties, and we tend to get that intel PDQ. I've also put a call in to Michael Gordon. We have a pretty good working relationship with him in this office, so if he knows anything, he'll call back. I'm sorry I can't give you more at this point in time."

After asking a few more questions but not really learning anything new, Jackson thanked the officer and hung up, even more frustrated than before.

Jesus, much more waiting and he'd be booking the next flight out to Jordan and go find Maggie himself.

Not that he'd be able get a visa.

Not that the US Marines would let him go.

Jackson shook his head. He didn't believe in lying to himself, so he knew that his reaction to Maggie's disappearance meant that his feelings for her were deeper than he'd first thought.

Which meant he had another problem: the woman he suspected he loved was in one of the most dangerous places on earth.

And now she was MIA.

"Christ, Maggie! Where are you?"

Chapter Eight

FOOTSTEPS IN QUICKSAND

The moment the RPG exploded, I dove for cover. I heard rather than saw my phone shattering on the hard packed dirt of the tent I shared with Marc Le Buin, a French-Swiss journalist that I'd met several times over the years.

As more grenades whined overhead, I crawled under a cot and rammed my helmet on my head, thanking the Powers That Be that I was already wearing my body armor.

I squeezed my eyes shut, cringing every time a shell exploded, wondering how much or how little protection the thin mattress and metal frame of the cot would give me. And with my eyes closed, I could picture the horror on Jack's face, a second before we'd lost contact. His beautiful dark blue eyes had widened with shock, and I think he'd been about to say something to me, but now I didn't know what it was ... and I was beginning to be afraid that I'd never know.

Another explosion sounded even closer, and I could smell the harsh scent of burning fuel, the stench filling my nostrils, choking me. One of the RPGs must have hit a car. The ground shook as more explosions rained down, and it felt like I'd fallen into Hell.

I pushed my face into the dirt as tears pricked my eyes.

The people in this camp were no threat, they had no weapons, they were refugees! We were under UN protection, weren't we? *Why? Why!*

The question pounded through my head in time to the shuddering earth, the concussion of compressed air crushing the breath from my lungs. And I knew there was no answer on earth or in heaven that I would ever understand.

The RPG attack went on and on, and my life seemed to flash past, year after year, until I finally heard the deep *thurg-thurg* of the heavy machine guns from the Jordanian Army returning fire.

Jet fighters streaked across the sky with an angry roar, and more distant explosions burned the air.

And then suddenly ... nothing. It was the eerie silence of people too stunned to cry out. It was as if the tens of thousands of people living in the refugee camp were holding their breath. And then, like a wave crashing over a stony beach, the sound returned with the thin wail of a baby's cry. Then the screams started, the howling and yelling, a thousand orders shouted in a dozen languages, the desperate pleas of the wounded, the shrill, pitiful ululations of the newly bereaved.

I ordered myself to sit up, my body stiff and weak as I peered past the heavy canvas flaps of my tent. I realized that my hands were shaking. I hadn't known.

Then I forced myself to take a pace forward, kicking the shattered pieces of my useless phone under the bed.

I should have been doing my job, reporting on the scenes of carnage, but instead I went where I thought I was needed most.

The hospital tent was a scene from Hell. Men, women and children were milling around outside, their clothes spattered with blood, their screams of agony instantly ingrained in my mind, and something I could only pray I'd never hear again. The worst injured were silent, too weak to utter a sound, their bodies shutting down, their eyes draining of life even as I passed by unable to help.

A child, a boy of about four, sat in shocked silence, his clothes costed with dust, his tears streaking through the mask of dirt. His tears were silent too, his mouth open in an agonized 'O', but no sound came out. Even if his physical injuries were a few cuts and bruises, I knew that the damage would go far beyond that. I could only guess the horrors that he'd seen. I wondered if he still had a family. Maybe he'd find them later. Maybe.

A whole generation was growing up knowing only despair, death and destruction. How could there be lasting peace when children were encouraged to carry guns? How could life return to normal when these children had never experienced it? The problem seemed too big, too difficult, too impossible to solve.

And here and now, we were all suffering the effects of lives lived in hate.

Doctors and nurses worked with strained detachment as they attempted to triage a thousand people at once. Chaos was too polite a word for everything that I witnessed.

"Can I help?" I asked, a nurse rushing past.

She raised her shoulders in a helpless shrug, then pointed at a teenage girl who had a wound on her leg, bright red pooling around her.

"Apply pressure," she shouted as she ran toward a child whose robes were dark with blood.

"Then what?" I yelled after her.

"Pray!" she shouted over her shoulder.

I turned to the girl whose jet-black eyes watched me without emotion. She'd wadded her dress, pressing it against the wound while blood soaked into the sand around us. I pressed down on her leg, trying not to gag as blood seeped between my fingers.

All around me, people were crying and begging for help, most of them young, so young. I knew that over half of the refugees at this camp were children, but seeing them like this...

I stayed with the girl, helpless to do anything except apply pressure to a wound that wouldn't stop bleeding. I pressed down, pressed down, and I talked to her—trivial nonsense that meant nothing, important things that meant everything. I told her about Jackson. I told her all about the man who'd stormed his way into my life, his eyes blazing. I told her my hopes and fears, and when I'd told her everything I could think of, I prayed, reciting Bible verses that I'd last heard at my father's funeral.

She didn't understand me, of course, but maybe she understood the tone. Maybe she knew that I was praying for her.

And finally the blood flow slowed and I stopped talking. There was nothing more to say because the girl was dead, her dark eyes open and accusing.

And what could I do? I wasn't a doctor, I wasn't a nurse. I wasn't even a fighter. All I could do was write about what I'd seen and heard, said and done, and hope that somebody cared. Maybe even someone who cared enough to help end the madness.

But when hatred is your birthright, hope seems a very long way away, and I wondered if God had heard my prayers.

I didn't know what to do. I couldn't just leave her. I wanted to close her eyes, but my hands were sticky with her blood. I wiped them on my jeans, and then, carefully, I pressed her eyelids shut.

I don't know how long I sat there in the scorching sun. I do know that sweat had matted my hair under my helmet, and my body was soaked, salt marks staining my clothes, and my mouth was as dry as the desert that surrounded me. And I waited.

Eventually, a team of men came to claim her body, treating her with a weary respect.

"I didn't leave you," I whispered brokenly. "I'm sorry I couldn't save you."

Once she was gone, her body tiny as they wound a cloth around her, a funeral shroud, I stepped into the clapboard hospital, walking among the wounded, looking for some small way to help, to give meaning to my presence in this pit of despair.

Hours flowed into night as I stumbled around, helping where I could, praying when I couldn't. I don't know why I prayed, because God or Allah had never seemed further away.

I thought about Jackson and how he must be feeling, hoping that he wasn't worrying too much.

Thinking of him brought me a sense of calm in the sea of chaos, because if I had died today—yesterday—if his face had been the last that I'd seen in life, it wouldn't have been so bad. But now that I was alive, all I wanted was to find my way back to him, one slow step at a time.

Finally, the hospital quietened, an air of desolation as the dead were removed, the worst wounded operated on and given painkilling medication. Many less badly injured still lined the corridors, but the weeping was softer now, as if exhaustion and hopelessness had replaced fear and anger.

On leaden feet, I staggered back to my tent.

Marc was sitting on his cot, typing furiously into his laptop. I stared at him tiredly, knowing that I should be doing the same, doing my job.

He glanced up, and I saw the unbearable defeat and misery on his face.

"*Mon Dieu!* I thought you had been hurt, *ma belle!* But you are safe I think."

"I'm okay, I guess."

He stood up to hug me, then stared at the blood on my clothes.

"I've been helping at the hospital."

He nodded, his expression grim as he kissed my grimy cheek and squeezed my shoulder.

"Fifty dead so far, and there'll be more by morning. I managed to send out one report. The MSF team let me use their satcomms to get out a short bulletin. I'm writing this in case I can get it on the wire later." His eyes were red as he gazed at me. "You should rest, MJ."

I shrugged.

"I need to take a shower."

Marc grimaced.

"Those aren't working either. One of the RPGs hit the water tower. They're conserving everything they can."

Sighing, I stripped off my helmet and armor, and Marc turned his back while I peeled off my bloody, sweat-soaked clothes.

It was nice of him to do that, not that I cared. I was too tired and I wasn't his type.

Standing in my underwear, I used babywipes to clean myself as best I could. Then I sat on my cot, and typed out an impassioned report. Then I read it back and turned it into a proper journalistic piece, one with more facts and fewer tears. I'd learned from experience that my editor expected the truth, but truths that couldn't be refuted at a later date. And besides, I owed it to these people, these suffering people, to do my job as professionally as I could.

By now, Marc was stretched out on his cot, but when I glanced up and saw his face illuminated by the blue light of my computer screen, his eyes were open. I didn't think many people would be able to sleep well tonight.

Dawn was already breaking when I finally fell into an uneasy and fitful sleep, jagged dreams and ugly images torturing me for the hour that my eyelids were closed.

My eyes felt gritty when I peeled them open reluctantly, and my body was already sweating from the boiling heat in the airless tent.

Marc was sitting bare chested on his bed, typing rapidly.

"*Chérie*, the satcomms at MSF will be online in an hour if you want to file your story."

His words were the spur I needed.

I re-read what I'd written the night before, corrected a few typos, then dressed quickly. I needed to speak to some of the people in charge of the camp to get a quote. I took my camera, too, snapping pictures of the RPG damage and the long lines that still snaked around the hospital.

It took 45 minutes of my precious hour to get the quote I needed from a harried Major in the Jordanian army. I'd hoped to get a short meeting with Kilian Kleinschmidt, the UNHCR's Senior Field Coordinator, but he was too busy coordinating the arrival of water tankers to speak to me.

The Camp's staff sometimes had an uneasy relationship with the Press. They needed us, needed us to tell the world about the enormous scale of suffering, but they also guarded against exploitative and voyeuristic stories. Plus, we were a drain on scant resources.

So I hurried to the MSF satcomms tent and filed my report and photographs. I also fired off a quick email to Allison, my PA, and to Jack, telling them both that I was okay and would be in touch when I could.

"Miss Buckman, I have a message for you," said the French-

Canadian woman who'd let me use her computer for a few precious minutes. "A Michael Gordon? From your newspaper."

I knew Michael. Not well, but enough to like and respect him. He was our military correspondent and a seasoned veteran of more wars than he cared to count.

"What did he say?"

"He wanted to know if you were okay after the RPG attack. I told him that I didn't know, but asked him to call back this morning."

"Okay, thank you. He might not call back now seeing as I've filed my report. He'll see it as soon as it lands with the desk editor and he'll know that I'm ... alive."

I was touched that Michael had gone to so much trouble.

"I got the impression that he was asking on behalf of someone else," said the woman. "Your husband, perhaps?" Then she glanced at my bare ring finger. "Or your boyfriend?"

In the midst of all the heat and horror, I couldn't stop myself from smiling. My boyfriend? My intense Marine who would move heaven and earth to protect the people he cared about? Yes, I could only imagine the strings that Jack had pulled to get all the way to Michael Gordon.

"Ah, look at that smile," said the woman, her pleasure in my happiness wiping away her exhaustion for a second. "I'm happy for you."

I thanked her again and walked away.

I spent the day interviewing as many people as I could, scribbling furiously, then typing up my notes into more reports. I watched the slow progress as the mobile phone mast was rebuilt, tied together with old pieces of wire and rope, and as soon as it was working, I borrowed Marc's cell phone to call Jack.

His voice was terse when he answered the unknown number.

"Connor. Who is this?"

"Jack, it's me."

There was a long silence.

"Jack? Hello?"

"Maggie..."

His voice cracked, and suddenly all the effort of holding myself together, of being strong, was over, and I had tears in my eyes.

"Yes," I whispered. "It's me. I'm okay."

"I thought..."

"I know, Jack. I know. But I'm okay, I promise. It was ... rough here for a while."

"I've read your article ... Jesus, Maggie!"

"I'm okay," I repeated weakly. "I'm coming home. The newspaper has pulled all personnel back to the capital, Amman. I've got one interview to do there, then I'm on the first flight out, the day after tomorrow."

I'd be back in New York, but I didn't know when I'd see Jack again. I knew he was visiting with his mother. I couldn't expect him to jump on a plane just because I'd be back in the city.

"I know," he said. *"I spoke to your PA and bugged the hell out of her until she told me what was going on."*

I laughed.

"You must have really charmed her if you got her in a good mood in the office on a Sunday!"

"Yeah, um, don't get mad, Maggie..."

He sounded uncharacteristically reticent.

"Why would I get mad?"

"So, I kind of got Allison to do another favor for me..."

"Go on."

"I asked her to get you a connecting flight to Biloxi," he said in a rush. *"Allison agreed with me that you needed a vacation after ... everything. You don't have to stay here, I can reserve you a hotel room, but Mama would love to meet you."*

I blinked, overwhelmed by everything that he was saying.

"Slow down, Jack. Let me make sure I've got this straight. You asked Allison to get me a flight to Biloxi and you want me to meet your mother?"

He chuckled, and I imagined his dark blue eyes crinkling, his even white teeth flashing a grin at me.

"Yeah, that about sums it up."

"You've got some fast moves there, Sarge."

"Too fast?" he asked softly.

Perhaps I should have been irritated by his high-handed behavior, but I wasn't. God, no. It felt so good to be cared for. I'd been alone long enough to know that independence can sometimes be very lonely.

"Thank you, Jack," I said sincerely. "It sounds wonderful. And I'm sure your mother can't wait to meet her only son's Yankee g— friend."

This time his laugh was deeper and carefree.

"You can say 'girlfriend', Maggie. She'll love you," he said.

And I wondered if he'd be prepared to say the same words to me one day.

Our relationship had been born from the most desperate of situations, warmed by friendship and respect, heightened by our physical attraction, and tempered with the threat of losing it all in an explosion of dust and violence. I couldn't help thinking that I'd be saying those special words to Jack soon, whether he was ready to hear them or not.

Being close to death, I knew that I wanted to live. I wanted to experience it all. With Jack.

"I expect you to meet me at the airport, Sarge," I said, my voice husky with more tears.

"I'll be there, Maggie," he said gravely. "I'll always be there."

We talked for another minute before I had to hand the phone back to Marc, a warmth of happiness filled me.

It seemed almost obscene when I was surrounded by so much misery.

By the time I arrived at Gulfport-Biloxi International Airport, I'd been traveling 29 hours. I was beyond exhausted and suffering from severe reverse culture shock. Flying into New York, we passed over the fields of upper New York State, the brilliant green a shocking contrast to the harsh, sunbaked plains and deserts of Jordan. The Atlantic seemed too blue, the people too colorfully dressed, and there was just so *much* of everything. Precious water was wasted on washing cars, and it was startling to see the vast amounts of consumer goods at both Amman's Queen Alia Airport and JFK.

I felt sticky and dirty, wearing my comfortable old jeans and tennis shoes that were still stained a dull orange-brown from the Zaatari sand.

My laptop case was slung over one shoulder, and my carry-on bag on the other. I waited at the baggage carousel in a daze, almost missing my dun-colored duffel as it slowly circled around.

I managed to drag it off at the last second.

As I stumbled like a sleepwalker, trudging through the airport, I thought again how lucky I was to be born American and therefore, in theory, free. Despite the losses I'd weathered over my thirty-one years, I'd won life's lottery. But seeing Jackson waiting for me, I felt like I'd won the greatest prize of all.

He was frowning, his intense gaze pinned on the passengers filtering past. I took a moment to drink him in.

He was wearing a plain white t-shirt that stretched over his broad shoulders, tightening on his biceps as he crossed his arms across a powerful chest. Khaki shorts hung from his narrow hips, held in place by a worn, leather belt.

And then his head swung in my direction and his eyes snapped to mine. I saw relief and an explosion of joy on his face, and I couldn't help smiling so wide I was afraid I'd scare small children.

He pushed his way through the crowds of people and gathered me into a tight hug, his face pressing into my neck, soft kisses pressed against my skin.

My hands slid over those broad shoulders and down his back. As I touched him, I felt the tension slide from his taut muscles. I relaxed into his chest, letting him take my weight, sharing the burden. My throat tightened and tears pricked my eyes.

"It's okay, Maggie," he whispered as my shoulders shook. "You're home now."

Tears soaked his t-shirt, but with his arms around me, I truly felt that I'd come home.

Eventually, I had myself under control and Jackson dropped a sweet kiss on my cheek before gathering up my bags in one hand, and holding my fingers tightly with the other.

I breathed deeply, calmly, letting my emotions settle like a pile of feathers that fluttered slowly to earth. As each one landed, a tiny piece of my life dropped exquisitely into place with it.

As we left the airport, the road shimmered in the heat, and beyond, the Gulf glittered in the late evening sun.

I stared out of the window in a haze of weariness that was bone deep.

We passed through the city and I kept expecting Jackson to pull into one of the hotels that lined the road from the airport, until it dawned on me that we were heading out of town.

"Jack, did you get me a hotel room?"

His eyebrows rose.

"No, sugar. You're staying at my place. Mama wants to meet you. I thought you were okay with that?"

I glanced down at my dirty, crumpled clothes. It certainly wasn't the way I would have chosen to meet Jack's mother.

"You'll be fine," he said, catching the direction of my quick glance. "She knows where you've been and what you've been doing. She's seen me in worse shape."

"Your compliments are overwhelming, Sarge," I said drily, making him laugh. "So ... how many of your girlfriends has she met before?"

His shoulders tightened fractionally and I glanced at him curiously.

"Just one."

"Care to give me a little more?" I asked gently, wondering why this was a sore topic for him.

"I was engaged once. Emmy. Her mama is friends with mine. Her younger sister is friends with Lucy."

"The kissing cousin you mentioned?"

"The same."

"I didn't know you'd been engaged."

His lips pressed into a thin line.

"It was a while ago."

"Can I ask what happened?" I paused as his expression darkened. "You don't have to tell me."

He sighed.

"It's okay. Same old story, I guess. It can be hard to hold down a relationship in the military. Emmy wasn't cut out to be the wife of an active duty Marine. She was too needy, too dependent. Not like you, Maggie."

He glanced across at me, but I wasn't sure what to say to that.

"She gave me an ultimatum: her or the Marines. She called it off after I re-upped." He looked at me again. "What about you? You ever been married?"

"No, I never wanted to."

He looked surprised, but it was the truth. I'd never met anyone who'd made me want them that way. I didn't see the point of marriage when nearly two-thirds ended in divorce. It seemed like an exercise in hope over expectation, rather than being realistic. What I didn't, couldn't, say was that I'd been re-evaluating my standpoint in a fundamental way.

Finally, Jackson made a left turn into a short U-shaped driveway in front of a colonial-style house with white painted pillars. I hadn't expected something so grand.

"I think you might have left out a few salient facts about your upbringing, Jackson," I muttered.

He winked at me.

"I tell good bedtime stories, Maggie. Ask me later."

I appreciated his enthusiasm, but I thought it was more likely that I'd pass out for 12 hours, given half a chance.

I was surprised when the door opened and two women walked out. One was clearly Jack's mother, sharing the same cobalt blue eyes, but the other was younger, and very beautiful.

"What are you doing here, Emmy?" Jack snapped out.

"Why, Jackson Connor!" said the older woman, eyeing me carefully. "That's no way to talk. You apologize."

"That's okay, Mama Connor," the younger woman said with a silvery laugh. "He's just being his usual ornery self."

Jack took a deep breath, and I sensed that he was reining in his annoyance.

"Mama, Emmy, I'd like you to meet my girlfriend Maggie Buckman."

"Hello," I said, holding out my hand, grimacing at my cracked and torn nails as I cast an eye over Mrs. Connor's perfect manicure.

"Delighted," she said, pasting on a quick smile.

Emmy gave me a cute wave, then kissed Jack on the cheek.

"Catch you later! Enjoy your visit," she said sweetly.

Mrs. Connor waved fondly, then escorted me inside, telling Jack to show me to the Primrose room, whatever that was.

As he carried my bags down the hallway, I glimpsed a guestroom decorated in pastels and primrose yellow wallpaper.

I glanced at Jack with a bemused smile as he continued walking.

"I'm assuming this isn't where you're sleeping?"

"Nope, and you won't be either. My room is down the hall."

He dumped my bags on a bed with a dark comforter and a room that was decidedly more masculine, if more suited to a high school football player than a grown man.

"Are you sure she'll be okay with this? I don't want to upset your mother."

Jack shrugged.

"I'll talk to her. After what I've been like for the last 72 hours, I'm not allowing you out of my sight."

I didn't want to talk about that right now—it was too raw. Instead, I changed the subject.

"So, that was your fiancée?" I said, smirking at him to lighten the suddenly tense atmosphere.

"Was," he grimaced. "*Was* my fiancée."

I glanced out of the window at the woman driving away, the woman with the perfect sundress, perfect hair and perfect makeup—a pageant princess. And then I looked at Jackson, hard and rugged, a core of steel running through him.

I couldn't see them together, although obviously he had. Once.

Other than the man in front of me, I had nothing in common with a woman like her, but I didn't feel threatened. Jack was a man more than capable of making his own choices. I was the one he'd asked to stay.

Besides, we'd both learned that it was pointless to worry about things that hadn't happened yet and maybe never would: you had to live for today. Control was an illusion.

"Do you miss her?"

He didn't answer immediately and I respected that. He'd loved her once and the words he said next would matter.

"I miss being part of something bigger than just me. That's what I love about the Marines. With Emmy, I would have been part of a marriage—I miss the idea of what that meant to me ... the dream. I know it wouldn't have been like that. We weren't right for each other. But I learned from her, too. So now I know what it looks like when something good comes along. And I'm not going to walk away from that, Maggie. Not for anyone."

His words were thoughtful and decisive, and I wasn't sure I was in the right frame of mind to hear him talk about marriage like that. So I fell back on my usual defense of humor.

"Does that mean I've got to put up with you?"

He grinned.

"Who said I was talking about you?"

I wrapped my arms around his neck and pulled his head toward me, pausing when our lips were an inch apart.

"Are you thinking about me now?"

His eyes darkened dangerously as his lips hinted at a smile

That sultry knowing look that said, *I'll make you beg for forgiveness ... and I'll enjoy every second of it.*

He kissed me the way a hungry man drools over all-you-can-eat buffet. I felt needed and wanted and desired, and all my tiredness fell away.

But then his mother called us, saying supper was ready.

His eyes met mine, hot and amused.

"You want to take a quick shower, Maggie, while I ... uh ... calm down."

I winked at him, then unzipped my duffel, trying to find something to wear that was as close to clean and unwrinkled as possible. I finally came up with a pair a shorts and a tank top that would have to make do, for now.

Five minutes later, with wet hair and damp skin I sat at Jackson's mother's table.

I didn't think she liked me much, tutting about "career girls like you" but when she saw how truly tired I was, her eyes softened, and it wasn't long before she was shooing me upstairs to bed.

Jackson followed a minute later, locking his bedroom door behind us. Despite my tiredness, I ran my hands over his body, feeling his arousal straining against his shorts.

"Thank God you're home safe, Maggie," he said seriously.

That evening, he loved me with an urgency and neediness that was new, and I returned it in full.

With our bodies pressed together in the dark, he opened up to me in a way he never had before.

"I was going out of my mind," he said softly. "When I couldn't get in touch with you and I imagined the worst. It was a dark place for me. And ... I get bad dreams sometimes. Wondering what had happened to you ... I'm not blaming you, hell no, but ... sometimes..." and he cleared his throat. "Sometimes I wake up screaming. The Marine shrink said that the invisible injuries are the ones that are hardest to heal."

I tightened my arms around him.

"Oh, Jack. I understand, I do. I had a lot of flashbacks after Afghanistan. I feel so powerless in my dreams. I don't have a gun, I can't run ... and sometimes ... sometimes, Jack, you're not there in time."

His body tensed for a moment and then he pulled me closer.

"I'll tell you one thing, Maggie—I wasn't scared of death until I met you."

I stared at him, his eyes glittering in the moonlight.

"I used to think that if I die and find out that Heaven exists, I'll have friends waiting for me ... and my pa and grandpappy. If it doesn't exist, I won't know anything about it."

I smiled.

"You have a way with words, Jack."

"But now I've met you, I'm afraid I'll lose you. The last few days..."

"Shh," I said. "Don't talk about that now."

I snuggled down under the sheet. Jackson felt solid, like a tree trunk warmed by the sun, his chest firm against my back, his arms heavy and wrapped around me, his scent of soap and clean sheets and hot, sexy man.

And I knew that no scary dreams would touch me tonight.

Chapter Nine

A NEW PATH

When I woke up, the sun was high in the sky and next to me the bed was empty.

The sheets on Jackson's side were cool but a single red rose lay on his pillow, and I smiled.

I'd seen Jack happy, worried, angry, intense and focused. I'd seen him with rage in his eyes and a rifle in his hands; I'd seen him sweet, and I'd seen him loving. But I'd never experienced the romantic man that was masked by the warrior's austere demeanor. And I'd never been with a man who left a beautiful, long-stemmed red rose on the pillow. In fact, most of the men I'd dated from Manhattan seemed to think they'd done me a favor when they offered to split the check with me.

This was new. And I liked it a lot.

I stretched, feeling the ache in my body. Not only from the long flights in cramped seats, but from the times in the night when we'd come together and washed away the intensity of the last few days in an ocean of kisses, a torrent of touching, and a new and different emotional depth.

When I first met Marine Sergeant Jackson Connor, I'd seen a stern, taciturn man. I'd assumed that he was the strong, silent type. But that was just one facet of him. Since we'd been together, ours seemed to be a non-stop conversation, and we talked all the time about everything and nothing—our hopes and dreams, our deepest fears.

But perhaps Jackson was at his most eloquent when we were alone in bed together. All the reserve of his training, his years as a Marine were left behind in these most private of moments. And I knew he showed me a side that very few people had ever seen.

I wasn't naïve. He'd admitted that in his twenties, co-eds at the beach were his favorite prey, and he was a predator honed to perfection by training, looks and natural charm. But I also understood that those sort of encounters no longer satisfied him. What we had was real and surprising and new. It challenged us both.

I swung my legs out of bed and padded to the bathroom, but as my hand touched the door handle, Jack's voice drifted upward.

I peeked out of the window and found him by the patio talking to his mother who was seated under a sun umbrella.

"She seems very ... independent, darlin'. Older than I was expecting."

Great. They were talking about me. With two strikes against me already, apparently,

"You'll like her when you get to know her," came Jack's confident voice.

"I can already see that my son approves," she teased gently.

"She's different from any other woman that I've met."

"That she is."

"Now, Mama..."

"I'm not saying that's a bad thing," she said briskly, "but how are you going to turn this into a relationship with grit and roots? I can see how much you think of her, Jack, I'm not blind. But do you really think she's going to give up her career as a journalist and follow you around while you build your own life in the Marines? Don't misunderstand me, I'd like nothing more than for you to tell your mama that you're leaving the Corps and going to settle down and make babies so I can be a grandma at last, but is she the right girl for that?"

And wasn't that the question?

I didn't want to eavesdrop anymore. If Jack had something to say to me on the subject, I wanted to hear it from him.

I forced myself to step away from the window and turned on the shower.

Jack

I thought about what Mama said. She knew me better than anyone. Or she had, until I'd met Maggie. I didn't think a civilian would ever be able to understand my job or what it meant to me, but she did.

It felt like she'd been created just for me, she was so goddamn perfect.

Mama knew how I felt about her, but she was worried, too. Every time I tried to pull Maggie closer, she'd get that look in her eye as if I was trying to hold her too tight. And damned if I didn't want to tell her that she couldn't take anymore assignments like that last one. But I knew she was waiting for me to say something, and from what she'd told me, it had been the reason that her relationships had failed in the past. So I kept my mouth shut and smiled.

But it made me understand Emmy a little better, too.

It had been painful seeing her again, more than I'd thought it would be. Honestly, I hadn't spent much time thinking about her over the last couple of years, only if Mama mentioned her when we were talking on the phone.

But I could see it in Emmy's eyes. She might have been the one to break it off, but she'd never thought her ultimatum would have me walking away for good.

A month after we'd broken up, Emmy had flown out to San Diego, begging to try again, saying she'd made a mistake. I'd tried to be as gentle as possible when I'd told her there was no chance of it. She'd become hysterical, sobbing and then screaming at me. I hadn't wanted to hurt her, but I knew our relationship wasn't right. If I was honest with myself, I'd known for a while, and when she'd broken up with me, it was a relief.

But now, maybe just a little, I felt a soft breath across the embers of feelings that I'd thought had died. Yes, I still cared about her, but it was nothing like the fire of emotions that Maggie made me feel.

Maggie scared the crap out of me because I felt so much, so

quickly. It was like jumping out of a C130 transport plane and realizing that I'd forgotten my 'chute.

But when I held her in my arms, she made me think of summer afternoons in Mama's garden—her warm skin, the sultry heat in her eyes, those sexy lips made for long, languid kisses.

I'd do whatever it took to hold onto her.

Even if that meant letting her go.

MJ

I took my time showering, deep in thought. If anyone understood how much my career meant to me, it was Jack. He'd *seen* how much it meant to me. And even though I could imagine a future with this man, a beautiful future, I wasn't ready to give up everything I'd worked for either. At least, not yet.

There weren't many married people who did the work I did, and even fewer were women. Most of those were either single or had families already grown up. It was rare to find a foreign correspondent who juggled childcare and frequent overseas travel. It happened occasionally, but it was tough.

The shower revived me, but did little to wash away the sad realization that the worlds that had brought us together were going to push us apart, and soon.

Standing with a towel wrapped around me, I opened my duffel bag and stared critically at my clothes. Everything was wrinkled, even the few clean clothes—which wouldn't have mattered if I'd gone back to my apartment in NYC. Instead, I was standing in a serene, sun-filled room, with the scent of honeysuckle drifting up from the garden, and a timelessness quality that made me feel grubby, like a hobo wandering into a black tie event.

I pulled out a cleanish pair of shorts and a plain t-shirt, shoving my body armor and dirty panties to the bottom of the bag.

This was as good as it was going to get. I didn't even have my full makeup case with me—just a lip gloss, concealer and a nearly empty tube of mascara. Oh and a comb. Happy days.

I slipped on a pair of flip-flops and made my way downstairs to the patio.

"Hey, sugar!" Jack said, standing up and taking my hand, kissing me sweetly on the cheek.

I felt a faint blush heat my skin, very happy to see the broad smile on his face. At least the conversation with his mother hadn't put him in a bad mood.

"Good morning, Maggie. Did you sleep well?" his mother asked politely.

"Too well!" I said, sinking into a comfortable cane chair. "I'm usually awake at sunrise. I'm sorry it's so late."

"You were beat," Jack said, pouring me a cup of coffee. "That's why I let you sleep."

My eyes flitted to his mother, wondering what she thought of us sleeping together under her roof, but she didn't bat an eyelid.

"It's good to see you looking so refreshed," she said. "Jackson has told me a little of what you went through in that terrible place." She hesitated. "I read your newspaper article: it was very … vivid. Heart-breakingly vivid."

My smile slipped. It was impossible to believe that this peaceful place existed on the same planet as Zataari.

"Thank you. It was … difficult."

She nodded.

"Jackson never wants to tell me about what he's doing," she said, her gaze moving between us, "but what you do … you're very brave."

I was surprised, but when I looked at her, I saw beneath the polite southern hostess to the mother who could create a man like Jackson Connor.

"I'm not brave," I said, as Jack squeezed my hand. "I write about brave people, and I write the stories that need to be told, that's all."

There was a long silence, and I tried to think of something to say that would ease the uncomfortable atmosphere.

"You have a very beautiful home here," I said sincerely, if somewhat abruptly.

"Thank you, dear. We're very fond of it."

I wondered if her words had a double meaning. Was she trying to imply that one day Jack would want to come back here to settle down? And why wouldn't he? It really was lovely.

"Well now, Jackson," she said, changing the subject, "did I mention that Cousin Laura is having her baby shower today?"

"No, I don't reckon you did. When did she get knocked up?"

I could tell by the glint in his eye that his language was a deliberate goad to his mother. She gave him a look that said she knew exactly what he was doing.

"Laura was lucky enough to *become pregnant* a couple of months after the wedding," she said, raising an eyebrow. "The baby is due in the Fall."

"I guess John is pretty excited about that."

"Yes, he's looking forward to being a father at last," she said meaningfully. "Anyway, John thought that you'd like to catch up and have a few beers." Then she turned to me, "and Cousin Laura has invited you to her baby shower. Isn't that lovely? She really is the sweetest girl. Unfortunately, I'm volunteering at a fundraiser or I'd have been there, too. She wanted Lucy to go, as well, but summer school is keeping her busy and can't get away this weekend."

"That's very kind of your cousin," I said. "But when I packed, it was for a quick assignment to a refugee camp. I don't have anything suitable to wear to a baby shower, and to be honest, I'm not sure I'm ready to be let loose in the civilized world yet. It can be hard to ... adjust."

Jack's mother surprised me by leaning forward and taking my hand.

"My dear, that's the exact reason you should go: you need something innocent and joyous, something to remind you that life goes on. I may not have experienced what you have, but I have seen my boy return from deployment time and again, so I do understand a little."

Tears started in my eyes. Her warmth and compassion felt so much like having a mother. Her words echoed what my own mother had said to me when she was in hospital for the last time—words about looking for the light, even when you experienced the dark.

Jack's mother squeezed my hand as I looked down to hide my feelings.

"And as for what to wear, I'm sure I can find you something of mine that would be perfect for you."

Then with another kind look, she stood up and excused herself. I brushed a few stray tears from my eyes as Jack moved his chair nearer to mine.

"You doin' okay over there, Maggie?" he asked tenderly.

"I was, until your mother started being so nice to me," I said, laughing a little.

"Yeah, she's kind of great," he said warmly. "She really likes you."

He leaned across and kissed my lips gently, then settled in his chair, his arm resting along the back of mine.

"You don't have to go to any damn baby shower," he said. "You should rest some more."

I thought about that. The offer to lounge in this beautiful garden, eat, drink and be peaceful sounded much nicer than being with a bunch of excited women that I didn't know. But on the other hand, it was really kind of them to invite me. Jack's mother had even offered to lend me something to wear—I didn't want her to think I wasn't grateful.

"Actually, I think your mother is right. It might be just what I need."

He threw me a skeptical look.

"You don't have to. No one is going to think the worse of you," he said, showing again how astute he was.

"No, it's fine. And it'll only be a few hours."

"Well then, I'll come with you."

I laughed out loud at the thought of this tough-talking, hard-drinking Sergeant of Marines getting gooey over baby clothes.

"You realize, Sarge, that crashing your cousin's baby shower will expose you to dangerous levels of estrogen. You'll have to do lots of macho things just to hold onto your man-card."

Jackson grinned, his smile white against the tan he'd developed in Afghanistan and topped up on the Gulf coast during the last week.

"I can handle it. Maybe I'll chop wood and wrestle alligators before driving my truck listening to Van Halen."

"You think that will be enough? Maybe you should bite the tops off bottles with your teeth."

He nodded thoughtfully.

"And then I'll crush beer cans against my forehead, just 'cause…"

"You're a goofball, Jack!"

"You bring it out in me," he grinned. Then his smile slipped. "You really doing okay, Maggie? You've been through a lot in the last few days."

"Honestly? I don't know. My emotions are all over the place," I admitted. "It usually takes me at least a week to start feeling…"

"Normal?"

"I was going to say, feel I can move on with my life. Those weeks are almost like being in limbo, or … as if I have to go through it to come out the other side. You know what I mean?"

"Yeah, I know, Maggie. We have to stay on the base for the first two weeks after coming back from a deployment. We're debriefed and wrap up what we learned or did. They figure if we don't do it then, we'll get drunk and forget it all." He gave me a tired smile. "We all get to see the base shrink as well. I prefer the way it used to be."

"Which is?"

"I hate talking about the bad stuff. Every Marine meets a shrink these days. We all have the 'cure' when we're back from deployment. I preferred the old-school method: three bottles of beer and a 48 hour pass to Vegas."

"I'm not sure that's a particularly healthy response, Sarge," I said gently.

He glanced at me sideways.

"I don't remember ever having a boss, an officer or anyone else, tell me to drink less. It's cheap therapy. "

"That's pretty cynical."

Jackson shrugged.

"It's the truth. Any improvements to our mental health, they've been led by a few individual senior commanders, but there's nothing consistent. The rest has been led by the public. They don't like the way their heroes are treated."

His voice rose sarcastically on 'heroes' and he threw me a look.

"I guess reporting the issues has helped. But it doesn't really come from the military—guys would lose their careers if they told the truth about what it's like."

"But surely you can talk to your CO about it?"

He shook his head.

"Not really. You're not supposed to have feelings. You're supposed to be a good little Marine and do as you're told." He shook his head. "I don't know what I'd be if I left. You're a hero while you wear the uniform. But as a civilian? Just another damaged person to ignore."

I heard the pain and confusion in his voice, but his cynicism saddened me.

I also knew that this expression of vulnerability was his way of supporting me, of showing me that he understood how hard it was to come back, to pretend that I hadn't seen the awful things I'd seen, to pretend that I hadn't been soaked in the blood of another human being. A child.

I closed my eyes, but that didn't stop the horrific images. It never did.

"I get it, Maggie," he said softly. "You don't have to hide anything—not from me."

I stood up and shifted onto his lap, my hands winding into his short hair. I buried my face into his neck, breathing in his scent, soothed in those strong arms.

He held me, rocking me gently, and we didn't speak because words weren't necessary. A deeper tie of understanding and shared experience bound us together.

I didn't want to let him go. I didn't ever want to let him go.

But then I heard the soft click of his mother's sandals, and I pulled away from him. He held onto me for a moment, then let me go.

I slid back into my chair, but from the tender expression on her face, I knew she'd seen us.

"Well now, honey," she said, smiling gently at me. "I have two or three summer dresses that would look pretty on you. Why don't you come with me and choose whichever you'd like."

"That's very kind of you, Mrs. Connor."

"Oh, please! Mrs. Connor was my mother-in-law. Call me Evelyn."

Jackson grinned at his mother, and I couldn't help thinking that I'd passed some sort of test—maybe with both of them.

I followed her into the house, and she took me to her bedroom which was furnished lavishly and decorated with a pale violet theme.

Two photographs sat on her dresser: an older man who was the spitting image of Jackson, and a beautiful black-and-white photo of Evelyn with a baby Jack.

"My two boys," she said, touching the frames of each reverently. "I'm so happy he's found you, my dear. Be kind to each other."

Her words left me speechless, but before I had a chance to digest her meaning, she pointed at the dresses.

"Now, here are three sweet outfits that I think would look darlin' on you."

She pointed at a pretty sundress with pink frills that was more suitable for a girl like Emmy; a pale blue shift dress; and a mint-green floaty, slightly hippy dress that was much more my style.

"Oh, good choice," she said, as my eyes fell on the green dress. "That will look perfect with your lovely complexion. It belongs to my daughter, Lucy. I wish she could have been here to meet you."

"Jack said she was studying at Ole Miss?"

"Yes! At least one of my children decided to go to college," she smiled. "Now then, I have the cutest sandals to go with it."

"That's so kind of you, Evelyn," I said, testing out her name and finding that I wasn't uncomfortable being so familiar with her. "Thank you very much."

"Oh pish! Any woman who can put a smile like that on my boy's face ... well, I think I should thank *you*."

She passed me a pair of flat, strappy sandals that were simple and elegant but also comfortable-looking, and patted my hand.

I didn't quite know what to do with her kindness after having overheard her conversation with Jackson this morning, but I decided to take it at face value.

I went back to Jack's room and changed into my borrowed dress. I was pleased how much it suited me, and even more pleased when I heard Jack's appreciative whistle.

"You sure scrub up nice, Maggie," he teased. "You look different when you're not up to your knees in mud and dust."

"I could say the same about you. And your bedroom smells a lot better than your sleeping quarters in Now Zad."

He pulled a face.

"You try sleeping with twenty other sweaty grunts. Scratch that! I don't want you ever to know!"

I laughed and kissed his freshly shaved cheek.

"I'll take it under advisement."

He gave me a lopsided grin as he peeled off his faded USMC t-shirt, swapping it for a pale blue polo shirt that made his eyes pop, and a pair of khaki chinos.

"You look like you're about to go and play golf," I teased. "No one would ever believe that you're a leatherneck."

He rubbed his hand over his short hair and grinned at me.

"I happen to play a pretty mean round of golf."

"You are full of surprises," I said, dropping a light kiss on his lips. "Now take me somewhere I can buy a gift for a baby shower."

"Yes, ma'am," he said grabbing me by the waist and spinning me around. "Did I mention that I love it when you give me orders?"

"Later," I laughed.

The only person I knew at the baby shower was Emmy, which felt a little awkward. But to hand it to her, she was nothing but friendly, introducing me to the other women as Jack's girlfriend.

Everyone there was beautifully dressed, pearls being a favorite accessory, but with my borrowed outfit, I didn't feel too underdressed.

Emmy was wearing a gorgeous shantung silk dress in a rose pink that perfectly complimented her strawberries and cream complexion.

I caught her staring at me several times during the afternoon, a perplexed expression on her face, as if she couldn't quite work me out or what Jackson saw in me. And I don't think she did get it. For one thing, I was several years older than all these women; and for another, even though they'd all gone to college and gotten their degrees, only two of them worked full time, and one of those admitted that she'd give up work as soon as she was pregnant, which she planned to do as soon as possible.

Lisa, the only woman there who had no plans to reproduce in the immediate future, threw me a sympathetic look and came to sit next to me, explaining that she was a lawyer, specializing in criminal law. We had an interesting discussion about world politics until the others deemed it "too miserable" for the current occasion. They were probably right.

The rest of the women were friendly, inquisitive, but really I had nothing in common with them. I smiled at the baby clothes and made the appropriate appreciative noises. I drank iced teas and laughed at the 'guess the baby food' games.

When Jack arrived by taxi to take me to dinner, I was very ready to leave. Two hours of small talk had left me feeling like the outsider I was. But as soon as he walked into the room, several of the women came over to hug and kiss him, and it was only then that I realized it had been more than two years since he'd paid a visit to his home town.

Emmy was one of the ones to greet him. She was friendly, but not over-friendly, although she couldn't completely hide her disappointment that he was with me.

Jack gave her a quick kiss on the cheek, and passed on his mother's good wishes.

Then, with a sigh of relief, we climbed in the taxi and drove away.

"How'd it go?" he asked.

"Very polite," I said with a smile. "Very friendly."

"You hated it, didn't you?"

"No, honestly I didn't. We don't have much in common, but they were very sweet."

"You're sweet," he said, his gaze slightly unfocused. "You'd make a great Marine."

I couldn't help laughing at his non sequitur.

"Is that right? A Marine, huh?"

"The British Army used to have *WRACs*," he said, grinning broadly.

"Excuse me? Racks?"

"Yeah, Women's Royal Army Corps—WRACs. You know, racks ... which means..."

"Let me guess: you screw them against the wall."

Jackson burst out laughing, I guess he really was pretty drunk.

"How many beers did you have while I was at that baby shower?" I chuckled.

"I kinda lost count," he murmured into my ear. "Let's go home and fuck."

"Are all you southern boys such gentlemen?" I laughed.

He grinned sloppily and tickled my neck when he kissed me.

"Oh boy, I think I'd better find a restaurant and feed you," I said.

"I sure could eat," he smiled, raising his eyebrows and licking his lips.

"Behave," I said. "Let's get you fed, then you can take me home and misbehave as much as you like."

"God, I love you, Maggie," he said.

And I wished with my whole heart that he'd said the words when he was sober.

I stayed another week with Jackson and his mother. I became truly fond of Evelyn, grateful that she was willing to share his time with me, a stranger who'd been thrust on her. But during those days, I saw where Jackson got his insight into people from. Behind the soft-looking southern woman was a steely reserve born of early widowhood and bringing up two young children by herself.

I also gathered that Jack had been something of a rebel in his younger years, and instead of going to college and law school, which is what had been planned for him, he'd left home at eighteen years of age to join the Marine Corps.

But time was passing too fast, and I needed to get back to New York and to my life. I had work to do, and Jack's leave was nearly through. In another two days, he'd be flying back to San Diego.

"We couldn't be much further apart," I sighed. "Me in New York, you in California."

We were curled up together in bed, delaying the moment when we would have to get up so Jack could drive me to the airport.

"We'll make it work," he said, a mixture of confidence and despair etched on his face. "If we both want it, we'll make it work." He paused. "Do you want to, Maggie? Because I'll understand if it's too hard. Fuck, I know it'll suck giant monkey balls being away from you."

"Of course I want it to work," I whispered, cupping his unshaven cheek. "More than anything."

His smile was full of relief as I kissed him on those soft, sensitive lips.

"Three thousand miles is just an inconvenience," I said, trying desperately to make light of a miserable situation. "I'll fly out as often as I can."

"Twice a month?" he asked hopefully.

"Yes, if I can. Lots of people make long distance relationships work."

He kissed me back, an edge of desperation in that tender, heated, questioning kiss.

But as it turned out, I was tempting fate.

Chapter Ten

LAUGHING AT FATE

Back in New York, the sidewalk was hot beneath the thin souls of my sandals and the heated air smelled like burnt paper. I'd been telling myself that I could put up with missing Jack for another two weeks until I flew out to see him. I wasn't sure I believed myself.

Feeling glum, I'd arranged to meet up with an old friend, a fellow journalist, to cheer myself up. I was also hoping that she'd have some insight into my current situation.

Lee Venzi had been a war correspondent and written some amazing articles during her embedment with troops in Sudan, Iraq and Palestine. Like me, she'd met a Marine out in Afghanistan while she was working, and now he was her husband and they had three children. The difference was that her husband was no longer serving.

She was already in the coffee shop when I arrived, and she waved when she saw me.

"Got you a caramel latte Frappuccino waiting!" she smiled. "How are you, MJ?"

"Great, thanks! And you look amazing. I don't know how you do it when you're holding down a full time job, running a house, and you've got three kids."

"Having a young husband helps," she laughed, tossing her long dark hair over her shoulder. "Although Sebastian is more trouble than the rest of them put together."

I couldn't help laughing with her. I'd met Lee's husband once and had to admit he was pretty darned hot, but these days I thought that he looked more like a surfer than a Marine, with his curly blond hair and year-round tan. He was a personal trainer, and worked with a lot of injured vets and people with disabilities, something he had personal experience of since he'd been badly injured in Afghanistan and still walked with a limp. I also knew that he did some modelling on the side for charity. He was certainly good-looking enough.

The man was a hot mess and a force of nature, but anyone who'd seen him and Lee together knew that they adored each other despite the difference in their ages.

"How is Sebastian?"

"A pain in the ass," she laughed. "And wonderful. Wonderfully annoying, annoyingly wonderful. Take your pick. He's been working with a photographer named Michael Stokes on a new book, pictures of wounded vets."

"I know him. His photographs are amazing, really moving."

"Yes, they are. Sebastian hates showing his wounds, but that's the focus of the book after all. Actually, that was something I wanted to talk to you about. Can you help with publicity at all?"

I nodded.

"Sure, no problem. I'll get a piece in the news section as well as Lifestyles & Entertainment. That work for you?"

"Perfect, thanks. By the way, great work on the Zataari story—it was so vivid. I just hope it does some good."

I closed my eyes and breathed out slowly.

"Thank you. I hope so, too, but compassion fatigue, well, that's another story. Oh, Marc Lebuin was out there. He says hi."

"Dear Marc! How is he?"

I smiled, remembering the stresses and strengths of sharing a tiny tent with him.

"The same. Totally focused, married to his work, although there was mention that he's seeing a guy he met in Geneva. Could be the one. I get a good vibe from what he says."

"Ooh! Interesting! I'll have to email him and find out. Now, what's this I hear about you seeing a guy you met in Afghan?"

I huffed quietly.

"Where did you hear that?"

"I talked to your PA, Allison. She couldn't wait to tell me that there was a rather yummy new man in your life. So come on, spill."

I smiled and shook my head.

"Okay, fine. I met him in Helmand. He saved my life, then chewed me out for putting myself and his team in danger. We got in a massive argument. We both apologized. I said I'd buy him a drink if he was ever in New York, and a couple of weeks ago he showed up out of the blue to collect on that."

She narrowed her hazel eyes at me.

"That is a terrible story! Call yourself a writer? Don't write romance novels, MJ, because you'd stink at it."

I laughed.

"Okay, that's the short version," and I sighed, my smile falling away. "How do you do it, Lee? How do you handle being married to an ex-Marine? You've spoken about Sebastian's issues with PTSD and that sounds really tough at times. I've never dated a guy in the military before. It's unknown territory, and I have to say it's a little scary. Or maybe it's scary because he's..."

"Special?" she said gently. "You don't have to say it, MJ, I can see it in your eyes. You really like this guy."

"I do," I admitted. "I think ... I *know* that I'm falling in love with him." I gave her a wry smile. "Slightly inconvenient seeing that he's 3,000 miles away in San Diego."

Lee gave a commiserating laugh and squeezed my hand.

"Okay, well, here's what I've learned: being a Marine wife 101. First, you don't 'handle' a Marine. They're a breed apart, different from any other man you'll ever meet. They're trained to be single-minded and focused, self-reliant to the extreme. That can make it hard to get through to them, difficult to make them share what they're thinking or feeling. Can *you* handle *that*?"

I thought about what she said. Lee had been married to Sebastian for several years and I knew that they had their ups and downs. It wouldn't be easy, but I suspected I was already in too deep with Jackson to walk away.

"Yes, I think so. Jack's actually pretty open about what he feels. It's … refreshing."

Lee's eyes widened.

"Then you're already ahead of the game. Nice going, MJ. And I have to say, their single-minded focus has an upside, too."

"I think I can guess," I grinned at her, "but tell me anyway."

She leaned forward, her lips pulling upwards in a conspiratorial smile.

"It makes them very skilled lovers," she said.

I walked back to the office with a smile on my face. Talking things through with Lee had really helped clarify my thinking. She and Sebastian made time for each other and worked at being a couple, taking nothing for granted. So although she didn't sugarcoat anything, I felt more confident that I could make things work with Jack, even though we were a long way apart. Yes, I worked for the *New York Times*, but these days, lots of correspondents worked from home rather than the office. Technically, I could work from anywhere.

I was still thinking about that when I walked into the boardroom and took my seat for the monthly meeting with the editorial board.

Dean Baquet, the Editor, called the meeting to order, and we discussed the way the paper was handling the Presidential elections and the coverage it was giving to both candidates. Then we moved onto overseas stories.

At the end of the meeting, I had half a dozen assignments to organize and delegate to other, more junior writers, but as I left the table, Dean stopped me.

"A word, please, MJ."

"Sure, Dean," I said, surprised.

"Good work on the Zataari stories. Very passionate. I liked them a lot."

"Thank you!" I said, glowing with pleasure at his praise.

Dean was a hard man to please, so hearing him say that he enjoyed my work was a big deal.

"Did you hear that David Kirkpatrick is leaving the Cairo desk?" he asked, cutting to the chase.

"No, I hadn't heard that."

I knew David slightly. He'd been the Middle East correspondent for several years now, and he was a fine journalist, very well respected.

"Yes, he's coming back to the US—family reasons. He'll be home by November." He gave me a sharp look. "So ... I've been following your work for a while now. Very impressive. The job is yours if you want it: Middle East correspondent, Cairo desk."

My mouth dropped open.

"You're offering me David's job?"

He gave a thin smile.

"Yes, I am. Some say it's not job for a woman—I say you're just the woman for the job."

I swallowed, my emotions thrown into chaos. It was everything I'd worked for, everything I'd ever wanted—until I'd met a certain blue-eyed Sergeant of Marines.

"I ... thank you," I stammered. "Can I have some time to think about it? It's a big step."

His lips thinned with disappointment.

"Yes, of course. Think about it over the weekend. But don't wait too long to say yes, Ms. Buckman. Opportunities like this don't come along every day."

We shook hands and I left the office. My first instinct was to call Jack and tell him the news, but then I hesitated. I felt the foundations of our fledgling relationship shift, and I wasn't sure what would happen next.

Chapter Eleven

MILES TO GO BEFORE I SLEEP

I needed to see Jack.

We'd already planned for me to fly out to San Diego two weeks from now, but I couldn't wait.

I'd made a split-second decision, bought a ticket, and now I was packing a bag ready for my first trip out west to see Jack.

When I phoned him with my flight details so he could meet me at the airport, I couldn't keep the tension out of my voice.

Three times he asked what was wrong.

Three times I laughed and said, "What could possibly be wrong?"

His tone was serious when he replied.

"I don't know, Maggie. You tell me."

We'd been apart for just over a week, and it had been one of the longest of my life. And now I had this huge decision burning a hole in my heart.

"Jack, I'm coming to see you this weekend," I said lightly, swallowing past the lump in my throat, "and I intend to spend as much naked time with you as possible."

He knew I was being evasive, but he didn't try to force an answer out of me, although I could tell that he was disappointed. I *wanted* to tell him about my job offer, but face to face, not over the phone. I wanted to see his eyes when he heard my news. And ideally, I wanted to have made up my mind about what I was going to do before I saw him.

Which sounds harsh, but I needed my head to make this decision, even though my stubborn heart kept shouting louder and louder.

Eventually, he sighed and gave in.

"I'll be counting the hours, Maggie," he said softly.

"Me, too."

Because I knew how short time could be.

My flight was delayed by over an hour, which wasn't a great start to the weekend. But when I saw Jackson, my gut tightened with apprehension.

He wasn't in uniform, but there was no mistaking that he was military, a warrior.

His arms were folded across his chest, and his lips were pressed together in a thin, hard line. And he looked pissed. Really pissed.

He seemed tough and unapproachable, more like the man I'd met in Afghanistan than the one who'd worshipped my body with soft kisses and gentle words.

The tide of travelers flowed around him as he stood granite-like, an island in a vast ocean of swirling humanity.

I took a deep, shuddering breath as I watched him from a distance, my small suitcase weighing heavily in my hand like my doubts.

I'd only brought carry-on luggage with me, so I'd be able to go right to him without wasting precious time, but now I wished I had a few more minutes to prepare.

As soon as I took my first step forwards, Jackson saw me immediately, his eyes narrowing. There was no smile of greeting or happiness to see me.

Time's up.

He unfolded his arms, his expression grim as he strode forward.

"Did you fly three-thousand miles to break up with me, Maggie?"

I froze, taken aback by the aggression of his words, by the pain hidden behind his expressionless face.

I swallowed and forced myself to man—woman—up.

"No. But you might want to break up with me."

He didn't even blink, just the same stony stare boring through me. "And why's that?"

"Can we go get a coffee? And I'll tell you everything."

"I think I'd like to hear it now."

A flare of irritation rushed through me, but I pushed it back.

"Jackson, I've been on a stuffy, overheated plane for nearly eight hours—ninety minutes of which was spent sweating on the tarmac at JFK. I'm tired, gritty, and thirsty. I'd like to get a drink before I discuss my news with you."

His eyes softened and his head drooped.

"Shit, I'm sorry, Maggie. I promised myself I wouldn't do this. But I've been standing here wondering if..."

"I'm not breaking up with you," I said gently. "But I do need to talk to you. And, if it's not too much to ask, a hello hug would be nice."

He wrapped his arms around me, nuzzling my neck through my hair.

My eyes drifted closed and my whole body sank into him, the feeling of being in his arms, just held. No questions, no judgement, just Jack. For a second, I felt peaceful, as if nothing else mattered but this moment, this man. As if the world wasn't waiting to claim us again.

"It's so fucking good to see you, Maggie. I'm sorry I was a jerk."

"You're forgiven."

And he was. How could I blame him when he cared? He cared so much.

I ran my hands over his t-shirt, feeling his muscles tremble from my touch. His eyes slid shut and he breathed deeply. I felt a little of the tension drain from his stiff shoulders, and he pulled me toward him more tightly.

"I've missed you."

His words rumbled against the soft skin of my neck, and I felt the weight of them, understanding what they cost him.

"I know. Because I've missed you, too. Now buy a girl a cup of coffee, Sarge, before she expires from thirst."

He loosened his grip and kissed me lightly on the lips, lingering for a second before he stood upright.

"Yes, ma'am!"

Then he scooped up my small bag with one hand and wrapped the other around my shoulders.

His ride wasn't a car, of course, but a Jeep—something that looked battered and bruised, as macho and masculine as Jack himself.

He shrugged sheepishly when he saw me eyeing the rust bucket. I wouldn't have been surprised to see duct tape holding it together.

"Not a Sedan, then," I teased.

"It's got character," he muttered.

"I don't know, Jack. Is it possible to have too much character?"

I raised an eyebrow, and he mumbled something under his breath as he tossed my bag into the back seat.

"Buckle up!"

His order was gruff, but I hadn't missed the smile tugging at his lips.

It took twenty minutes for Jack to fight his way through the San Diego traffic and out across to Mission Beach. We didn't say anything important. Even though there was much to say.

I was so thirsty by the time he pulled up outside a tiny beach-hut café, that I would have considered drinking seawater. Well, maybe not, but when the waitress brought us each a glass of iced water before taking our order, I could have kissed her.

"So, what's this big news?" Jack asked, unable to hold himself back any longer.

I looked into his dark blue eyes, wishing that I had different news to give him, and took a grateful sip of cold, cold water.

Then a longer one, gulping the water as it streamed down my dry throat, ignoring the cool trickle over my chin from drinking too fast. Jack reached across the table and caught the stray drip with his thumb.

It was a gesture so tender and caring, so natural and loving that I wanted to cry.

Instead, I gave him the respect he deserved by telling him everything.

"I've been offered my dream job. Foreign correspondent. Cairo office."

He sucked in a deep breath as he fought to hold back the riot of emotions that ghosted across his face. He certainly wasn't as impassive as he'd seemed at the airport.

"Cairo, huh? Congratulations, Maggie. You deserve it. I know how hard you've worked," and he forced out a smile. "How long you goin' to be there?"

How long? I didn't know.

"It's a permanent position," I said softly.

His eyes widened and then he looked down. Still avoiding my gaze, he picked up his water and took a long drink before placing the glass carefully on the table.

"Permanent?"

"Yes."

He nodded, absorbing the information as my heart catapulted around inside my chest and my fingers fisted under the table as I fought to remain calm.

"I won't be allowed to visit you, Maggie," he said, looking over my shoulder at the ocean and rubbing his eyes. "They'll never give me permission to travel there, not to the Middle East. All movements have to be approved, and if you get caught lying, it's a court martial. Hell, I can't even go to TJ."

Of all the things he might have said to me, I hadn't considered that his being a Marine would restrict his travel. I really, really should have. *So stupid. So naïve.*

My lips started to tremble, so I pressed them together. My dream job was turning into a nightmare.

Jackson sat with his head bowed, his hands held loosely in his lap.

He was still staring at the table when he began speaking.

"I'll be honest with you, Maggie. I want to tell you not to go, but I have no right to do that." He looked away and shook his head. "All the years I've been a Marine, I've listened to the guys bitching about their wives and girlfriends hating it when they're deployed." He gave a wry smile. "It got old. And I can't tell you how many Dear John letters I've seen burned, torn up or pissed on. Some women can't handle it, you know? One guy had gotten divorce papers sent to him because his wife found ants in the kitchen and he wasn't there to get rid of them. Just a grain of sand too many, I guess. I used to think those women were weak, shallow even. But I kind of get it now, because I want to tell you not to go. I want to tell you to stay in the US where you'll be safe ... safer. I want to tell you it's too dangerous. But I can't. And I'm choking on it, Maggie."

His voice had turned harsh and rough.

I reached across, touching the back of his hand, but he didn't react. He was holding himself so tightly.

Then, slowly, his eyes turned toward me.

"I'm not sorry for saying any of that."

I nodded, my throat dry and my eyes wet.

"Thank you for telling me what you're thinking."

Jack breathed out a long sigh, and tapped a tanned finger against the side of his head.

"I gotta say, Maggie, a lot of thoughts were rattling around in there since last night. I knew there was somethin' that you weren't saying, but I didn't think you'd be telling me that you were going to live in Egypt."

"I haven't said yes definitely yet."

He gave a faint smile.

"But you're going to."

I curled my fingers around the back of his hand, squeezed gently and pulled away.

"Yes, I am."

Because all that he'd said was about men risking their relationships to protect our country. And in my own small way, that was what I was doing, too—risking my relationship with Jack because my work was about something bigger than myself, my life. To me, journalism isn't just reporting the news, it's about telling the stories for people who have no voice. And that was important to me. It drove me, fired me up; it mattered to me.

If anyone understood that, it was Jack.

I hoped. I hoped that he understood.

Finally, he nodded.

"You *should* say yes. Hell, I'm the last person who'd say you couldn't go. I can be away for six months, a year. More, maybe. And I have been. In the twelve years I've been a Marine, maybe seventy months have been on US soil. I'd be one hell of a hypocrite if I tried to tell you how to live your life. Even if I want to."

"You're not mad?"

"No. But I'll miss you like hell."

The knot of unease that had solidified inside my chest began to loosen.

"So, you still want to do the long distance thing?" I asked hesitantly. "Even more long distance? Even though we might only see each other two or three times a year? Living our lives on email and Facetime?"

It sounded even bleaker said out loud.

Two years, I told myself. I'd give it two years—twenty-four little months.

Broadly speaking, there are two types of foreign correspondents: the ones who live their whole lives overseas, and the ones who burn out quickly after one or two postings, preferring to live in the US and make short trips abroad. After Zaatari, I'd begun to suspect that I belonged in the second category. Maybe I should have realized that earlier.

Jack sat upright and held both my hands across the table tightly.

"Long distance? Hell, yeah!" he said softly. "I've waited too long to find you. I'm not letting you go now. I want to try. I know it won't be easy..."

A relieved smile spread across my face.

"Jackson Connor, have I told you lately how amazing you are?"

"No, you've been slacking on that," he grinned.

"You. Are. Amazing."

"And not just in bed."

"No. You're pretty amazing all around."

We finished our coffees in companionable silence, gazing out over the ocean, knowing that soon, too soon, I'd be even further away with an ocean, a continent, and a river of red tape between us.

The sun's heat seeped into my skin and Jackson's thoughtful expression washed over my senses. Somehow, and I didn't yet know how, somehow it was going to be okay.

We climbed back into the rattling, rearing bucket of rust, and Jack drove us an hour north to a large, Spanish-style hotel near the pier in San Clemente. The palm trees outside rustled in the breeze and the perfect blue sky was gilded with warmth, even at this time of the year.

"This looks very upscale," I smiled at him.

"Not as upscale as you deserve," he said sweetly. "But it's pretty nice. A lot of guys from Camp Pendleton use it when families come to visit."

"Do I get to see your barracks as well while I'm here?"

He shrugged.

"Sure, if you like. There's not a whole lot of interesting stuff I can show you."

"I'm sure you'll think of something."

Heat flared in his eyes.

"There are one or two things, now I think about it."

Jumping out of the Jeep, he grabbed my suitcase and tugged me to his side as we walked into the hotel.

There was something slightly desperate about the way he kept touching me, pulling me close to him all of the time. We were counting down the seconds to goodbye again.

Guilt washed over me, because this time I was choosing a path that led me away from him. And what was my excuse for that?

Jackson

I haven't been entirely straight with Maggie. She thinks she knows what I do in the Marines, and I've let her carry on thinking that. I've been vague, not only because there are things I can't tell her, but because there are things I don't want her to know.

My MOS, military operational specialty, is Marine Corp Recon. We're elite forward-operating troops, the eyes and ears for our battalion. We collect intel, and lead clandestine, unconventional attacks against the enemy: my Marine Specialty Occupation.

When I was in Afghan, Maggie thought I was with some sort of public relations remit who just happened to be around to rescue her when the shit hit the fan. Well, I do my best. The Brits out there call it a 'hearts and minds' op—winning over the civilians, but that wasn't my first duty then and it isn't now. And when you're a Marine, your sense of duty overshadows every other priority, whether it's your uncle's funeral or watching your first kid come into the world. If the Marine Corps says, *Jump*, you'd better have springs in your shoes.

I'm Team Leader for Scout Snipers, which is a polite way of describing what I do. Yeah, we collect a lot of intel on missions, but our real purpose? We're long-range assassins.

Do I think Maggie would ditch me if she knew that? Maybe, at first. I think, like me, she's in too deep now to do that, although I don't want to test that theory just yet. Especially given her bombshell news.

My specialty is over-the-horizon warfare, which seems pretty ironic given that Maggie will be far, far out of sight.

But here's the thing: I reckon I'm due a promotion any day now. At 30, I'd be pretty young for a Gunny, which is the next rank up, but I think it's coming. And my CO has suggested that I step back from operations and take up more of a training role. I've got eight years left to go in the Marines, then I'll have done my twenty. I could stay longer, but there are other things I want to do with my life, too.

I've had twelve years of being on live ops, but I'm not greedy. I'd be okay ... mostly ... with handing that over to younger guys coming up behind me. I don't think it's a coincidence that I've been having these thoughts since I met Maggie. A year ago, I re-upped. I applied for three duty stations, and then there are four places that good ole Uncle Sam sees fit to train snipers: right here at Camp Pendleton in sunny Southern California; Marine Corps Base Hawaii, which every motherfucker wants; and back down in North Carolina at Camp Lejune, which is where I started this journey.

Just before I met Maggie, I learned that I'd be at Pendleton as we usually stay with our units, but since I met Maggie, the pull eastward has been stronger.

Yeah, I said four places, I know. They also train snipers at Marine

Corps Base Quantico in Virginia. Yep, Virginia. Just four hours from New York City. Just four hours from Maggie.

Life is just one fucking joke after another. I could have been moving three-thousand miles nearer to her, but she's just told me that she's moving five-and-a-half-thousand miles in the other direction.

I want to tell her no fucking way. I want to tell her that I'm thirty years old and finally ready to make a commitment to one woman for the rest of my life. I want to tell her all of that.

But I can't.

She's been offered her dream job in Egypt. And what kind of bastard would I be if I tried to stop her? I'm not even sure I could, which makes me feel like shit. But even if I could stop her, I know it would be the wrong thing to do. She'd resent me, and resentment would turn to hatred, then disappointment and indifference.

I've seen it happen.

Life in the military isn't for everyone, and it's particularly tough on families. It's not a coincidence that with units who get deployed regularly at short notice like SEALs, they're made up of a higher than usual number of orphans and foster kids. True story. And if I wanted to be real cynical about it, I'd say the military likes it that way. They want the baddest motherfuckers on the earth running toward the enemy because they've got nothing to lose, not running away because they've got a family to get back to.

So now I don't know what to do.

With Maggie being in the field in the Middle East, I don't want to go into a training role. I want to be out there, with her, which I know is dumb because I'm not going to get deployed to Egypt. Well, probably not. Although I did have some EOD friends who were out in Libya helping get rid of landmines.

My CO is a good guy, but if I went to him and asked to be transferred to Quantico because of Maggie, he'd laugh at me. We get our orders and we stay for three years, no matter what. So I go where they send me—and hope that Maggie will come back to me one day.

The motto is: *Home is where the Marine Corps sends you.* But I can't help thinking that home is where Maggie is. Either way, I've got at least three more years on the west coast.

All these thoughts have been buzzing around in my brain since she told me her news.

I kind of want to be mad at her, but when I look into her beautiful eyes, I can't do it. I'm not going to spend this weekend being a dick. I don't know when I'll see her again, and I'm going to make every second count.

"How you doing over there, Jackson Connor?" she says, all soft and sexy. "I can practically see the thoughts churning around in that busy brain of yours."

"Is that right?"

"Yes, but I have a tried and tested method of distraction that I think could help."

She stretches out on the white sheets of the king-size bed and smiles up at me.

"I don't know, I'm trained not to get distracted but to complete the mission. You sure you can help?"

"Hmm, let me see..."

All it takes is one light touch of her fingernail running down the bare skin of my forearm and I'm so turned on, there's fucking stars bursting behind my eyes.

"Is it starting to work?" she laughs gently.

"Yep, definitely taking effect," I agree, laying down on the bed next to her, and covering her slender body with mine.

But even as her tongue presses into my mouth, starting a wicked conversation that burns right through every molecule of my body, part of me is thinking, *God, I love you, Maggie. So much.*

But I don't say the words out loud.

Chapter Twelve

A ROCK AND A HARD PLACE

Jack was reading the newspaper while he waited outside his CO's office, but he only got as far as the headline before he tossed it aside in disgust.

It didn't help. In fact, folded on a desk a few feet away, it taunted him.

Finally, he leaned across and picked it up again, reading avidly, a tense frown creasing his forehead. As he continued to scan through the black columns of ink, his blood pressure began to rise.

74 journalists killed in line of duty this year

The organization Reporters Without Borders has stated that nearly three-quarters of the journalists killed were victims of "deliberate, targeted violence".

Five female journalists were also killed, including 32 year-old Anabel Flores Salazar, a crime reporter for the Mexican newspaper El Sol de Orizaba.

"The violence against journalists is more and more deliberate," said Christophe, the secretary general of Deloire Reporters Without Borders. "They are clearly being targeted."

Jack's heart was racing and he felt the need to point his M40 sniper's rifle in the direction of...

But that was the problem: he didn't know where the enemy was hiding. Probably in plain sight. Probably within a dozen clicks of where Maggie was currently doing her job.

His knee began to bounce and sweat broke out on his forehead.

He pulled his cell phone from his breast pocket, desperate to hear her voice, desperate to know that she was okay. Or as okay as she could be, given the tightrope of danger she was walking.

He rubbed his sweaty palms over his camouflage pants and took a deep breath, forcing himself to calm down, then tucked his phone back in his jacket pocket. She wouldn't appreciate being woken up just to stop him from having a meltdown.

Get a fucking grip, Marine!

This was hard, really hard. In some ways, mentally tougher than boot camp. The Marines didn't have a 'Hell Week' like the Navy's BUD/S training to become a SEAL, although there was a 'Crucible' phase at boot camp. Nope, no single Hell Week, just thirteen really shitty ones.

He'd been a skinny, towheaded kid when he'd gotten through basic training, and he'd believed that he'd survived the worst that could be thrown at him.

That kid didn't know that being separated from the woman you loved grew more hellish every single day.

Maggie had only been gone for two weeks and Jack had hated every single second of them. They'd agreed to spend Christmas together with Maggie flying out to California for the holidays, but that was still three months away. Three long, lonely months with nothing but memories to hold, memories that slipped through his fingers like mist.

"Staff Sergeant Connor, you may go in."

Jack's head jerked up when he heard his name, embarrassed to have been caught daydreaming.

He nodded at the young Private First Class who was waiting to usher him in to see his Commanding Officer, Captain Joe Richmond.

Jack marched into the office and stood at attention.

"At ease. Have a seat."

"Thank you, sir."

"Well, Jack, you and me have been down a long road together, haven't we?"

"Yes, sir. Nine years, sir."

"So long? And before that?"

"Just your average grunt, sir."

Captain Richmond gave a brief smile.

Jack thought back to those early days when joining the Marine Corps had felt like the greatest adventure on earth. He'd assumed that it wouldn't be long after boot camp until he rolled right into scout sniper training, since he could outshoot every recruit he'd ever met. Instead, he'd hit his grunt unit and got hitched in a line company for his first deployment to Iraq. So it was almost two years before he got a shot at a scout sniper screening.

By then, he'd realized that there was a lot more to being a sniper than simply being a good shot. And besides, there was only one scout sniper platoon per Marine Corps infantry battalion—maybe only sixteen men among a thousand Marines and Sailors. A scout sniper had to be at the top of his game, not just physically, but mentally and professionally. Maturity was key, as snipers were trusted to operate outside the wire, sometimes well outside the range of friendly support. Every member of the team had to know their job backwards, forwards and inside-out with a strong core set of infantry skills.

And he'd done it and was proud of it, but now Jack was at a crossroads: professionally and personally. And the two important paths in his life weren't necessarily going in the same direction.

"Well, Jack, you made Gunnery Sergeant. Congratulations."

His mind jerked back to the present and he felt the wash of relief and pride flood through him. He'd hoped to hear that news, and all his colleagues had assured him that his promotion was in the bag, but still, it was fucking fantastic to hear it at last. Jack's smile was genuine and large as he stood to salute his CO.

"Thank you, sir."

Jack's head was spinning. He'd gotten his promotion. But in some ways it felt like a hollow victory without Maggie being there to share it with him.

His CO offered a brief smile.

"Here are your orders, Gunny. Do us proud."

"Yes, sir."

"Dismissed."

Jack snapped a salute and turned around, marching out the door and into the future.

Whatever that would be.

Maggie

Sweat clung to my forehead as I scraped my hair into a ponytail, feeling a momentary coolness on the back of my neck.

It didn't last. The humidity was at eighty percent and the weather app on my cell phone said 32°C. I converted the figure in my head: double it and add thirty, making ... holy shit 94°F.

And the air conditioning didn't work.

But Cairo was very different from the city that I'd expected to find. I'd read stories about Western women being harassed and foreigners being cheated, buying goods at double or triple the prices locals paid, but that hadn't been my experience so far. On the whole, I found a fascinating, bustling city where history exploded in a thousand colors, accents, religions, languages, skin tones, dress styles, car exhaust fumes and spice.

Yes, I had to remember to check the expiration dates on food and not to drink the tap water, but I found the people friendly and welcoming, eager to share their beloved city with me.

Five times a day the call to prayer rang out simultaneously from minarets across the capital, starting with *azan* at sunrise. The song-chant rose sonorously in the warm air calling the faithful, and I found it beautiful.

Cairo itself was beautiful and ugly, timeless and ruthlessly modern, and even after two weeks, it was still loud and confusing, but I was beginning to find my feet, aided and abetted by my predecessor's fixer, Asim, whom I'd inherited along with my tiny office and creaking desktop computer.

Fixers were an essential part of my new world: a local guide who could think on his feet and had hundreds of connections to make things happen. He knew who to talk to and who to avoid, who could be bribed and who shouldn't be approached. He could find a plumber or a politician and the means to get me access to them. In short, without him, I would have already failed.

Asim was a tall, slim man in his early forties who slid seamlessly between my world and his own, sometimes wearing a turban with the ubiquitous *galabiya*, a loose fitting ankle length robe, or more usually dress pants with a short sleeved shirt. Once he wore jeans, but apologized all day for being so informal.

He'd also helped me find an apartment, a tiny one-bed place, but newly decorated and without rusting pipes, which Asim seemed particularly pleased about. It was in the busy, metropolitan district of Masr el-Gedida, which reminded me of Manhattan with its restaurants, bars, gyms, and of course, a McDonald's. It was near the office too, and, Asim assured me, a safe district with low crime. It was all relative, of course.

The previous Christmas, a church next to the Orthodox cathedral in Abbaseya was attacked by Daesh supporters, killing twenty-five people. The shadow of terrorism was everywhere and I couldn't become complacent. Not when my life depended on it.

Women's clothes were more conservative and less westernized than the men's, of course, so I was cautious. I wore slacks and loose-fitting cotton shirts, and carried a headscarf in my purse at all times. Not every woman wore them, but the majority did, and it saved being stared at all the time.

Without Asim's careful guidance, life would have been a lot trickier.

Only the day before, we'd been driving through a suburb when I heard the sound of firecrackers. At least, that's what I thought it was. Asim scooted down in his seat and told me to do the same. Somewhere nearby, guns were being fired. I pulled my headscarf out of my purse without being asked and I saw Asim's dark eyes flash to me in the rearview mirror.

The gunfire started again. It was probably another riot, more people protesting against the present regime.

Asim put his foot down and got the hell out of there. I'd been a journalist long enough to know that you didn't drive into gunfire unprepared. But I didn't run away from a story either. I checked out Twitter while Asim made a quick call on his cell. Fast, accented Arabic poured from him, his eyes flicking to me the whole time.

Twenty minutes later, he'd secured me an interview with eye witnesses to the riot, a guy in his early twenties who'd managed to snap photos of armed police assaulting men with placards protesting about Russian involvement in Syria.

I paid a small fee for the pictures, then interviewed a second person to corroborate the story. My Arabic was spotty, but I was learning.

When Asim took me home, the report was sent to the *New York Times* within ten minutes.

Modern technology had its benefits.

But even with all the new stimulus and the new life, with all the hustle and bustle, and the energy needed to get up to speed with my new job, I missed Jackson. I missed him horribly. Cairo was ten hours ahead of California, so I'd be going to bed when he was taking a lunch break. His favorite time to talk was when he was finishing up for the day and I was still in my tiny apartment before leaving for work.

"Hey, baby!"

Just hearing his voice put a huge smile on my face.

"Hey, yourself! How are you?"

"Good. Missing you. How's it going?"

"Not bad. I have an appointment to interview a General in the Egyptian Army today."

"Is Asim going with you?"

"Yes, for the first part of the meeting. Probably not for the interview itself."

Jack sighed.

"I wish that guy was armed, Maggie. I can't believe that they haven't given you armed protection."

It was a constant grumble, but I knew it stemmed from Jack's concern, from his love, even though he never said the word.

"What's new in Pendleton?" I asked, changing the subject.

There was a pause and I could hear the smile in his voice when he spoke.

"I got my promotion: Gunnery Sergeant Jackson Connor, at your service."

I screamed into the phone.

"OHMIGOD! OHMIGOD! That's fantastic, Jack! Congratulations! I'm so proud of you!"

"Yeah, it's pretty good," he understated calmly.

"Pretty good? It's wonderful! Thirty is young to make Gunnery Sergeant, even I know that. It's amazing! You're amazing!"

He laughed, happy I was happy, happy to share good news.

"How does it work? Do you have a ceremony?"

"Yeah, but it's not a big deal." He paused. *"Mama and Lucy are going to fly out."*

It was a big deal, it was a huge rung up his career ladder, and I felt the leaden weight of sadness press on my chest. It was an important day for him and I wasn't going to be there.

"That's great," I said, trying to keep up my previous level of excitement and enthusiasm. "When's it taking place?"

"A week from Thursday."

I fantasized about being there, but knew it wasn't possible. I couldn't leave Cairo so soon after arriving. Besides, I had scheduled interviews with a senior politician, and it would look very bad to reschedule that at such short notice.

I tried to be happy for him. I was happy for him. I was also kind of miserable.

He picked up on my mood instantly.

"Maybe you can come to my promotion ceremony if I ever make it to Master Sergeant," he teased gently.

He was trying to make me feel better. Master Sergeant was the top rank a non-commissioned Marine could make, and it was rare. There was no guarantee he'd ever get there, although I had faith that he would.

"It's a date, Sarge," I said softly, and I meant it.

His voice held a warm, rich longing when he replied.

"You have to call me 'Gunny' now."

I tested out the word.

"Nah, sounds too much like 'gummy'. You'll always be Sarge to me."

There was silence on the other end, and I wondered if I'd insulted him without meaning to.

"I do have some other news," he said tentatively.

"Okay?"

"So ... months ago, before we ... before you left, I asked about taking leave at Thanksgiving so I could visit with Mama and Lucy. But they usually give it to the guys with families, so I didn't think I'd get it. But I did ... yeah."

"Oh!"

It would have been wonderful to spend Thanksgiving together at his mother's, sipping iced tea on the terrace, elbow to elbow, making love in the twilight. My voice wobbled when I spoke again.

"Your mother will be so happy to see you for the holidays."

He sighed.

"I didn't want to tell you before you left, because I didn't think I'd get it."

He laughed without humor.

His words trailed off and I heard his heavy exhalation of breath. I wondered if he'd been nervous about telling me. He shouldn't have been; I was happy for him, and I was going to see him at Christmas. Besides, the Cairo posting wouldn't be forever. I'd do two years—that was a reasonable amount of time.

God, *two years* without Jack.

As if he'd followed my train of thought, Jackson spoke again.

"And there's one more thing, Maggie..."

"More surprises? You do know how to give a woman a rush of blood to the head."

"Just to the head?"

"Stop it! I have to leave for work in five minutes. I don't have time for ... that."

We'd become very inventive during a couple of our late night calls. Well, late night for one of us.

He laughed heartily.

"Okay, no time for that. Well, I have a seventy-two hour pass for Thanksgiving..."

"That's wonderful, Jack! I'm so pleased they gave you time off for the holidays. You obviously weren't expecting it."

"*Kinda. But, I was wondering, how easy is it for you to get to Paris? Paris, France, not Paris, Texas, that is?*"

My breath caught in my throat.

"It's a four hour flight. Jack, what is this?"

"*I could meet you in Paris,*" he said. "*With that three-day pass, I could be there for thirty or forty hours.*"

My heart leapt with hope and longing. And then dived again. I couldn't ask that of him.

"Jack, I ... but that's so much traveling for you. And your mother will be so disappointed."

"*Just say yes, Maggie.*"

"But ... your family...? Oh, Jack! I feel terrible. I can't ask you to..."

"*Don't, sugar. I'm not sorry. I'll be able to see Mama and Lucy at my ceremony. I want to be with you for Thanksgiving. Are you in?*"

"Yes!" I said happily. "Yes! Yes, definitely! Yes, yes, YES!"

And that's how I ended up on a date with a sexy, hot Marine in one of the world's most romantic cities.

Chapter Thirteen

HOPE AND HOPELESSNESS

Seven weeks later, November

When I told Ben, the division editor for overseas correspondents that I'd be spending Thanksgiving in Paris, he sent me on a detour via the Netherlands to follow up on a story that had surfaced in Reuters the international news agency, and he wanted a more in depth exploration.

After the crazy chaotic color of Cairo, it was a different sort of culture shock landing at Schiphol airport, close to Amsterdam's city center. The wide concourses and plethora of luxury goods took some getting used to.

I hopped on the local train, which was a twenty-five minute ride downtown, scanning the posters for the Rijksmuseum and the Van Gogh Museum, wishing I was here for a little longer, but also wishing this job was out of the way so I could be hours nearer to seeing Jack.

We'd hardly managed to speak to each other at all during the intervening weeks. He'd been on exercises, with a comms blackout for much of the time. Sometimes I woke in the morning to find a short text or sometimes an email waiting for me. Mostly, I woke to the disappointment of not hearing from him at all.

I was becoming addicted to Jack, but instead of the cravings fading the longer we were away from each other, they intensified, doubling in strength every week we were apart. It wasn't a good recipe for a long-distance relationship, and that worried me.

I checked the address I'd been given, then entered the coffee shop, pulling my small wheeled suitcase behind me, and glanced around.

I immediately caught the eye of an older woman whose round smiling face was welcoming.

My interviewee was an older Dutch lady named Jacoba, living on the southern edge of the Zuidplaspolder, one of the huge manmade polders that held back the North Atlantic, less than an hour from the city.

I knew that she was seventy-three, but she looked a decade younger with her bright eyes and mostly dark hair. She stood to shake my hand, towering over me.

She caught my surprise and laughed.

"I'm the little one in my family."

I thought she was joking.

"All my sisters are taller. I'm only 1.78 meters."

I squinted, working out that she was about 5' 10".

"I'm Jacoba Visser. Thank you for coming. I was surprised when I got an email from such a prestigious newspaper as the *New York Times*. But please, call me Coby."

Her English was excellent and I keenly felt my lack of linguistic skills.

"Well, we really are interested in world news," I said, smiling at her to soften the words.

"I'm glad to hear it."

We ordered our coffees and Jacoba told me to try the *oliebollen*, the Dutch version of donuts, but with dried fruit and lemon zest, then sprinkled with powdered sugar. Heaven. I couldn't help thinking how much Jack would have enjoyed them. Despite his denial, that man had a sweet tooth.

I sat back in my chair with a pen and notepad, as well as recording our conversation on my phone, ready to hear her story.

"I was born during the War," she said. "I was very young, so sometimes I'm not sure if it's my memories or the stories I was told growing up. But we were an occupied country, the Nazis controlling us with an iron fist, and my father had a wife and baby daughter to feed. He was a blacksmith and also skilled with metalwork, an enormous man with hands like hams, very strong. The Germans needed men like him, so we were better off than many because he was of value, but by the time I came along, many of the people were starving. It was five long years before we were liberated. I've heard the stories a thousand times from my parents.

"My father used to pretend to like the Germans. By day, he'd fix things for them and by night he'd be with the Resistance blowing them up again. Very dangerous, and all the time he'd be stealing food from the Nazis. My mother told me that one time he came home with a pocketful of butter that he'd taken from the plate of SS officer at an outdoor café while his back was turned. My father could have been shot for that, but we were hungry."

Her eyes tightened as she talked, the old memories crowding out her smile.

"I was only four by the time the war ended, we were all as thin as beanpoles, skinny ghosts with bad teeth. But I do remember the casual violence, the daily struggle for survival. And I still remember the two Jewish families who lived in the village and disappeared one night, never to be seen or heard from again. I've often wondered whether they fled or were taken. Now I'll never know." She sighed. "I promised myself then that I would always support those in need, and I have. I raised my children to be givers not takers." Her large hands folded in her lap. "I supported the asylum seekers when they first came. We all did. We welcomed them, housed them, clothed them, but now ... we have too many immigrants," she said sadly. "We are a small country. We have to build polders to make new land, and we are always afraid that one day, one storm, and the sea will take our land back. But they keep coming, hundreds every week. We house them, clothe them, feed them and give them money to live. I was one of the first ones volunteering at the shelters, before we became more organized."

She shook her head.

"But now I sound like Geert Wilders, that awful man."

"What do you mean?"

Until now, I'd just listened to what she had to tell me. A good journalist knows when to ask and when to talk. Coby had a story to tell.

"Wilders is a right wing politician. He says all the migrants should go home. I used to ask, to what? To broken cities? To killing? But now ... I don't want them here anymore."

"What changed your mind?" I asked gently.

She pushed her chin out.

"It happened this summer. I was on my bicycle. It was warm out and I had shorts on. I was going to pick up vegetables from a friend who grows them. There were three of them lounging by the bus stop, drinking. And they called me a whore as I rode past. A whore! Because I had bare legs! I'm seventy-three years old! No one has ever spoken to me like that my whole life!"

Anger and hurt warred in her bright blue eyes, and she sighed.

"Where I live, it's not a remarkable town, or even very interesting. But now it's exceptional for the large numbers of dark-haired, dark-eyed young men huddled together in groups, watching the passing cars. It's not because they're Muslim," she said tiredly, "It's because they're young men without roots. They've left behind their families, their community leaders, everything they've known, and all they carry with them is their fear and anger. Go anywhere in the world and take a group of homeless young men, and you will see the same thing."

Then she looked up at me.

"But I'm old and this scares me. I don't want this in my home town. I want to cycle in my shorts in summer as I have always done. I don't want to be called a whore. They shouldn't be here if they can't respect our ways."

Her face sagged, her youthfulness drained by strong emotions.

"It's not much of a story, I know. But I am not the only one. Other women started telling me that they were afraid to travel by themselves now. I have survived a war, Miss Buckman, but now I feel like the war has come to my land again."

We talked a little more and I thanked her for her time. I didn't want to be late for my next appointment, but her words about being rootless struck a chord.

As she'd hinted, the problem wasn't just cultural dissonance, it was the lack of roots. These young men—and they were 99% young men —had been sent away to make better lives for themselves and eventually their whole families. But here, in a strange country without their traditions or their community ties, or even a common language, the guidelines for acceptable behavior had been torn away. There were few older men to govern them, no mothers, grandmothers or sisters who could remind them that half the world was female. They couldn't work and were reliant on state benefits, stuck in a cycle of boredom and frustration while Europe decided if it was possible to assimilate the 13 million migrants who had arrived over the last seven years.

I also suspected that Coby was right: large numbers of unsupervised young men of any nationality would be equally untamable in similar circumstances. Even children—I'd read *Lord of the Flies* in high school.

My next stop was to interview some of those young men in one of Amsterdam's many shelters.

I met with Pieter, one of the volunteers who worked with migrants in the city.

"I want to show you two places today, Miss Buckman, so you can see what we're up against."

The first place he took me was an abandoned office building not far from the central area near Dam Square.

"Thirty-two men live here," he said. "They moved in because otherwise they would be out on the street. We don't know the real figures, but the government says that there are 100,000 refugees and asylum seekers in my country. It could be double that—we just don't know."

He pulled aside a battered tarp and led me into the darkened building.

"There's no heating or electricity, but they have access to running water and toilets. That's all. There's nowhere to cook, so they survive by begging on the streets and on what organizations like mine can give them." He gave me a sideways look. "Sometimes they steal because they are driven by hunger. It is terrible, Miss Buckman, to be hungry."

He shook his head.

"Internationally, we are seen as a tolerant, liberal country. But the anti-immigration party is popular in the opinion polls, and the government doesn't want to attract more asylum-seekers. Now they have implemented a harsh policy, very tough, especially cruel during our freezing winter months."

"Can the men here apply for asylum?" I asked.

"One or two of them, perhaps. But the others, they're all men who have had their claims rejected. They are supposed to go back to their country of origin. But they are afraid, so they run away from the official shelters, and now they live here."

The building felt cold and damp. I saw piles of cardboard boxes that had been dragged inside to give some insulation from the coming winter. Piles of newspapers were scattered like straw, and the stale air stank of despair.

"They can't work, so they have no money. We bring them food, but there's so little we can do."

His frustration and anger bled through his words.

"Will they talk to me?" I asked, as I snapped some photographs.

Pieter nodded.

"I have arranged for you to speak to Tareq. He came from Libya, and walked or hitched from Italy. When the Jungle was torn down in Calais, he ended up here."

I'd heard about the infamous Jungle, a massive migrant camp in France, filled with thousands of men, women and children, desperate to get to Britain, but stuck on the coastline, just twenty miles from their goal. Britain didn't want them and neither did the people of Calais. Eventually, the Jungle had been torn down and the people rehomed throughout France, although I'd since read reports that many were drifting back to live rough, in the continuing hope of finding a way to slip past the guards and get to Britain. Most tried to hide in the back of trucks returning from continental Europe; a few tried to walk through the Channel Tunnel, risking being killed by the trains that thundered through—all in the belief that the streets of England would be paved with gold, or state benefits. They were often disappointed in both, but at least it was safer than where they'd come from.

Pieter rattled out some guttural Dutch to one of the men who'd been watching us with dispassionate eyes. He shook his head twice before standing up and leaving.

Frustrated, Pieter tried another man, with the same result.

He rubbed his forehead and turned to me.

"I'm sorry, Miss Buckman. They say Tareq isn't here. I don't know if that's true, but they're scared to talk to you. I've told them you're a journalist, but they're afraid it's a trick."

"None of them will talk to me?"

Pieter shook his head.

"I'm sorry, no. But I've arranged for you to visit one of the established shelters, too. Perhaps you will find a story there."

His voice was tired and cynical. I couldn't blame him for that.

He led me outside into the daylight, and I dragged the crisp, clean air into my lungs.

"No one would choose to live like that," he said bitterly. "But it's better than being sent home to die."

I watched as his hopelessness hardened into determination.

"Even though many are economic migrants and not fleeing warzones?" I questioned him.

He shrugged.

"Yes, they wish for better lives. That's all. That's why we will never stop helping them, why we push the government to do more. They run regulated emergency asylum centers, but the refugees are not allowed to cook for themselves, they have no privacy, and it is very hard for them to mix with locals. That breeds fear, on both sides. But in our shelters, run on contributions from the public, they can lead as normal lives as possible. But we are small, we only help a few and there are many."

The second place could not have been more different. The first thing I noticed was the smell of cooking and the spicy scents hanging in the air. The second was children's drawings tacked to the walls. And then I saw them, dark-eyed boys and girls whose ready smiles and rapid chatter showed their contentment. Their parents, however, seemed tired and defeated, but still proud to show me how they gained a little privacy by hanging blankets to create small rooms.

They had cooking and washing facilities here, but their frustration at being reliant was apparent.

"I was a civil engineer in Raaqa," said Nizar, speaking through an interpreter. "But when Daesh swept into the region, I was afraid for my family and for my life. We took our car and left, but when we ran out of gas, we had to leave the car. We had to leave everything. We are here with only our memories and the clothes on our back. I feel I have failed my family as a husband and father."

Tears reddened his eyes, and he wiped them away angrily.

"All I want is a future for them, but we are waiting here, waiting to see if a future will be given to us."

I thought a lot about what both Coby and Pieter had said as I took another train, heading south to Paris. I thought about what Nizar had told me and what I'd seen at both shelters. So as I wrote my story and downloaded the photographs I'd taken onto my laptop, I hardly saw the countryside as the train rushed past, until we rolled into Paris Nord station. I emailed the story to my editor, but there was no answer to the problem, no conclusion, and very little hope.

I rubbed my forehead. There's a certain dichotomy required when you're a journalist. You have to care about what's happening, you have to care about the news that you're writing, but you also have to be able to switch off. It's always a fine line between protecting yourself emotionally without suffering from compassion fatigue. I wasn't sure I'd ever got it right.

I needed a dose of my sexy Marine to bring the joy back for a few, precious days.

Chapter Fourteen

LA RUE DÉSOLÉE

Our hotel was situated halfway along La Rue Désolée, two minutes from the River Seine and a short walk from the Louvre gallery. One of my colleagues had recommended it, and I fell in love from first glance.

It was an older building, some four or five hundred years old, hidden on a back street, and as I entered, the red and gold décor mixed with old beams was at once gaudy, stylish and oddly welcoming.

The woman at the front desk greeted me.

"Bienvenue au Grand Hôtel Dechampaigne."

"Merci. Parlez vous anglais?"

"Yes, of course, *madame*. How may I help you?"

I gave her my reservation, and she smiled.

"Your friend has already arrived. Maybe one hour ago."

Shivers of desire mixed with anxiety and urgency spread through me, my heart fluttering.

She gave me the room number and a key. Not a key card, a good old fashioned key. I gripped it tightly as I entered the tiny elevator which rumbled and coughed its way up three floors. The doors wheezed open and I stepped out into a narrow, carpeted corridor with dim lighting and muted sounds, giving it a soft, romantic feel.

My heart began to beat faster as I approached our room and slid the key into the lock. The heavy door swung open silently.

Jack was lying face down on the bed, his sneakers hanging off the end, as if he'd been dropped from a great height, or perhaps too tired to kick off his shoes. I knew he'd been traveling twenty hours.

I realized with a start that one of his beautiful dark blue eyes was watching me, then he rolled over onto his back and smiled.

"Maggie."

That was all he said, my name, but spoken with such love, such peaceful joy infusing those two short syllables that it brought tears to my eyes. I climbed onto the bed and slipped into his waiting arms, snuggling against his broad chest, safe and content.

"I've missed this," I sighed.

His arms tightened around me as a reply, and we held each other, washing away the weeks apart, the longing and regret.

He dropped two soft kisses into my hair before I turned my face toward him and found his lips with my own.

Kisses turned to caresses, and touching turned to tasting, and when that wasn't enough, we shed our clothes and I felt the warm press of his skin against mine. And when he lowered himself so I felt his weight on me and in me, I felt wanted, loved and protected.

Long, languid thrusts, intense blue eyes gazing into me as I clutched his shoulders and wrapped my legs around his back.

Sweat broke out across my skin as delicious friction lit my body and I began to tremble around him, digging my nails into his deeply tanned shoulders.

His jaw tightened as he fought to bring his own body under control, but it was a battle he wouldn't win.

His hips began to thrust aggressively and my knees were pressed toward my chest, and when he slid in further, hitting a new angle, reaching a new depth, the sex went from fantastic to overwhelming as I flew apart.

He shuddered and became rigid, our bodies pressed tightly together, and then, with a satisfied sigh, he relaxed, kissing my throat and breasts affectionately as he pulled out.

I curled against his shoulder, chuckling as he mumbled something about not needing PT with me around.

My fingers trailed down his ribs, drawing thoughtful circles over old scars by his hip.

I felt lazy and satiated, content to lie here and stare out at the darkening sky.

"Waal, I gotta say," Jack said with a smile, "Paris is livin' up to its name as the most romantic city in the world."

I laughed.

"Mr. Tough Marine is getting all soft on me! Is the world still turning?"

"Not tonight, sugar. Tonight the stars will stay exactly where you hung them and the moon will do as it's damn well told."

"Spoken like a true Devil Dog."

"Ooh-rah!" Jack shifted so he could look at me. "Although I may just have reserved two tickets to go see the Eiffel Tower at night. You want to hunt down some dinner first?"

"Oh my God, yes! That sounds perfect! Thank you, Jack."

"Thank you for being you, Maggie Buckman."

I had no words for that, so I kissed him.

We couldn't see the Eiffel Tower from our room, but as soon as we stepped outside, it was like a beacon, drawing our gaze upwards. Spotlights bathed it in a pure white light, and from this distance it seemed ethereal.

"Makes a helluva radio mast," mused Jack, before taking my hand and strolling toward the river.

"That's slightly less romantic," I smiled as he grinned down at me. "Were you always like this, romantic one minute, calm and practical the next? I mean, before the Marines."

"I don't think I've changed that much. Mama would say that I'm tidier and more organized, and that the romantic side comes from her. But yeah, pretty much, although the Marines taught me a lot about patience. There's a lot of waiting. You know: *Hurry up and wait*. That happens all the time. Plus, running around screaming doesn't get the job done. We're taught not to let our fears freeze us—you gotta work through them, or work with them. You have to trust that the guy next to you has your six. That's the way it works. Shit happens," he blew out a breath. "Shit happens and then you deal."

I didn't reply because I was trying to avoid serious tonight, so I squeezed his hand and pointed out a sidewalk bistro that looked appealing.

We dined well and drank cheap Beaujolais, then walked hand in hand along the riverbank as a cool breeze blew across the water.

When we crossed the river to the Left Bank, the sidewalk was lined with artists selling everything from handmade jewelry to watercolors to large canvases in vivid Impressionist styles.

We feasted with our eyes and enjoyed every moment of intimacy as we created special memories together.

The lines at the Tower weren't long, and we were soon gliding up to the second landing place, then gazing out at the Paris landscape.

We watched the red and white car lights flowing down the wide boulevards, and gazed at the classical lines of the Louvre splendidly lit, and the gothic beauty of Notre-Dame cathedral. Then we shuffled round to the northern-facing platform and a guide pointed out the Moulin Rouge and Arc de Triomphe.

There was so much history here, so many centuries of stories told and lives lived. It made me nostalgic for something I'd never had and vividly alive at the same time. I leaned into the safe circle of Jack's arms as we shared this moment of magic.

"It's really somethin'," he said, "but I can't help thinking it's even better seeing it with you."

And this time I had no witty comeback, because I felt exactly the same.

We kissed at the top of the Eiffel Tower, making more memories that would last a lifetime.

Then we made our way back down, stopping at the base of the tower to drink bitter black coffee and buy matching tourist t-shirts that said, '*Je t'aime Paris*'.

Living in New York, I was used to walking around a city at night, but Paris was different. The streets weaved in and out, and few were built on straight lines. Every block revealed something new and wonderful, an old building, an art gallery, kebab stands and Moroccan cuisine, or shops selling French chocolate. Each was new and wonderful, and I could have spent weeks exploring every nook and cranny.

We wandered back across the river and thought about going to the Folies Bergère, but decided strolling around was more enjoyable.

We were heading toward the Pompidou Centre, renowned for its curious modern construction, when we found ourselves outside the Bataclan theater. I stopped and stared, realizing what the floral tributes meant.

The theater was really nothing more than a large café-bar with a concert venue and dance hall. It was so pretty, decorated in a colorful Chinoiserie style, and I knew it was over 150 years old. But now it was most famous as being the place where eighty-nine music lovers were gunned down in an appalling act of terrorism on Friday 13th, November 2015.

Jackson's lips pressed together and he pulled me tighter against him.

I shivered, a tremor that was nothing to do with the creeping cold.

"Sometimes it seems like the whole world is on fire," I said, my voice low and despondent.

Jack didn't speak, because what was there to say?

We stood in silence, paying our respects, then walked away, his arm around my shoulders, keeping me close.

When we made love again that night, we clung to each other fiercely, and I wondered how our lives would continue after this moment. Would we travel together, or were our roads leading us in different directions?

I didn't have the answers. I wanted love to find a way … but I was beginning to think it would need a helping hand.

I'd never thought I'd choose a man over my career, but the powerful feelings that coursed through me every time we were together, they were growing louder and more demanding.

In that Paris bed, with Jack sleeping peacefully beside me, I knew.
I knew.
I'd met the love of my life.
And I wasn't letting him go.

Chapter Fifteen

CITY OF PEACE, BAY OF TROUBLES

Of course, life doesn't work like that—'work' being the operative word. We both had lives to return to, our real lives. Being in Paris, painted with the romance of the city, it was a perfect, rose-tinted bubble, but it couldn't last. Less than forty hours after Jack had arrived, he had to fly back to San Diego, and I flew in the opposite direction, home to Cairo.

The heat seemed even more oppressive after the cool, crisp air of Paris in the fall. The changing leaves in the City of Lights had suited our increasingly somber mood. I wondered if we'd ever visit there in the springtime. I wondered how Jack and I could ever have a real, lasting relationship.

Something would have to give.

But for now, at least, I was back at work.

My next assignment was in Sharm El Sheikh. A city on the southern tip of the Sinai Peninsula, it had been one of the jewels in Egypt's thriving tourist trade.

With glittering white buildings, soft breezes and a perfect climate, Sharm sat prettily on the Red Sea, a favorite place for beach vacations and those who enjoyed snorkeling, scuba diving and any variety of watersports. The sea sparkled, sunlight glinting on the water, a picture-postcard turquoise lapping up to pale, gleaming sand.

Millions of visitors from all over the world arrived every year, boosting the tourist industry profits to record heights.

Until Flight 9268 exploded midair on October 31st 2015, with the loss of 224 lives. Crash investigators eventually agreed with the clamoring and bereft relatives of the many dead that an improvised bomb aboard the aircraft was responsible for the disaster. ISIS, known locally as Daesh, were proud to accept responsibility.

All across the world, flights to this popular resort were canceled and the grand hotels with their beautiful beaches stood empty.

Thousands of local people lost their livelihoods, and to date, more than eighty hotels had closed.

A few intrepid tourists were beginning to drift back, many from Saudi and Kuwait, but the Europeans were far fewer in number. Immediately after the terror attack, a worldwide travel ban had been sanctioned by nervous governments. Most countries had now lifted that, although the British were still banning flights to Sharm.

I had been invited to stay at the magnificent Four Seasons, a large building of white stucco and elegant Moorish arches, its tall palms providing shelter across the broad, baking sands. But the four swimming pools were almost devoid of visitors, and everywhere small discreet signs revealed the guilty truth:

20% off diving activities
30% off boat trips
40% off watersport activities.

Their desperation for business was palpable, hungry for every tourist dollar that came their way.

I dined alone that night, and even though the food was exceptional, a painful hollow in my chest made my stomach ache, and I missed Jack painfully. Too many waiters hovering around me, urgently wishing me a pleasant and relaxing visit, left me irritated and depressed. Once word went out that I was a journalist, they begged me to write a story about how beautiful, how special, how cheap it was to vacation here. Which was all true. But with armed guards patrolling the resort, it was hard to say that I felt truly safe. What I would have given for Jack's calm, reassuring presence beside me. But he was many thousands of miles away, and I felt more alone than ever.

My assignment was to interview the Egyptian minister for tourism, a round-faced man in a Western business suit with a ready smile.

His eyes tightened at the mention of the continuing British ban.

"More than 1.5 million British visitors came to Egypt in 2010," he said, visibly aggravated. "This year we expect it will be fewer than 300,000 persons."

He insisted that security had been increased, private firms hired to protect the intrepid who dared to travel; but still visitors didn't return in their previous numbers. And I could see the effects of that loss of income all around.

Everyone was so desperate to tell me what a wonderful place Sharm was, how friendly, how perfect for a relaxing vacation.

But I couldn't help noticing that the few vacationers I met were loath to move beyond the secure and gated resort. In fact, to move beyond the city limits into Sinai required a separate visa.

The few British I did meet were all repeat visitors and had been coming to Sharm for years. They were aware that they traveled without support of their Foreign Office and hadn't been able to purchase travel insurance.

"I feel more secure in Sharm than I do in London," said Ken, a fifty-two year old taxi driver. "How many terrorist attacks have there been in Paris? No one's stopping me from going to France."

I admitted that I'd recently been there, and Ken fixed his eyes on me.

"Is anywhere really safe?" he asked.

He introduced me to his friend Emad who owned a café in the resort that could seat a hundred people, where tourists used to come to sip ice-cold fruit juice or puff on a *shisha* pipe. Only two tables were taken.

"Everything has slowed down. We have no income. Prices have gone up and our currency has been devalued twice."

He shook his head and went on to tell me that the family business of producing rice, honey and sugar had foundered. There was no hard currency to purchase the raw materials they needed.

Everywhere, ordinary people were struggling. And they were angry: angry at the government, angry at Daesh, angry at the tourists for not coming back. I wondered, not for the first time, whether that resentment and lack of money allowed ISIS to fill the vacuum of desperation and need.

The visit left me even more depressed and also doubtful of the value of my work. The slow, dragging disease of hatred seemed to seep into everything. And yet, it was truly a beautiful resort with a wonderful climate, and the people I'd met were genuine, warm and friendly. In the months that I'd been here, I'd grown to love Egypt.

Love: that little word with the largest meaning.

I thought once again that most people just want to live a good life, a full life, with their family safe around them. Was it so much to ask?

And what about me? What about my life? Was my career worth keeping me away from Jackson, the man I loved?

I thought back to the conversation we'd had just before leaving Paris.

We'd spent the evening walking along the Champs Elysée and drinking in a tiny bar where tourists seldom ventured. Then, slightly less than sober, I'd taken Jack to bed and showed him how an American in Paris behaved in the City of Love.

And then Jackson had flipped me onto my back with ease and had come with pounding, staccato thrusts that reminded me of Berlioz's *Symphonie Fantastique*. Although at the time, I wasn't able to think so clearly or make the comparison: that was much later.

Then, when I was weak and vulnerable, he'd ambushed me.

"Do you want kids, Maggie?"

His question caught me off balance and a little fearful. We'd never discussed this before, and his question seemed to have come out of the blue. But I also thought that it was perhaps something he'd been mulling over, and surprised himself by blurting it out a second after pouring himself into me and rolling from my overheated body.

"I've never thought much about it," I answered cautiously, still out of breath.

Before I'd met Jack that would have been an honest answer, but being with him had made me think all sorts of things I'd never considered before.

He seemed disappointed and looked away, sitting up and taking a long drink of water from the glass sweating on the bedside table.

"I'd always imagined having a large family," he said mildly, before swinging his penetrating gaze my way. "Life is short, Maggie."

I hadn't known what to say, so I gave him a weak smile and made some dumb comment about his kids having great genes.

He smiled back, but it didn't reach his eyes. We both knew that I'd deliberately chosen my words when I said '*your* kids'.

He hadn't mentioned it again, but he wasn't the kind of man to sulk either, and he didn't show through word or deed that he was disappointed in me. Maybe I was disappointed in myself.

I was rarely an impulsive person. I was a thinker and a planner. That's not to say that I was too rigid to follow a story when it went in an unexpected direction. And Jack had very neatly hacked a new path to my heart, flailing aside all my careful plans. His words stayed with me, and I mulled them over, letting them sink inside.

As I sat watching the enormous globe of sun setting behind the glowing waters of Sharm El Sheikh, I turned his words over and over, like pebbles on a beach, searching for the perfect one, the most beautiful. They terrified me and charmed me, the future becoming misty. Was that what he truly wanted? A large family? Did he imagine a house full of children, a minivan, and a dog? Did he imagine camping trips and backyard barbecues?

All things I'd never had and never wanted.

I had a one-bedroom apartment in Greenwich Village and didn't even own a car. I'd never had pets, not even a goldfish, and plants died regularly with lack of watering, by reason of forgetfulness or absence.

What he wanted, what I thought he was offering, was so different from the direction I'd assumed my life would go.

After he'd mentioned children, I'd avoided having 'the talk' while we were in Paris, and it was entirely due to my own cowardice. It was all so wonderful, so perfect, so utterly romantic, that tackling the thorny question of our future—and possibly uncovering new holes in our relationship—wasn't something I wanted to do, risking spoiling our brief time together.

But I knew that conversation was coming. I wasn't a naïve 18 year old. I'd seen too much, experienced too many things, and I did want to get to the bottom of what Jack really wanted, what I wanted. But maybe because I'd seen so much of misery, pain and poverty, I was happy to spend our time in Paris in an unassailable bubble of love and hope.

Returning to Cairo alone, I'd sought distraction in my work, immersion in the problems of the Egyptian people and the wider Arab world.

But I couldn't deny that my heart was no longer my own, instead hovering in the care of a blue-eyed US Marine, a man who challenged and tested me, who loved me.

I was in one of the most beautiful places I'd ever visited, an all-expenses paid trip to a five-star hotel, doing my dream job and hoping to make a difference as I did it. But I was sitting alone, and while that had never felt lonely before, it did now.

And when I thought about it, didn't that tell me everything I needed to know?

Maybe I could be a mother and still work as well. Others did it. My good friend Lee was a successful journalist despite having three children and a husband who was a veteran of the Marines. Sebastian had settled down and now ran his own thriving business. So why couldn't Jack?

The difference was that Lee had always wanted kids.

Part of me insisted on burying my head in the sand. *We'll cross that bridge when we come to it*, I told myself.

Because more than anything, I wanted Jack.

More than anything.

I sighed.

My editor would be so disappointed. And part of me was disappointed in myself, too. After all, I'd achieved everything I'd been working for my entire adult life, only to find that the achievement was not as fulfilling as it should be, as I wanted it to be.

It wasn't an easy decision, because my head was fighting my heart, but in the end it was an unequal battle.

I'd give Dean Baquet a month to find my replacement. Then I was going home.

To Jack.

I arrived back at my apartment in Cairo hot, tired and longing for air conditioning that worked. While I'd come to love Egypt, there were a lot of things that I missed about home—reliable utilities being one of them.

I dropped my bags in the corner and pulled a bottle of water out of the fridge, relieved that the ancient device was still working as it grumbled and complained, coughing at irregular intervals.

My phone was dead, the 'no service' message tucked into the upper corner of the screen, which meant the local transmitter was probably being repaired again, but at least my Wifi was working, thank God.

And when I checked my emails, there was a message from my old friend and colleague Marc Lebuin. I'd only had one short message from him since our dramatic exodus from Zataari, and it would be great to catch up with him.

He was in Cairo for a couple of days and he'd reserved us a table at *Abou El Sid*, an upscale restaurant that catered to locals as well as visitors seeking an authentic, if refined, experience.

I wasn't thrilled with the idea of showering and going right back out into the heat again, but talking everything over would be useful. And Marc was a good friend.

When I arrived, late and rather sweaty, Marc leapt to his feet, hugging me happily and kissing me three times in the European style.

"*Ma belle,* MJ! How are you?"

He looked elegantly casual in light linen slacks and a long-sleeved white shirt. When I'd last seen him in Jordan, he'd been covered in dirt and lined with grief after our horrendous experiences and close call with the Grim Reaper.

Now he looked like he'd stepped out of a *GQ* fashion shoot.

Sometimes the contradictions of our lives were hard to reconcile.

We caught up on each other's news, chatted about old friends, and dined on *Kafta* and Shrimp *Rajin*.

I didn't have room for dessert, but Marc ordered *Fetir* with mixed nuts and honey.

And then I told him about my thoughts, my plans for the future.

Marc's eyebrows went through his carefully arranged hairline.

"MJ, what you're talking about is career suicide!"

I bristled at his disapproval.

"Maybe I just want to live my own life instead of writing about other people's."

He shook his head.

"It won't be your own life: if you follow him to San Diego, it will be *his* career, *his* friends, *his* life, not yours."

His words blasted holes through my newborn certainties.

Sensing my hesitation, Marc sniffed blood and went for the kill.

"*Mon Dieu!* Have you worked so hard all of these years to build up your portfolio, earn the respect of your colleagues, your editor and your readers, to go bury yourself in a military life with a man you've just met? Has *he* offered to give it all up? Has *he* offered to stop being a Marine?"

"No, but..."

"Then why should you?"

"I don't have to give it all up. I can write just as well from the west coast."

"Can you? And what about Cairo? This is your dream job? This is what you've been working for! Ever since I first met you, this was your goal!"

I gave him a small smile.

"It's not my dream anymore."

He tossed his napkin onto the table in disgust.

"Bah! Love makes fools of us all. I suppose it is God's way of leveling the playing field."

Which, I think, was Marc's acquiescence.

"At least tell me that your Marine is good-looking," he grumbled.

"Very."

And I showed him a picture on my phone.

Marc's eyebrows shot up again, and this time they stayed there.

"*Quel beau gosse!* Does he have a friend?"

"Yes, but not your type."

"I disagree. All men who look like that are my type."

"I'll tell him you said so."

"Well then, I approve. Go be Mrs. Marine and live that life, but don't forget your old friend Marc when you invite all those beautiful military men to your beach parties."

When I arrived back at my apartment, there was no electricity, no wifi and still no phone signal. Sighing, I lay naked on top of the sheets, sweltering in the sultry heat as I listened to the voices on the busy street outside, calling in Arabic, French, and some African languages that I couldn't even guess at.

The power came on at 3AM, forcing me to get up to turn off the lights. And it was only then that I saw a text message from Jackson on my phone.

Hey, Maggie,

I hope the Sharm trip was good. Did you get any snorkeling in? Can't work all the time, sugar.

I really wanted to hear your sexy voice, but your phone is off, so I'm doing it the old fashioned way and texting. Why do they make keyboard screens so damn small on these phones?

Call me any time. I got my phone right next to me just so I can hear your sweet voice.

Gotta run.

Love you, Jack x

I smiled, stupidly happy to read his words.

But just as I was calculating the time in California and I'd picked up my cellphone to call him, a bulletin from Reuters news agency popped into my inbox.

. . .

GUNMAN ATTACKS U.S. MILITARY BASE.
THREE MARINES KILLED.

Horrified, my heart hammering, adrenaline shaking my body, I dialed Jack's number.

The phone rang and rang and rang. Then I got his voicemail.

I called back, nerves tightening my throat as the phone continued to ring. This time I left a message.

"Jack, it's Maggie. I need to know you're okay. I just heard about the attack on a US military base. I need to know you're safe. Please call me as soon as you can. I love you."

But he didn't call back and I didn't hear from him.

I turned to my computer, jittery as I scanned the news agencies for updates.

All I could learn was that a lone gunman was killed after he'd gunned down three Marines at a military base in California. Oh my God, in California!

But which Base?

And which Marines?

I searched the growing number of reports for an hour as I tried to find out more details. I learned that the attack had happened at Camp Pendleton, Jack's base ... and he still wasn't answering his calls.

Hands shaking, I bought a ticket to San Diego.

Chapter Sixteen

TRIAL BY FIRE

I waited impatiently for a cab to take me to Cairo International Airport, clutching my phone and passport in one hand, and a small carry-on bag in the other.

The talkative taxi driver ignored my rudely monosyllabic answers to his friendly chatter.

Behind me, the sun was climbing above the horizon, suffusing the light with a soft pink haze as heat began to rise from the dusty sidewalks.

In the driver's rearview mirror, my tanned skin looked pale, my eyes huge, my mouth etched deeply with lines of fear.

I glanced at my phone, constantly refreshing the news page, but none of the news was good.

The death toll had risen to four and there were reports coming through of several wounded. When I saw a live news report from Pendleton, my heart skipped a beat and I felt a sudden swooping sensation in my stomach.

I swallowed down the panicked tears that threatened and I clutched my phone tighter, feeling the edges digging into the palm of my hand as I forced myself not to faint.

If I pass five red cars, Jack will be safe...

If I see two camels on the way to the airport, Jack will be safe...

I'd tried to make the same sort of deal when my mother was dying of cancer in the hospital. It hadn't worked then, but maybe now...

I prayed once more.

Oh God, I'll never take life for granted again if you'll just save Jack...

But you can't make deals with God, the Angels, or Death himself.

Security at the airport was tight. Improved drastically in the last two years, as well as soldiers with rifles there were armed private security, the men hard-eyed, with fingers resting by their triggers. They reminded me of the first time I'd met Jack, his skin yellowed with Afghan dust, shouting orders to his platoon as he saved my life from a baying mob. Later, calm and detached, and then back at base camp, thunderous with anger that I'd put myself and his men at risk.

Amidst death, I had found life; I'd found a man who cared. And yet, afraid to commit completely, I'd let the miles between us increase.

Oh God, please let me see him again. Don't let the best part of my life be behind me.

As my cell phone, coat, shoes and carry-on bag trundled through the airport's X-ray machine, I strode confidently through the scanner, only to hear it beep loudly.

Perplexed, I put my hands in my pockets in case I'd left change in them that could have set off the alarm.

A security guard shouted at me to raise my hands and pointed his rifle at me threateningly. Shocked, I thrust my hands in the air as a second guard approached me cautiously, his black eyes narrowed with distrust.

Then a female security guard in a black *hijab* was summoned and proceeded to pat me down roughly, feeling around my waistband, armpits, thighs, the under-wiring of my bra and backs of my legs.

When there was nothing to find, the woman stepped back, staring at me unsmilingly.

Then they forced my hands into another scanner. I thought at first that they were checking my fingerprints, but they weren't.

Again, the scanner beeped, and the rifles swung towards me. By now, I was sweating, looking guilty as hell, and watching the clock tick down toward the time my flight was boarding.

"I have to catch a flight," I said, my voice shaking.

"One minute."

"It's important."

"One minute."

The guards muttered to each other, then one of them stepped forward and swabbed the palms of my hands.

"We look for bomb-making chemicals," he explained curtly.

I didn't know what to say. Wisely, I kept my mouth shut. If the worst came to the worst, I could use my connections at the *New York Times* to get me out of here.

A careful search was made of my bag and shoes. The lining was cut out of my coat, the seams minutely examined.

I had seven minutes to catch my flight.

Despite the air conditioning, sweat dripped into my eyes, making them sting, my t-shirt was soaked and my hands shook.

And then they found something, their voices louder and excitable, and suddenly my travel-size hand lotion was seized and tossed onto the table. More swabs were taken, and the guards relaxed as they read the results.

I could have cried with relief when an unsmiling guard told me that some of the chemicals in the lotion, probably the glycerin, mimicked bomb-making equipment.

How many miles had I traveled with that in my bag?

I didn't know whether to be relieved, amused, or furious, but when I was permitted to leave, I didn't bother to argue. I scooped up my torn jacket, bag and shoes, and sprinted in my socks across the terminal to my gate, arriving just as the last passenger was boarding.

Gasping for breath, still trembling, hot and sweaty, I settled into my seat next to a man in a *jalabiyyah* robe and headscarf. He certainly wasn't happy to see me or to be seated next to a woman who was also a foreigner, and complained loudly to one of the air stewards until he was moved to another seat.

I was too relieved I'd made the flight to care.

Now, I had the unbearable task of waiting for news of Jack: twenty hours of traveling ahead of me with two stops before I reached San

Diego. The Turkish Airways flight had a stop-over at Istanbul and I also changed planes in Los Angeles.

The engines rolled like thunder and I was ordered to turn off my phone. I hoped that there would be wifi once we were in the air. I hoped for a lot of things.

Jackson

Ten hours earlier...

Jack sat at his desk, glancing at his phone every few minutes, willing it to ring, willing Maggie to call. He was aware that his behavior was both amusing and annoying the guys in his platoon, and he'd had to endure a lot of cracks about being pussy-whipped. Not that he cared. He told them that they were all a bunch of damned losers and jealous as hell. Which was half true.

The men who'd been with him in Afghanistan all admired Maggie's bravery and the fact that she hadn't crumbled or cried when they'd been tasked to extract her from a life-threatening situation. They appreciated even more that she'd come to thank them personally for saving her life. The fact that they thought she was hot also gave Jack brownie points, although he'd threatened them with immediate pain followed by punishment duties if they mentioned her tits or ass again.

At the time, naturally, there had been a lot of grumbling about dumb reporters being where they shouldn't be and expecting a bunch of grunts to save their asses, but it was mostly pretty good-tempered.

Seeing their Sergeant (now Gunnery Sergeant) fall head over heels in love with her was an added bonus. But they all agreed he was definitely pussy-whipped.

Jack sighed, unenthusiastically punching his keyboard with two fingers and willing the pile of paperwork to self-combust. He hadn't joined the Marines to be a paper-pusher. Unfortunately, the higher up he was promoted, the more paperwork seemed to be involved. He'd known long ago that he'd made the right decision not to apply for officer training school—he'd have drowned in paper by now.

He decided it must be some sort of hubris that had gotten him hitched to a lady journalist—someone who made their living with words and reams of paper.

Jack frowned. He wasn't hitched to Maggie, not in the legally binding sense of marriage, but he'd certainly been thinking about it a lot.

He'd planned to pop the question in Paris, but when he'd impulsively asked her about having kids, she'd made it pretty clear that it wasn't on her agenda. Jack had made a tactical retreat and kept the ring that he'd bought with his last month's wages in his pocket.

Not a man usually given to self-doubt, Jack had begun second-guessing Maggie's every phone call, text and email.

She said she loved him, but then so had Emmy. He found himself wondering with surprising bitterness whether Maggie would turn out to be one of those women who loved the uniform, who loved the idea of having a Marine for a boyfriend, but when faced with long months apart, decided that a man on civvy street was a safer bet.

Maggie had never seemed like that—it was one of the things that had attracted him to her in the first place—that and her bravery, the way her dark eyes flashed when she was angry, the passion hidden behind the professional appearance. It seemed inconceivable that he'd misread her, but ever since Paris, a dark cloud of doubt had hung over him and consequently over their relationship.

Now she wasn't even answering her damn phone and he'd left a text message hours ago.

He'd never wished his judgement was unsound before, but he'd woken up with a bad feeling in his gut. His gut was rarely wrong.

The temperature was in the high sixties, but the humidity was increasing and the air zinged with electricity, thunder threatening in the distance.

Droplets of sweat beaded his forehead in the stuffy office, and he stared with distaste at the mountain of paperwork still to climb.

Morning PT had been the highlight of his day so far. He'd hoped to speak with Maggie, but there'd been only silence stretching dully throughout the whole day. It was nine in the evening in Cairo—surely she was back from her assignment by now?

He poked his phone again, glaring at it moodily when there was still no word from his woman. The screen dimmed and he frowned as he realized that the battery life was down to five percent. Damn thing was always running out of juice. He really needed to get a new cell phone, one whose battery life was longer than a PT session. Searching for the charger in the desk drawer, he cursed furiously when he couldn't find it, then remembered he'd left it in his room after using it the night before.

Edgy and miserable, Jack forced himself to focus on form-filling and filing.

Two minutes later, he yawned, stretching his tanned arms above his head and deciding a stroll around the base in the winter sunshine and an early lunch would improve his outlook. And he'd pick up his charger. Nothing to do with hoping to hear from Maggie. Of course not.

Suddenly, a too familiar, too ugly noise tore the air ... *ak-ak-ak* ... *ak-ak-ak* ... the distinctive, unmistakable sound of a Kalashnikov. Without thinking, pure instinct driving his movements, Jack threw himself face down on the concrete floor as the echo of exploding bullets sang close by.

His brain could barely compute hearing an enemy weapon fired on home turf, although his body had recognized it instantly and responded.

The concrete was hard and cool as he listened to the relentless clatter of bullets, stunned.

"Christ, it's on auto mode," he whispered. "About four hundred yards away. Shit, that's the main gate!"

Keeping his head down, he sprinted to the locked metal weapons room where he kept his rifles and sidearm. His fingers hovered lovingly over his M40 sniper rifle, but it would be less useful in close quarters. Instead, he snatched up the M4 carbine, loaded in a magazine and put another four in his pocket. *I still miss my M16*, he thought irrelevantly.

He slapped on his OTV outer tactical vest and helmet before he ran toward the noise. By now he could hear fire being returned and the wail of an alarm.

Then there was a pause of maybe a minute before he heard more

AK47 shots from a different direction. He already knew what that meant: the enemy was mobile and on the move.

Jack changed direction and ran toward the gunfire.

He was close now and he sucked in his breath when he saw the body of a young Private, blood pouring from a chest wound, arms flung open as his sightless eyes stared at the massing clouds.

Jack swore softly and even though he knew the kid was dead, he knelt down and pressed two fingers to his throat, searching for a pulse. Nothing.

He locked down his emotions, training taking over.

Moving cautiously now, using every inch of cover, he eased forward.

Then he saw the enemy: a man in green fatigues and dark glasses, jumping from a Marine-issue M1163 light strike vehicle and strolling across the baking tarmac of the parade ground.

"Halt! Lower your weapon!" yelled Jack.

The AK47 swung toward him, the muzzle looming largely.

Jack didn't hesitate. He squeezed off three rounds, watching with cool professionalism as the enemy's weapon jerked, emptying a bloom of bullets in his direction.

Jack turned to take cover, slipped in blood and crashed to his knees.

Maggie

I couldn't sleep during the long flight from Cairo. After ten years as a journalist, I'd learned to catnap anywhere, but this time my brain whirred and spun as I searched every news website, trying desperately to find out if Jack was okay. But the news was grim and gave me no comfort.

Logically, I knew the odds weren't bad—tens of thousands of Marines were stationed at Camp Pendleton, but my stubborn heart feared the worst as well as desperately hoping for the best.

There were now four confirmed dead and multiple wounded mentioned in the news reports, but as with standard reporting practice, no names had been circulated to the Press until the families had been informed.

I had horrified visions of a Casualty Notification Officer waiting on the porch at Evelyn's house, a folded flag in his hands. I tried to assess how much time had passed because I knew it was a standing rule that the family had to be informed within four hours. That window was long gone, but still no names were being released.

What did that mean?

As I finally staggered off the plane at San Diego International Airport, dry eyes scratchy in the winter sunshine, I switched on my phone and immediately dialed Jack's number. Once again, it rang and rang and rang. When I still couldn't reach him, I was desperate enough to call his mother. I punched in Evelyn's number, but the line went to voicemail, and I left an incoherent message, begging her to call me back.

I hurried over to the car rental desk but had to wait twenty agonizing minutes while the clerk slowly tapped on her keyboard, yawning and taking sips of coffee, telling me happily that all the midsize and larger cars had already been taken by journalists flying into town, and that she'd try to find me a compact.

Fuming, but refusing to lose my temper, I drank a cup of coffee from a machine and waited while she filled in form after form, until she finally took my credit card and handed over the keys to a tiny Toyota.

I wouldn't have cared if it had two wheels, as long as it had an engine. I flung my bag onto the back seat, set up GPS on my phone and headed north.

The muggy heat was oppressive after the air conditioned airport. I gripped the steering wheel, pushing the speed limit as I sped up the I-5. I nearly swerved into the concrete divider when my phone rang.

"Evelyn! Thank God! Is there any news?"

Her softly modulated voice was strained.

"No, darlin'. Jackson isn't answering his phone and I can't get through to anyone on the base. I even called his friend, Gray, hoping he might be able to help. He promised to call all their mutual friends, but he says the base is on lockdown, and so far, nothing. I'm so sorry not to be able to tell you more. It must be awful for you being so far away. What time is it in Egypt?"

"I'm not in Egypt, I'm in San Diego."

"Excuse me?"

"I flew out as soon as I heard the news. I'm on my way to Camp Pendleton now. I should be there in thirty minutes."

I heard a sharp intake of breath and then her voice cracked as she struggled to hold in tears.

"You'll find out for me, Maggie? You'll tell me that my boy is going to be okay?"

"I will, Evelyn, I promise."

"Thank you, sweetheart. God bless you."

As the call ended, I accelerated past a BMW, the line on the speedometer touching a hundred.

I only took my foot off the accelerator when I saw a sign for Camp Pendleton, and only then because I was following a convoy of three news vans.

Camp Pendleton was built on a wide strip of coast by the mouth of the Santa Margarita River. Beyond the base stretched dunes and bluffs, sage scrub and chaparral. With seventeen miles of coast and over two-hundred square miles, the place was massive.

A hot wind blew off the ocean and black clouds rumbled ominously, reflecting my mood.

I parked the Toyota at the side of the road and clipped my Press badge to my jacket. A small crowd of outside broadcast journalists were standing around making notes, or speaking on their cell phones. Several were giving live on-camera reports. A short distance away a news chopper hovered well outside the base's no-fly zone.

"What's the latest?" I asked a woman whose perfect makeup told me she was a TV journalist. "Have they announced the names yet?"

"Nope," she said, glancing appraisingly at my wrinkled clothes. "The whole base is still on lockdown because of the bomb."

Blood drained from my face and I felt icy cold.

"What bomb? I haven't heard anything about that—I've been on a plane for the last twenty hours."

She raised her eyebrows and flipped open her notebook to check her facts, although I suspected she knew them off by heart.

"The suspect killed two Marines on duty at each gate, smashed through the barriers in a military vehicle—we're not sure what type yet, or whether the vehicle was stolen or belonged to the suspect. He then drove around the base, killing two more Marines and wounding a dozen. Three are in a serious condition with life-threatening injuries and..." she paused. "Are you okay, honey? You're awful pale."

I blinked back tears as I gritted my teeth. Breaking down wouldn't help anyone. But her unexpected kindness had pushed me to the edge.

"I ... my boyfriend is here. I can't get through to him."

Her eyes widened with concern, and she took my arm gently.

"Why don't you sit in our van for a moment, it's cooler in there. I'll get you some water. Where have you traveled from?"

I sat on the passenger seat of her team's Outside Broadcast truck and gratefully gulped down some water.

"I'm with the *New York Times*," I said once I'd cleared the dust from my throat and swallowed the lump that was constricting it. "I'm stationed in Cairo, but when I heard and couldn't get through ... I had to come ... I had to."

She smiled sympathetically and patted my arm, her forehead creased with concern.

"All I can tell you is that there was a report that the suspect's vehicle had some sort of improvised device attached. There weren't any explosions, but there's sure been a lot of movement. Should I go on?"

I nodded so quickly I must have looked like my head was on a spring.

"Yes, please! God, please!"

"So, one of the Marines took out the suspect, killed him. But when they went to check his vehicle, they saw it was filled with explosives, possibly some sort of fertilizer and God knows what else. We were moved back to here at that point. The bomb disposal team arrived in minutes from somewhere else on the base. It was several hours before the device was rendered safe, but they're checking the whole base to see if the terrorist, whoever he was, had time to plant any other devices. There's a lot of base to check. That's why they're still on lockdown, and that's why we're all waiting out here like bumps on a log. And now you know everything we do."

"Thank you. I appreciate that."

"The *New York Times*, huh? Do you know Lee Venzi? Her husband was a Marine."

"Yes! She's a friend of mine. Where do you know her from?"

"I did a piece on her husband and his charity work. We met then. Lovely couple."

She eyed me thoughtfully.

"How about I interview you? It would make a nice companion piece, the worried girlfriend who's flown halfway around the world. It's kind of romantic—our viewers would love that. And it might persuade the authorities to give you info on your man," she added craftily.

She certainly knew which buttons to press, but I couldn't blame her for that.

"Maybe later."

"Come on. It's not like you've got anything better to do. And it might help. Besides, if you can't get through on your cell phone, it would be a great way of letting him know that you're here. They're gonna be watching the news in the base, see how it's being played out, and if we've found any new information."

It seemed unlikely that Jack was going to have time to watch the news, but it was worth a try. Tired and worried, I gave in.

"Fine. I'll do it."

She brightened immediately.

"Great!"

She took some details from me, asking all the right questions. Even though I wasn't firing on all cylinders, I recognized a professional when I saw one, although it wasn't my style to do the emotional 'how are you feeling now?' stories.

Then she carefully combed her silky blonde hair and added a fresh layer of gloss to her already shiny lips before summoning her cameraman. Beside her I looked like a homeless person, but she said that would add to the pathos of the story and I was past caring.

"We good?" she asked the cameraman who nodded and started to record.

She pulled her face into the 'serious but sympathetic' expression that all TV reporters seem to know instinctively.

"I'm outside Camp Pendleton, scene of the appalling terrorist massacre of four Marines, and as the numbers of the wounded continue to rise, our hearts go out to the loved ones who are left wondering if it's their parent, brother or sister, or even their child who lies among the fallen. One of those awaiting devastating news is here with me today. And as a leading reporter on the *New York Times*, Margaret Buckman is usually behind the camera on a news story, since she's based in the Middle East, one of the most dangerous places in the world..."

She was really piling on the emotions.

"But Margaret ... known to her friends as Maggie ... has just flown for twenty hours, over 8,000 miles, because her boyfriend, Gunnery Sergeant Jackson Connor, is here at Camp Pendleton. Like many other families, she awaits news of her loved one."

She pushed the microphone toward me.

"How are you feeling, Maggie?"

"Shocked and worried," I answered honestly. "I know the military has protocols to follow, but not knowing ... it's unbearable." I took a deep breath. "I have to hope for the best."

"Where did you two meet?"

As I told her our story, her eyes grew bigger, pleased with the direction her scoop was taking her. I didn't begrudge her—she was only doing her job.

"Jack's mother Evelyn and his sister Lucy are at home in Gulfport, Mississippi, waiting for news, too."

She brought the microphone back to her mouth as the cameraman swung toward her.

"As the clock ticks down, we can only hope that Maggie's Marine comes home, but already knowing as we do that four families will be mourning the loss of their loved one tonight. This is Heather Lake, Camp Pendleton, San Diego for Fox 5 News."

Her words cut me to the heart. If Jack lived it was because someone else had died. I had to walk away as hot, angry tears leaked from my eyes.

Chapter Seventeen

THE ROAD HOME

Jack's eyes burned with tiredness but he had a job to do.

He'd taken a man's life. A man who wanted to kill him, a man who'd already killed four men, but a life nevertheless.

He felt empty, emotionless, with the great weariness that comes from running on adrenaline without sleep for too long.

He'd joined in with the EOD team and dozens of other men to search the base for any incendiary or explosive devices. As he had the clearest idea of the path the enemy had taken, he had to stay with the bomb disposal team the whole time, barely having a minute to take a piss, let alone eat a meal, although someone had brought him a cup of coffee during the long day and night.

Once the base was given the all-clear, and half a ton of fertilizer packed with nails had been neutralized by the EOD team, he'd also been interviewed by senior officers, MPs, and an incident team, telling the same story each time. And now he had to fill out a ton of forms to account for discharging his weapon. There hadn't been nearly so much paperwork when he'd been in Afghanistan, he thought bitterly.

Trudging back to his office, he glared at his cell phone, still dead and without his charger, unlikely to be resurrected any time soon. It was the first chance he'd had to pick up a phone in nearly twenty-four hours and he needed to call Maggie again, his mama and sister. He longed to hear Maggie's voice, but still uncertain if she wanted to talk to him and not sure what he'd say, he fired up his laptop instead and turned to a news channel to see what the reporters were saying.

He was stunned to see Maggie, red-eyed and exhausted, being interviewed by a busty blonde.

"I just need to know that he's safe. Jack, if you're listening to this, please call me. Evelyn and Lucy are desperate to hear from you, too. We all love you. Be safe."

He couldn't believe she was here, standing with the other journalists on the base's perimeter. He knew how many hours it took to fly from Cairo—he'd thought about it often enough. Hell, she must have gotten a flight within an hour of the attack.

With that realization, all his doubts melted away, and he felt furious and ashamed that he'd ever questioned that she was anything but sincere. Or that she loved him. Hell, she'd just announced it to the whole damn world!

His chest felt tight and full as he let her love fill him, as he let himself believe.

He picked up his landline and dialed, knowing her number off by heart.

"Maggie..."

"*Jack? Jack! Oh my God, Jack!*"

And then he didn't know if she was laughing or crying as choked sobs reached him.

"It's okay, baby. It's okay."

And perhaps for the first time in a long time it *was* okay.

"I can't believe you came all this way."

There was a long pause as she sniffed and cleared her throat.

"*I was so afraid ... there was nowhere else I wanted to be. I love you so much.*"

Jack's heart swelled with gratitude, love overflowing his tough demeanor. But it was several seconds before he could speak.

"I love you, too, Maggie. Christ, I'm so sorry, sugar. I forgot to charge my cell phone..."

This time she was definitely laughing, just one stop before hysteria central on the crazy train.

"*You didn't charge your cell?! I've been going nuts! Your mother ... Jesus, Jack!*"

"I know, I know. I'll get a new phone first chance I get. But the base is still on lockdown—I can't leave, I can't come to you. God, Maggie! I just want to hold you so I know that you're real."

"*Oh, I'm real alright, Sarge,*" she whispered, the stress and strain of the last twenty-four hours apparent in her voice. "*You're not getting rid of me now.*"

He hoped that was true. It was all that he hoped for. And when he'd faced down the enemy, faced death as the gunman's spray of bullets missed him by inches, it was her face he'd seen.

If I hadn't slipped, I would be a helluva lot dead about now. Luck. Sheer dumb luck had saved him. Or maybe, he thought in his most secret self, maybe he'd been saved. And even while he stared at muzzle flashes from the enemy AK47, he'd wanted to survive for her, for Maggie.

They talked for another fifteen minutes, but he could hear the exhaustion in her voice and tried to persuade her to check into a hotel to get some rest, but she was reluctant to leave the perimeter in case the lockdown was revoked. Finally, she only agreed when he promised to call her the moment there was any more news or he was allowed to leave the base.

After they'd reluctantly said their goodbyes, he called his mother and sister. Listening to them crying over the phone, he gave them as much reassurance as he was able.

Finally, alone again in the deep silence of his empty office, he swore at the pile of paperwork on his desk, gave it the bird, then stumbled back to his room and fell into a deep sleep.

He was woken four hours later by the CO's clerk knocking on his door and asking for the report that Jack should have emailed by now.

Wearily, he sat up rubbing his gritty eyes, remembering at last to plug his cell phone into his charger, frowning as it beeped at him in a long, angry jingling of missed calls and text messages. He listened to them all, his eyes clouding as he heard Maggie's increasingly worried words from Cairo, Istanbul, LA and finally outside the base.

He felt even guiltier that he'd ever doubted her and was determined to put that right as soon as possible. He was still a little overwhelmed that she'd flown 8,000 miles to be with him. She was an amazing woman and he was a lucky bastard to have her in his life.

Back in his office, he read the updates on the incident. The newspapers and TV were calling it a terrorist attack, but the military were carefully avoiding giving it that title.

The killer had been an unemployed 28 year old from Escondido with a police record for petty crime. No one knew yet why he'd decided to attack the base, but the authorities were working on it, going through his rented apartment, laptop and cell phone.

In little more than eight minutes, he'd fired over forty rounds from inside his vehicle, killing two Marines on the gates and two more inside. Seventeen others had been injured, and one of them had since lost an arm. Another two were in ICU and it wasn't yet certain if they'd survive. Men he'd served with, men he'd known.

Where did such hatred come from?

He rested his head in his hands, took a deep breath, then started punching the letters on the keyboard, stoically completing his report, doing his duty. Sometimes life was shit.

Then he remembered that Maggie was waiting for him.

Sometimes life was good.

Five hours later, the lockdown ended. But Jack, being the key witness, had to wait another two days before he was granted leave. Two excruciatingly long days while he waited to see Maggie. They spoke for a couple of hours both evenings when he was off duty—it was killing him not to be able to see her.

At least in his dreams he could hold her in his arms.

Maggie

I did a lot of thinking while I was stuck in my hotel waiting for Jack. I went for long walks over the sand dunes, lost in my thoughts, wondering what the future would bring, asking myself what I wanted from it: what I wanted and what I was prepared to give up, what I could compromise on and what I couldn't.

I was fairly sure what my decision would be, but not rushing in, weighing the evidence, those were the marks of a good journalist. But who is sensible when they're in love?

Each evening, we talked for so long that we were both yawning by the time we said goodnight.

I spoke to Evelyn, too, reassuring her that Jack was fine. I even chatted with Lucy whom I'd never met, and found her sweet and funny, proud of her big brother and very welcoming to me.

I yearned for Jack, I craved him. I wanted to feel his hands on my body, I wanted to be able to look into those cobalt blue eyes. I wanted his smile and his laugh, and I wanted to make love to him, to make up for all the nights we'd been apart since we met.

And I didn't want to say goodbye again. I was afraid that if I did, it would be the last time. Stupid to think like that because I'd never been superstitious, but when I'd learned that it was Jack who'd shot the attacker, a shiver of dread had worked its way into the very core of my being, into my soul.

I'd come too close to losing my love. The thought made me physically sick.

So I kept busy, filling those two long days, hardening my resolve and testing the words that I wanted to say to him.

So when he called to tell me that he was on his way to the hotel at last, I wanted to cry and laugh and hug him forever.

He was still driving his crappy Jeep when I saw him from the window. It tore up the driveway to the hotel in a cloud of dust, the exhaust even louder than I remembered.

I flew down the stairs and through the lobby, flinging myself at him, making him stagger back. And then I kissed him until neither of us could breathe.

I let my fingers rove his freshly shaven cheeks, the faint scent of soap clinging to his tanned skin. My hands stroked his regulation hair, the soft bristles tickling my palms, and I felt that strong body shiver as I clutched him to me, and he buried his face in my hair, hugging me so tightly I could barely draw breath.

Jack spoke first, brushing his thumbs over my mouth and cheeks, pushing my tangled hair out of my eyes.

"Why are we wasting time, Maggie? It could have been me. You know that, right? Or next time it could be you. We can't keep playing this game."

It wasn't the opening I'd expected, but Jack was nothing but direct.

"It's not a game, Jack," I said urgently. "Not for me. When I heard … when I saw … I couldn't … it wasn't … my life flashed in front of my eyes, Jack. Your life, my life. I want to be with you. Forever. No more goodbyes. We've said those words too many times. I don't want it anymore."

His blue eyes burned with an almost desperate passion, a need for certainty.

"I'm a Marine. That's what I do. I could be deployed again next year for six months, longer. There will always be goodbyes."

I nodded slowly, knowing he was right, and knowing I couldn't, wouldn't ask him to give this up, even when it put his life in danger. He had a strong sense of duty and he loved being a Marine. I wouldn't make him choose between his job and me.

I hadn't forgotten Marc's words about living Jack's life instead of my own, but I'd come to terms with them, too.

"I can live with that," I said quietly. "I won't like it. I'll never like saying goodbye to you, but you're a Marine and I'm so damn proud of you—and I always will be."

His eyes scanned my face, keeping his hope in check.

"Do you mean that?"

"Yes, I do. With all my heart."

He pulled back to look at me, gripping my shoulders almost painfully.

"What about Cairo?"

I thought carefully about my answer, wanting to explain it so he'd understand, so there'd be no uncertainty.

"My whole career I've wanted that assignment, to be a foreign correspondent."

Jack's shoulders slumped.

"I know."

"And I've achieved it. I think, in some small way, I've made a difference. Maybe that's arrogant, but I believe in my work, I do. Even though sometimes I feel like Canute, trying to hold back the waves, but in the end only proving that no one can stop the ocean from rolling in. What I'm saying, Jack, is that I'm done. I've achieved what I set out to achieve. I can't do it anymore. I'm finished. I'm leaving Cairo. I've already given my month's notice."

His eyes widened.

"But ... you did? When?"

"Two days ago."

"You ... you didn't say anything!"

"I was waiting to hear back from my editor. I wanted to be sure ... about everything."

"What did your editor say?"

I gave a wry smile.

"Well, he wasn't very happy, but he doesn't have a choice in the matter either."

"So..." Jack drew out the word painfully. "You'll go back to New York now?"

I lowered my eyes until I was gazing at his chest.

"That's certainly one possibility and my editor offered me my old job back ... but there's another option that I'm considering."

I glanced up, feeling his burning eyes on me.

"The International Rescue Committee is a small but growing charity. They're looking for someone to head up their publicity department—and they've offered me the job."

Jack gave a strained smile.

"That sounds real great, Maggie."

"It is. They do amazing work all over the world: health, education, famine, refugees—wherever they're needed, and I'll still have a chance to make a difference. There'll be some traveling, but I won't be living abroad, and..." I took a deep breath, "their offices are in Glendale. It's only 85 miles on the I-5 from Camp Pendleton. I looked it up."

Jack's deep frown smoothed slowly and his tanned cheeks lifted in a smile that grew broader and happier.

"That means we could..." I began to say.

Jack interrupted me.

"I know what it means, Maggie. Hell, yeah! Are we really going to do this? I'm not talking about dating, seeing how it goes; I'm talking about the whole tamale." He paused. "Because I love you, Maggie. I've been hiding from the truth for a while now. I know that being married to a man in the Marines hasn't been on your to-do list. I spend a lot of time away or on training, sometimes deployed at short notice. I could be away more than I'll be home. It's not much of a life for a Marine's wife and..."

I pressed my fingers over his lips.

"You can stop selling it to me now, Jackson."

He swallowed and straightened his spine.

"I want to marry you, Maggie, and I'm not taking no for an answer."

I glowed with love and relief.

"I'd better say yes then."

"Fuck, I'd better ask you then."

We both burst out laughing at the same time. Then his expression became serious and muttering under this breath, he tore off a thin sliver of silver paper that must have come from a candy bar and fashioned it into a ring.

His cheeks flushed red as he sank to one knee and held up the improvised ring.

"I got a real one back in my desk," he muttered sheepishly.

"You do?"

"Yeah, but this is kind of impromptu..."

He shook his head, staring up at me beseechingly.

"I can't offer you much. I guess this ring about says it all. I can't even give you my heart, because you've had it for quite a while now. But I promise to love you and cherish you, argue with you and make up with you, hold you and care for you every day of my life.

"You are the most frustrating and ornery woman I've ever met, but you're also brave and loyal and kind, and you fight for the world to be a better place. There's nowhere else I want to be but by your side fifty or sixty years from now, God willing.

"Margaret Jean Buckman, will you do me the honor of marrying me and being my wife?"

I nodded wildly as tears streaked my cheeks and I discovered that the woman I was, the one who was never lost for something to say, the woman who was paid by the number of words she hammered out couldn't find a thing to reply.

"Is that a yes?" he mumbled. "You sure?"

"My answer is that I love you, too. So I'm saying yes. Yes, I will marry you Gunnery Sergeant Jackson Connor. With all my heart."

Jackson slid that foil ring onto my finger and kissed my hand.

"Yes!" I half cried, half snorted. "That's a yes! Big, big yes! I love you."

And when we kissed, dusty, salt-stained, messy and clumsy, it was perfect.

Chapter Eighteen

REBOOT

I flew back to Cairo the next day wearing a beautiful diamond ring with a platinum band on the fourth finger of my left hand. I had a month to finish up current assignments, people to say goodbye to, and a few days in which to do a handover to my replacement.

Adam Arshad Richardson was a young, darkly handsome journalist in his late twenties. He explained that his mother was Iranian and she had come to the US when the Shah was expelled in 1979. His father was a high school English teacher and had been volunteering to teach English to the newly arrived refugees.

Adam was the youngest of three children, the only son and the only one of his siblings who'd ever been to the Middle East.

He was excited about his new posting, mentioning casually that he'd had a girlfriend back home but had broken it off when he'd been offered the job.

His faintly patronizing comments told me that he thought women weren't cut out to be foreign correspondents: "too emotional," he said. "You've got to be able to distance yourself from the story, stay professional."

I had to bite my tongue. It wasn't that I completely disagreed with his view, but understanding the emotions of the people I interviewed was what made a story relatable to readers back home. I was only five years older than him, but that was five years of experience on the front line.

Even so, he made me feel like a stereotype—the little woman who gave it all up to go home and get married.

When he asked me what I'd been working on, I showed him the stories from Sharm, Amsterdam and Zataari. He was a little more respectful after that.

I gave him my list of contacts too, and at first, there was some tension between him and my fabulous fixer Asim. I suppose it was competition to see who'd be top dog, but after a couple of days they soon saw that working together was going to be mutually beneficial. I had high hopes that they'd figure it out. Asim had been invaluable in smoothing my entry into Egyptian politics: Adam would need him.

Asim took me out for a cup of *Koshary* tea on my penultimate day. It was prepared the traditional way by steeping black tea in boiled water, letting it to brew for several minutes, then adding cane sugar and fresh mint leaves.

"It has been an honor working with you, Miss Emjay," he said. "I have told my daughters all about you. I have always believed education is important for girls. It's not easy for them to see that because female unemployment is so great. We had our first female cabinet minister in 1962, Hekmat Abu Zeid, but I am afraid progression is slowing down, even reversing. We have to keep fighting for our rights. Thank you for being a part of that."

I was surprised and touched by his words. Asim had always been very reserved with me, very formal. It felt good to know that he'd appreciated my efforts.

For the first time, I saw myself through his eyes: a Westerner, a woman, coming to his country to write about it with no previous knowledge of Egypt. I was proud that I'd been able to exceed his expectations, but I felt a twinge of guilt that I hadn't seen the assignment through.

I wished him and his family well and, as was the local custom, we exchanged gifts. For Asim, I'd bought a fountain pen with an eagle's head engraved on the silver nib. For his wife and daughters I played it safe and gave jars of American jelly and several boxes of hard candy. I'd also decided not to worry about the cost and bought five pairs of different Ray Ban sunglasses: Aviators for Asim because they were so macho, and a variety of Wayfarers for his wife and daughters.

As was socially acceptable, Asim's gift to me was ostensibly from his wife, a gorgeous dark blue leather laptop case from the Egyptian designer brand Wali's, and a small silver bracelet in the Nubian style.

"Come and see us again, Miss Emjay," he urged as we said our goodbyes.

I promised to stay in touch which wasn't the same thing at all because I already knew that it wouldn't be easy for me to get permission to travel here if I was married to a Marine. There were very strict rules about where you could visit abroad; one of Jack's friends had been denied permission to travel to Mexico, which astonished me. And I realized with a pang that there would be a lot of places I wouldn't be able to visit.

I'd already discussed this with my new employers and they'd promised they could work around it, but a sense of panic shot through me—I was giving up an awful lot to be with Jack.

Then I shoved the thought away. He was worth any restrictions his job made on mine.

My last night was spent with Adam, a slightly strained dinner, but the polite thing to do. Not only was he moving into my job, but he'd also taken over the rent of my apartment, so I was staying in a hotel. At least the air conditioning worked.

Gently, I tried to give him some tips, but he seemed more interested in finding out about local nightclubs. I wasn't going to lose any sleep about it. He'd find his own way—we all did.

And so I said goodbye to Egypt, a beautiful, uncertain country clinging to the north of Africa and a culture that stretched back thousands of years. I wondered when or if I'd ever return.

I arrived back in New York in early January to find it snowbound with worse weather closing in. Sidewalks were slick with ice, the daytime slush refreezing as temperatures plummeted with the sunset to well below freezing, and traffic crawled along slower than a caravan of camels.

Shivering, wearing all the wrong clothes, I lugged my suitcases and bags into the first cab that deigned to stop, returning home to an icy and empty apartment.

The radiators hadn't been on for months, and a friend who'd been looking after the place and watering my plants had left a message apologizing because she'd promised to turn the heating on, but had gotten stuck at work and didn't want to risk traveling across town in such bad weather.

The refrigerator was empty, too, and I couldn't face going out to buy milk, so I drank some aging instant coffee black and munched on a couple of slightly dusty-tasting Pop Tarts that were only a month past their eat-by date.

I pulled a thick quilt over my shoulders and gazed around the apartment, looking at the black and white photographs that I'd taken on assignments; the photograph of my parents, and another of me with my dad; one with Jackson at his mom's home, sitting on the porch like an old married couple. I remembered that photo because I was trying not to make it obvious to his mom that he had his hand up my skirt at the time. Even now, I could see the mischievous glint in his dark blue eyes.

I was dreading packing up another place, but my home was in San Diego now, with Jack.

Just as I was feeling a little lonely and a lot sorry for myself, shivering in my slowly warming apartment, my cell phone rang and Jack's photo lit the screen.

"Hey, sugar! Welcome back to the US of A. How are you?"

"Jack! Oh, it's so good to hear your voice. Yes, I'm okay. Cold, though! There's a foot of snow on the sidewalks and there's another storm coming in. It's going to be a complete whiteout."

"Sounds bad, and it's pretty cold here, too. I've been shivering through PT in thirty-five degrees. Last time I was here it was eighty-five degrees and the mosquitoes were as big as squirrels."

He pronounced it 'skwurls' and I loved the warmth of his southern accent. If I closed my eyes, I could almost feel the heat of his large, solid body.

I knew he was in a training class at Camp Lejune in North Carolina. I didn't know exactly what was involved in this training, although he sounded happy but tired.

"I've missed you," I said honestly.

"I've missed you too, sugar. But it won't be for much longer."

He was only 500 miles away and I was so tempted to hop on another plane and fly down to Wilmington, but we were working with a deadline of March 13th for our wedding and I had so much to do here.

I wasn't superstitious about the date in fact I welcomed it. Our love had begun in the most unprepossessing circumstances when I was nearly killed and Jack had saved my life. It seemed symbolic to me— there could be nothing worse, so why worry?

I knew that wasn't very rational thinking, but love isn't rational. The ancient Greeks believed that the fickle gods made humans fall in love for their own amusement, enjoying the chaos and disorder that would surely follow. Well, if that was the case, bring it on.

Besides, it would be a small wedding, Jack's mother the only parent we had between us, and with my friends spread all over the world, I wasn't expecting many to fly out to San Diego. The thought made me sad: Dad would have been so proud, so happy to walk me down the aisle to marry the man I loved.

I basked in the warmth of Jack's voice, so much closer now that we were in the same country on the same continent, but still too far away.

I fell asleep on the sofa listening to the rise and fall of his warm words and when I woke up hours later, my phone was stuck to my cheek.

Chapter Nineteen

STOP ALL THE CLOCKS

I spent the next couple of weeks boxing up my clothes and books, selling off furniture and bookshelves, contacting utility providers and having to run out to the local Abraço coffee shop every time the realtor had someone who wanted to view the apartment.

I'd also started my job with International Rescue Committee, so I was trying to get an understanding of the charity and the roles and responsibilities of my new colleagues, even though I was still in New York.

Over in San Diego, Jack was trying to find suitable housing for us, no more than fifteen miles off the base so he could be there quickly in an emergency.

As we had no dependents, we weren't eligible for family housing on the base, for which I was grateful. I was moving to Jackson's world, but I wanted to have a little normalcy, something non-military, too. Although as so many Marines and former Marines lived in the area, the chances were we'd have serving military or vets as neighbors.

I'd seen Jack's room at Camp Pendleton. Because he was a sergeant he'd been upgraded from three or four bunk beds, to a single occupancy room. His bed was narrow but comfortable. I knew that because we'd tested its limits rather athletically one day when I was visiting. I think he got a kick out of screwing in the barracks. I didn't want to know if he'd ever done it before so I didn't ask.

But he was finding it surprisingly challenging to locate an apartment or house somewhere that met our budget. After all, he'd never paid rent before and never even had to pay a utility bill. So self-assured in many ways, he'd never had to learn the skills that most of us do when we leave home at eighteen. He was catching on quickly, but I had to nix several pretty homes with enormous yards and glistening pools that were out of our price range.

And even though we didn't yet have a house, Jack had already treated himself to an enormous leather reclining chair for his man cave.

Time was running out and at this rate we'd be camping on the beach. Jack wasn't worried: at least we'd have a comfortable chair to sit on.

I was sitting in Abraço's, trying to get my head around writing IRC's annual report and praying that the latest viewing of my apartment would result in an offer this time, when Jack called my cell.

I was a little surprised, because he'd usually be taking PT at this time of the morning.

"Hiya! This is a nice surprise. How are you?"

There was a long pause.

"Not so good, Maggie."

"What's wrong?"

He let out a long sigh.

"It's Kevin Murphy's funeral tomorrow."

I closed my eyes, picturing Jack's distraught face. Eleven days ago Jack heard the news that his friend had been killed while on guard duty at the US Embassy in Baghdad. A suicide bomber in a bomb packed with explosives had driven straight at the security barrier, killing himself and three Marines.

There had been several delays, and the authorities had only just released his body to the family for burial after a long inquest.

Jack had been Kevin's sergeant in Afghanistan and that gave them an unbreakable bond, even in death.

"I'm so sorry, Jack. I wish I could hug you right now."

"*God, me too.*"

I heard the sounds of a marching song in the background and men's voices, so I knew that he must be standing somewhere close to the parade ground.

"*That's kind of why I'm calling, Maggie. Will you come?*"

I was momentarily taken aback.

"To the funeral?"

"*Yeah.*"

"But ... I never met Kevin. Would his family want me there?"

His reply was certain and immediate.

"*Yes, you're one of us now.*"

My lungs felt like all the breath had been squeezed out of them. It was almost as if Jack was right here, hugging me fiercely. I didn't have to think about my answer.

"Then I'll come."

"*Thank you, sugar. I love you.*"

He hung up and I used my phone to book the first flight out. Then I speed-walked back to the apartment, just in time to find my realtor locking the front door and talking to a dark haired man in a suit.

The man was in his early forties and looked tired. The journalist in me wondered if he was recently divorced. I just got that vibe from him.

"Oh, Ms. Buckman! I was going to call you," said my realtor smoothly. "This is Derek Johnson and he's just made an offer on your apartment."

"That's great," I smiled briefly. "Perhaps we can discuss the details later—I'm rushing to catch a flight."

"To San Diego?" she asked knowingly.

"Yes," I said flatly. "For a funeral."

Her professional smile evaporated, but it was the man who spoke.

"I'm sorry for your loss, Ms. Buckman."

"Thank you."

"I'll be in touch with Ms. Suarez about the apartment."

He took her by the elbow and guided her to the elevator. He seemed like a nice guy and I hoped he'd be happy in the apartment.

I hurried to pack a small suitcase, throwing in the usual things, plus my favorite black dress and a pair of heels.

Then I called a cab and headed out to Newark.

Eight hours later I stepped out into the blazing California sunshine, hopelessly overdressed in boots and a quilted coat.

Jackson was waiting for me, handsome and casual in blue jeans and a faded gray t-shirt that looked so soft I couldn't resist burying my face in it.

He held me tightly, murmuring over and over again, *I love you.*

Now the words had been said by both of us, he seemed to feel a need to say them every time we spoke, and to hear them every time we spoke.

That made me happy.

I'd spent too much time with the specter of death growing up, and later in my job, and now here I was at another funeral, this time for a man I'd never met.

A scorching blue sky was the pitiless backdrop to Corporal Kevin Murphy's funeral, mocking the sweating Marines in their Dress Blues as they marched solemnly to the *boom-boom boom-boom-boom* of the drummer.

Jack was a pallbearer, so I'd been left in the care of one of his brother's wives while he did his final duty for his comrade.

A shiny black hearse carried the coffin, with the Murphy family walking behind, heads drooping like wilting flowers. There was also an escort of four men following the pallbearers, two carrying the regimental colors and two with swords drawn.

The hearse stopped outside the base's Catholic church, and in eerie silence, like a movie that had been deliberately run at half-speed, the pallbearers slow-marched toward the coffin.

Then, to the accompaniment of a drumroll, the coffin was carried up the steps.

The church was filled with men and women in uniforms and an

equal number of civilians, like me, dressed in black. The uniformed Marines with their white covers and gloves seemed almost colorful.

When the eulogy had been read and the service concluded, some people sobbing, some stoic, we made our way to the graveside.

It brought back memories of burying my parents, and tears were close to the surface for a man I'd never met. He'd died doing his duty for his country and I hoped that his family could draw some comfort from that, however small.

I wondered how many funerals like this Jack had attended. Too many. Far too many.

I could see sweat mingling with tears on the faces of two of the pallbearers, but Jack's face was stony and grim, the emotions locked tightly away.

At least I could be there for him when he needed me later.

There was another drumroll, then the Honor Guard pallbearers briefly lifted the coffin to shoulder height, as if letting their fallen comrade see the sun one more time, before lowering him to his final resting place.

The mournful skirl of a lone bagpipe lay thickly on the burning air, and then 'Amazing Grace', the saddest of hymns, rang out across the graveyard.

Through many dangers, toils and snares
　We have already come.
　T'was grace that brought us safe thus far
　And grace will lead us home.

I wanted to believe that Marine Kevin Murphy was home at last, but it was hard when his death had been so senseless. Or maybe all deaths seem senseless to the ones left behind.

When Jack handed the folded Stars and Stripes to Kevin's mother, she clutched it to her chest, sobbing as her white-face husband wrapped his arms around her. They sagged and clung together, crumpled and despairing.

"May we who mourn be reunited one day."

The Priest's words rang out, calm and certain, and maybe—just maybe—a little of his faith seeped into me.

The three-gun salute made me jump and clutch the hand of the woman next to me. We held hands tightly, each wondering if one day we'd be mourning someone closer to us, wishing that words or prayers could ward the danger away.

Kevin's father stood on shaky legs, then kneeled next to the coffin, resting his head on it as he cried silent tears for his boy.

It's not right for a parent to bury their child, it's just not right.

The woman next to me squeezed my hand again.

"Freedom has a taste that the protected will never know," she said, whispering the well-known words.

"And I, one of the protected thank you deeply and sincerely," I replied.

The wake began with muted chatter and we paid our respects to the Murphy family, uttering meaningless words, awkward in the face of such grief. Kevin's father and sister shook hands with everyone, but his mother sat with her youngest daughter, inconsolable, until her husband urged her to take a sleeping pill and lie down.

Uniformed men and women stood in groups reminiscing about deployments they'd shared, recalling fond memories of sandflies and crotch rot. Then the alcohol started flowing and the noise level gradually grew. After a glass of wine I switched to water, knowing that I'd be the one driving us later.

I met some more of Jack's friends and chatted to a few of the wives about living in San Diego, making a mental note of their recommendations for which areas were the best to live in.

Somehow it seemed wrong to discuss this at a wake, but of course, life goes on.

Just not the life of Kevin Murphy.

Jack was drunk and weaving all over the place when I got him back to our hotel. He sat on the end of the bed fumbling with the multitude of buttons that made up his uniform, swearing with frustration when they defeated his uncoordinated fingers.

I had to help him out of his clothes, watching with sadness as he remained closed off, rolling onto his side and immediately falling asleep.

I undressed and had a quick shower before quietly climbing into bed next to him. I listened to his soft snores for a long time before I fell asleep.

I was woken by Jack's hands sliding over my body as the full moon bathed our room with silver. He made love to me with a silent intensity and desperation that told me he needed me, even if he couldn't say the words.

I knew he would, one day.

Chapter Twenty

THE ONE IN WHITE

Sixty days later...

Just four hours earlier, a stunning blonde with Jack's navy blue eyes stumbled into my arms sobbing her heart out.

"I'm so happy to finally meet you!" she cried, almost knocking me over with her enthusiasm. "Thank you for making Jackson so happy!"

Lucy was a force of nature who then proceeded to soak my t-shirt while she wept, and made her way through my handy-size packet of tissues, hiccupping and blowing her nose and telling me how awesome it was that I was marrying her big brother.

After I'd held her, stroking her narrow shoulders and patting her back for five minutes, she gave a small giggle.

"I think I'm a little drunk. Jackson flew me and Mama first class and they had free champagne."

"Don't worry about it," I smiled. "It's really sweet of you."

"Oh, don't be nice to me!" she wailed. "I'll start gushing all over again, I'm so ridiculous!"

I laughed and passed her yet another pack of tissues while my three other bachelorette party guests Lee, Allison and Jules eyed her with amusement.

"I'm so happy Jackson isn't marrying Emmy. She's okay but she's such a stuffed shirt—she never bitched about anyone, not even the appalling Coley Robson. He's the Reverend's son and used to wipe boogers under the pew. There's no way she'd have beer and a barbecue on the beach if she was getting married like you guys. She'd probably have a cotillion ball."

As I'd run out of tissues, she wiped her face on her sleeve.

"Oh God, I'm such a mess."

"You look lovely," I said almost honestly, if you ignored her red nose and swollen eyes. "Should I introduce you to my friends?"

"They must think I'm such an idiot," muttered Lucy.

"You're fine," I reassured her. "We're all a bit emotional."

"At least Mama's not here. She'd be so embarrassed by me."

Jack's mother had opted to spend the evening at the hotel. She said it was because she was tired after the flight, but I suspected she didn't want to cramp our style during my bachelorette party. I wouldn't have minded in the least—I was very fond of Evelyn.

"Lucy, you already know Jules. Come say hi to Allison and Lee. Al was my PA when I worked in New York—knows everyone and everything about everyone. And this is Lee who's also a writer and is married to a former Marine, so she'll be filling me in on all the gory details."

My other journalist friend Marc was supposed to be with us, but once he'd met Jackson and all his buddies, he'd decided to be 'one of the boys' for a change. I wondered how he'd get on since I suspected there'd be strip clubs involved at some point during Jack's bachelor party. Oh well, Marc had practically a platoon of Marines to take care of him, and he was tougher than he looked.

Since both Lee and Jules had opted to leave their children at home, my plan for the evening was a casual dinner and drinks at Ruby's diner on the pier at Oceanside, and cocktails on the terrace.

Unfortunately, that was deemed far too tame by Lucy. She insisted that dinner was just the start to an evening that ought to include a show and casino in downtown San Diego. Allison backed her up, and

Lee smiled and said she'd go with the majority. I was desperately willing Jules to say she'd prefer a quiet evening, but she winked at me, then reminded me that there'd be nothing quiet about Jack's evening.

"Gray promised he'd get Jackson back in one piece, although not necessarily conscious."

I winced and shook my head.

"I'm not sure I want to know."

Lee laughed.

"It's the best way. You know what these guys are like when they get together, they all revert to little boys, trying to decide who has the biggest ... weapon."

Lucy tossed her long hair over her shoulder and said she was going to get an Uber to take us into the city after dinner. Then she pulled a small piece of fabric out of her suitcase, insisting it was a whole dress and it was what I would be wearing. As she'd made the dress herself especially for me, I didn't have a choice but to grin and bear it. Or bare it.

It also came with a promise that she'd give me a makeover before we went out.

"It's so nice to have a sister at last!"

I couldn't veto her ideas after that, so I decided that Lee was right and I should go with the flow.

Two hours later, I'd been polished, buffed, primped and straightened, my chin-length hair looking glossy and full. Lucy had done a good job with my makeup, too, although I was probably wearing my usual quota for a month in a single night.

The dress though...

Oh my God it was so short, it was more of a pelmet than a skirt, barely past mid-thigh. Lucy's dress was even shorter. Neither of us would be able to bend over in public all evening.

Allison looked amazing in a slinky silver halter-neck, and Jules had glammed up in a pale blue bandage dress. Lee, older than the rest of us, was stunning in a dark red cheongsam that clung to her full curves.

"Sebastian chose it," she said, a faint blush coloring her cheeks.

"He has great taste," I said, hugging her.

Jack and Sebastian had only met this afternoon but they'd

immediately gotten along. Two tall blond guys who looked like models —they'd be breaking hearts tonight, I was sure. Marc had certainly thought so. He was also a friend of Lee's and had met Sebastian before —he said he was looking forward to catching up.

Dinner was enormous fun and it was lovely to see all my friends chatting and laughing. Lucy kept ordering cocktails for me, determined to loosen me up, as she put it. After a Cosmopolitan, Key West Cooler, Hendricks Fizz and two Mojitos, I was so loose that walking in heels demanded extreme concentration.

"I'm going to break my ankle," I mumbled to Lee.

"We'll look after you," smiled Allison, putting her arm around my waist while Lee locked her arm through mine.

The car, when it arrived, was a huge stretch limousine with a fully stocked bar.

Lucy smiled wickedly as she crawled onto the back seat.

"Jack always says 'Go big or go home', and anyway, he's payin'!"

The floor show at the casino was something else. A group of male strippers gyrated across the stage, while I clamped my arms to my chair and refused to volunteer for anything, despite Lucy egging me on.

When one of the men dressed in leather pants with the ass cut out started grinding on a Harley Davison, I took a long drink of my Sea Breeze. Lee leaned across to me and whispered, "Sebastian used to feel like that about his motorcycle."

I spat out a mouthful of vodka and cranberry juice, making her jump.

"I can't believe you just said that!"

She winked at me and demurely sipped her glass of champagne.

Then one of the strippers strode up to the microphone.

"I hear we've got a bachelorette party here tonight!"

I cringed in my seat as Lucy jumped up and down pointing at me.

The stripper was the color of a teabag, thanks to his fake tan, and so musclebound that I couldn't help wondering where he found pants to fit over his enormous thighs.

He vaulted off the stage and sauntered toward me.

"Hello, beautiful. Wanna take a ride with me?"

"No! No!" I squeaked at the same time Lucy yelled, "Yes! Yes!"

He smirked, pulling me up easily and tossing me over his shoulder as if I was a side of beef.

"Put me down!" I yelled, trying to scrabble free and hoping that I wasn't flashing my panties to the audience, but his back was so well oiled, I couldn't find anything to hold onto and slithered around helplessly.

He dumped me in a chair on the stage and then danced around, thrusting and grinding. I didn't know where to look, so I glared at my so-called friends who were laughing their asses off.

He leaned down, giving the audience a view of his smooth ass, as shiny and hard as teak.

"Your friends just want you to have a good time," he whispered. "Come and shake that cute lil tush for me."

"Oh alright!" I grumbled.

I stood up, grateful when he helped me catch my balance, then surprised the hell out of myself and everyone else when I showed some moves that I'd learned in a belly-dancing class in Cairo featuring the traditional hip lift, shimmy and figure eight, working it like a pro, and shakin' what my mama gave me.

"Holy shit! It's always the quiet ones," he yelled.

When he tried to copy me, the audience howled with laughter at both of us.

Ah well, what's a little public humiliation between friends?

I stumbled into bed about three in the morning, wishing that Jack hadn't booked us separate rooms for the night before our wedding, out of respect for his mother.

I fell asleep smiling because the man I was going to marry was so darned sweet.

I woke with a start when someone banged on my door. Dawn was seeping through the heavy drapes and my head pounded, reminding me exactly how much alcohol I'd had the night before ... um ... a few hours before.

"Who is it?" I croaked, my voice cracked and dry as a desert.

"'Smee!" came Jack's voice, slurred and happy.

I opened the door to find Sebastian and Gray holding up a drooping Jack.

"He wouldn't go back to his own room until he'd seen you," Sebastian apologized, looking none too sober himself, if his glazed expression was anything to go by.

"Hey, sugar," grinned Jack, a goofy smile on his face. "You have great tits. I really fuckin' love your tits."

As if my boobs had magnets attached to them, both Sebastian and Gray's eyes swung to my nipples, and I realized that the sexy nightgown I was wearing left nothing to the imagination.

Sebastian winced and looked away; Gray's mouth dropped open.

"Okay, you've seen her," Sebastian muttered to Jack. "Now let's get you back to your own crib. Sorry to bother you, Maggie."

"M'gee, M'gee. I wan' M'gee," slurred Jack, gripping the doorpost and refusing to let go.

"It's fine, let him stay," I laughed, despite my headache.

Looking relieved, Sebastian half dragged, half carried Jack to the bed and let him fall on top of it. I wanted to yell, "Timberrrr!"

"Love you, M'gee," he mumbled. "Lots 'n' lots. Love. You."

"I love you too, you big lush," I whispered, kissing him on his parted lips, and inhaling enough whiskey fumes to make me wrinkle my nose.

Within seconds, Jack was snoring softly.

"Sure you'll be okay?" Sebastian asked, trying not to look at me or my over-enthusiastic boobs.

At that moment, we heard a crash in the bathroom.

I rushed in to find Gray laying in the tub with his dick hanging free and the toilet unflushed. He was also out cold.

"Ah shit," Sebastian sighed, discreetly pulling Gray's pants up so he was at least covered. "Wake up, motherfucker!"

He shook Gray, but there was no response.

"Which room are you in, dumbass?"

Still nothing.

"Leave him," I said, yawning. "I'll just throw a blanket over him."

Sebastian shook his head, suddenly seeming sober.

"He shouldn't sleep with his prosthetics on or he'll be in a world of hurt tomorrow."

"Oh," I said softly. "I guess ... I guess we should take them off then."

We stared at each other. Somehow, removing his aluminum legs seemed far more intimate than covering up Gray's dick, as Sebastian had done just a moment ago.

"So, we just ... pull?" I asked doubtfully, staring at Gray's prosthetic legs sticking out of the tub.

"Let me check," said Sebastian, rolling up the pants leg. "Depends on whether he's got a shuttle lock or a vacuum or ... oh yeah, vacuum. I should be able to just ease it off. Pull gently here while I..."

Lacking the coordination of full sobriety, I tugged too hard and landed hard on my ass on the bathroom floor, clutching one of Gray's legs. I was appalled, but when Sebastian started to laugh, I couldn't help joining in.

"Holy shit! That's the funniest thing I've ever seen!" he grinned while gently pulling the thin fabric sheath covering Gray's stump. "Can you do that again?"

"I'll tell Lee you said that," I pretended to grump.

"Won't matter," he said cockily. "She loves me."

I smiled at the certainty in his voice. Plus, he was right—his wife adored him.

He turned back to Gray's other leg, carefully pulling off the prosthetic and the second lining.

"Mind you," he said quietly, "Jack is pretty damn crazy about you, too. Kept going on about how amazing you were. Wouldn't even let Charlene or Ginger..."

He ground to a halt, his handsome face turning pink.

"Uh..."

"I'll pretend I didn't hear that," I smiled.

"Thank Christ," he said, shaking his head. "I must be more hammered than I thought. I'm gonna go find my woman. I haven't had sex for nearly a whole day."

"Thank you for bringing Jack home safely ... mostly."

"No problem. See you at the wedding."

He waved over his shoulder, crashing into the doorframe as he left the room.

I found a pillow and spare blanket for Gray, making him as comfortable as I could and propping up his legs next to the tub so he could reach them in the morning.

While I was in the bathroom, I swallowed a couple of Ibuprofen and washed them down with a glass of water. One hangover averted, with any luck.

Then I untied Jack's sneakers and managed to ease them off his feet. I pulled off his socks, but I couldn't make headway with his jeans —he was just too heavy to shift. Sighing, I covered him with the quilt.

"I love you Jackson Connor," I said. "I'm so happy that I found you."

Then I crept under the quilt as well, enjoying the wall of heat that rose from his prone body.

I slept till mid-morning when I was woken by Gray's pitiful groans coming from the bathroom. I tried to go back to sleep but the sound of retching convinced me I ought to go check he wasn't dying.

He'd climbed out of the bath and was draped over the toilet seat, moaning and swearing.

I, on the other hand, felt refreshed and only had a slight headache that would be solved by drinking a few glasses of water.

"Morning, Gray!" I said cheerfully. "Good time last night? I'm just going to order sausage, bacon, eggs, fruit, toast and coffee. You want some?"

"You're evil," he whined, glaring up at me with a bloodshot eye.

"Suck it up, buttercup," I laughed.

Back in the bedroom, another of the fallen was sitting up in bed, clutching his head.

"Shoot me now," he croaked. "Put me out of my misery. I'm dyin', Maggie."

His misery was so abject, his expression so plaintive, I laughed out loud.

"Come on, Sarge, first to fight!"

He muttered something under his breath and fell back with his arm over his face.

I crawled onto the bed, kissed his chin, then dropped my lips to his ear ... and yelled.

"Time to get up, Marine! You've got a wedding to go to!"

He cringed, holding his head, his eyes wide and wounded.

"You're mean! Is this what married life is going to be like?"

"Only when you get tanked," I grinned at him. "Now, can you evict Gray so I can go shower?"

"Gray's here?"

"Yup. He helped Sebastian carry you back here last night, but Gray never made it out of the bathroom. He's in worse shape than you are."

"Don't count on it," Jack mumbled.

He staggered to the bathroom door and found Gray trying to put the wrong leg on the wrong stump.

"You dumbass," he chided. "Should I call Jules to come get you?"

"No!" whimpered Gray. "She beats me!"

"She will today, you dumb grunt."

He hauled Gray into a sitting position and helped him get his legs on right. Then he called Jules who turned out to be just five doors down the hall. If I'd thought about it last night, I might have remembered that.

Two minutes later, Jules knocked on the door, looking fresh and angelic in a pale pink summer dress.

She took one look at Gray, who might have hoped for sympathy, then gave him a bawling out that had me and Jack retreating to the balcony to give them some privacy.

"Is that what you're going to be like when we're married?" he asked, looking worried.

"Yep, it's in the manual. Shoulda read the small print."

There's nothing like someone else's hangover to make you feel chipper, I thought, smiling at my poor wounded soldier.

Then the shouts died away and the sounds of murmured endearments followed as the door slammed behind them.

"Can I get an aspirin now?" Jack begged, feeling sorry for himself.

"Sure," I said cheerfully. "In your own bathroom. You're not supposed to see me before our wedding, so get your cute lil ass moving, Marine!"

Muttering to himself, but not able to stop a smile creeping over his full lips, he staggered to the door.

"Meet you at the altar, Sarge!" I called after him. "I'll be the one in white!"

I had a leisurely breakfast sitting out on the balcony, staring at the ocean. Despite what I'd said to the guys, I could only tolerate a couple of pieces of dry toast and a lot of weak tea.

I was so nervous, my stomach swooped and lurched as if I was on a funfair ride, and my hands felt cold and clammy.

I wanted to marry Jack, but I was less sure about marrying into the Marines. I also knew I couldn't have one without the other.

I wanted my mom. I badly wanted to talk to her, to have her love and quiet wisdom. And even though my dear friend Marc was walking me down the aisle, I wished and wished it was my father.

Tears were always close to the surface when I thought about my parents, but my sadness was interrupted by a knock at the door.

I opened it to find Evelyn standing there, looking beautiful and serene in a blue silk skirt suit.

"Hello, Maggie darling," she said warmly. "Ready to marry my son?"

I nodded and wiped my eyes.

"Oh honey! What's wrong? You ... you're not having second thoughts, are you?"

"No," I sniffed, trying to find a tissue. "I just wish my mom and dad..."

She wrapped her arms around me, hugging me tightly.

"You want your parents here, of course you do. Oh sweetheart, I know how hard it is. I'd give anything for Jack's father to be here. He'd have loved you so very much."

Then she reached into her purse for a tissue.

"Sugar lumps! I promised myself I wouldn't cry this early in the morning," she murmured.

Snorting, laughing and crying, we dabbed our eyes and sat on the balcony, Evelyn in the shade while I soaked up some winter sun.

She leaned forward to take my hand.

"Let me just say this and I promise I won't mention it again..."

"Okay...?"

"When I first met you, I wasn't sure about this. I liked you, but I didn't think you were right for Jack."

I sucked in a sudden breath and tried to pull my hand free.

"No, hear me out. I knew that he was in love with you, any fool could see that, and I knew that you cared for him. But you've turned your life inside out and upside down to be with my boy, and that tells me everything I need to know. I admit, I was very wrong. It's been a long time since I've seen him smile so often or be so truly happy, and that's down to you. I hate the term mother-in-law; I always think it sounds like someone you'd want to arrest. But ... I'll be proud to be your mother-in-law. And although I can never replace your own dear mother ... if you feel you'd like to ... I'd be honored if you'd consider me to be your mama, too."

She squeezed my hand tightly as tears burned behind my eyes.

"Oh my dear," she said. "We'll both be needing waterproof mascara!"

Another knock on the door proved to be the hair and makeup team that Lucy had insisted was necessary.

Realizing I was in danger of running late, I threw myself in the shower, shaved my legs carefully, and moisturized every inch of flesh. Then I wrapped myself in an enormous fluffy robe and let Carrie and Shelby get to work.

Shelby slapped on something cooling to take the puffiness out of my eyes, dabbed a silky foundation cream over my cheeks, chin and nose, then gave me subtle, smoky eyes and glistening lips. Carrie curled my hair, weaving in a corsage made up of tiny white rosebuds and a silvery feather that I adored.

Allison, Lucy, Lee and Jules arrived looking gorgeous, Lucy wearing a pale apricot bridesmaid's dress that suited her peaches and cream complexion.

While I slid between the folds of my satin dress, the others opened a bottle of champagne, promising a couple of glasses would calm my nerves.

"How was Gray when you left him?" I called from the bedroom.

"Upright, front and center," Jules smirked. "He knows he'll be in the dog house if I hear so much of a whimper out of him today. Tough love!"

"Sebastian was suffering as well this morning," smiled Lee. "He swore blind that all they did was have a few drinks with the guys from Jack's platoon. He did have trouble explaining why a red leather thong had been slipped into his jeans pocket and a phone number from someone named 'Ginger'. I left him sweating."

We all laughed.

"Not going there! I'll be a happy woman if Jack never finds out about me shimmying on stage with Carlton the Cowboy."

"He had a great body," sighed Lucy.

"Jack's is better!"

"Ugh! Don't talk about *my brother* like that!"

Then I stepped out of the bedroom and Evelyn started to cry again.

"Oh, Maggie! You look so beautiful! Even more beautiful, honey!"

"You sure scrub up nice, boss!" smiled Allison as her voice cracked.

I stared at myself in the full length mirror, shocked to see a bride staring back at me.

Nothing would ever be the same again.

EPILOGUE

My white satin dress is floor-length, sleeveless, and with a scooped neckline. Tiny seed pearls have been sewn onto the bodice in the shape of miniature rosebuds, matching the corsage in my hair. I hold a bouquet of white and apricot roses, smiling at the happiness I see in my reflection.

"Jackson is gonna bust a gut!" Lucy whispers, dabbing at her eyes. "Oh my God, you'll make such pretty babies!"

"Hush," says Evelyn, watching me out of the corner of her eye as I blush. "No one has said anything about babies."

I smile at them, but don't speak. That is a bridge for Jack and I to cross in the future. But not very far in the future.

Everyone starts squawking when another knock raps on the door. The others hurry to find purses and fix their lipstick while I take one final gulp of champagne.

Marc is standing at the door, looking handsome in a tailored black tux with a dark apricot cummerbund and matching bowtie.

He takes my hand and kisses the knuckles gently

"You looking stunning, *ma chère*. I will be most proud to escort you to your waiting bridegroom."

Then he lowers his voice.

"It was heaven and hell being surrounded by so many beautiful men last night," he confides. "I can't wait to do it again tonight."

I laugh as he kisses me on the cheek.

"And I have a gift from your divine Jackson."

He opens a small jewel box, and resting against the blue velvet is a tiny EGA pin, a miniature eagle and globe, symbol of the Marine Corps, a small diamond twinkling in the setting.

"Oh! Oh, it's beautiful!"

Reverently, Marc pins it to my dress. My husband-to-be is a Marine, and I truly am marrying into the Corps.

Then arm in arm, we sweep out of the room.

Two limousines carry us to the Marine Memorial Chapel at Oceanside, where Jack is waiting for me.

As I climb carefully from the car, my bridesmaid and maids of honor crowd around me, smoothing the wrinkles in my dress, drawing out the small train. Wishing me luck, Allison, Evelyn and Lee tiptoe inside the church, while Lucy stands breathless behind me.

"Are you okay, *chérie?*" Marc whispers, unnerved by my silence and pallor. "The car is still here..."

I turn to him and smile, squeezing his hand.

"No, I'm ready."

I take his arm, longing to see Jackson. The few hours we've been apart have been too long.

The music begins, stately, formal, but joyous too, and slowly, we walk up the aisle. I know our friends are watching us, but I have eyes only for Jack.

He stands at the altar, tall and proud, his eyes matching the dark blue of his uniform, his smile as bright as the sun pouring through the stained glass windows.

There is no doubt, no fear, no shadow of uncertainty, only the complete knowledge that ahead of me stands the man with whom I will spend the rest of my life.

It's all there, shimmering in a beautiful future: a family, a home filled with children, working for something I believe in, Jack and I growing old together, living our lives shoulder to shoulder as we walk into eternity together.

Our story started in the churning yellow dust of an Afghan village and somehow, against all the odds, with shared scars of life's battles, it has led us here, to this moment. This perfect, wonderful moment.

But it isn't an ending, it's a beginning. Today, our wedding day, our story is truly starting.

My lips tremble as Marc places my hand in Jack's. I see tears of joy glistening on his long lashes and I know that our love will last a lifetime.

Jack, my Jack. My lover, my friend, my confidante, the love of my life, and soon, very soon, my husband.

THE END

REVIEWS

Reviews

I really hope that you enjoyed Jack and Maggie's journey—it turned out to be a longer short story than I'd expected. Originally, the first chapter was a short story, but so many of you said that you wanted more, I couldn't refuse. Not that I tried very hard, because Jack and Maggie had found their way into my heart, too.

Reviews are love! Honestly, they are! But it also helps other people to make an informed decision before buying this book.

So I'd really appreciate if you took a few seconds to do just that at the following links.

NOW READ TICK TOCK

romantic suspense by Jane Harvey-Berrick

If you enjoyed Jack and Maggie's story, I hope that you'll enjoy my military suspense/romance out now: TICK TOCK on Amazon

Swipe the page for the Prologue and first chapter.

<u>Synopsis for</u> ***TICK TOCK***

"What's the time, Mr Wolf?"

Forget SEALS, Marines, Fighter Pilots - I have the most dangerous job in the world. And I fucking love it.

James Spears is part of an elite group who lives and breathes danger. Where others run from it, he walks towards it, calm, focussed ice-cold. James is a top EOD operative.

Explosive...

Ordnance...

Disposal...

You'd call him a bomb disposal expert. Or crazy. A guy with a death wish. He's heard it all before and he doesn't give a shit. He's the best.

They say he doesn't have blood in his veins, he has ice. They say he has no nerves.

All that's about to be tested.

Amira is recruited by the CIA to infiltrate a terrorist cell living in rural Pennsylvania. She's the perfect plant, no one would ever suspect her. Because her brother was killed when a bomb was dropped on the Syrian hospital where he was volunteering as a medic. And now hate burns deeply inside her. She's perfect.

That's what they tell James when he's told to train her to be the best damn bomb-maker there is. In a secret camp, deep in the woods, James teaches her everything he knows about building bombs. He's not a praying man, but now he's really hoping that he's doing the right thing.

Can he trust her? Will she ever trust him? Who is playing who? And who will pay the ultimate price?

Codename: Hansel and Gretel

TICK TOCK **– the romantic suspense novel from best-selling author Jane Harvey-Berrick on Amazon**

TICK TOCK PROLOGUE

If you enjoyed Jack and Maggie's story, I hope that you'll enjoy my new military suspense/romance out now: TICK TOCK on Amazon

Swipe the page for the synopsis, Prologue and first chapter.

Synopsis for ***TICK TOCK***

"What's the time, Mr Wolf?"

Forget SEALS, Marines, Fighter Pilots - I have the most dangerous job in the world. And I fucking love it.

James Spears is part of an elite group who lives and breathes danger. Where others run from it, he walks towards it, calm, focussed ice-cold. James is a top EOD operative.

Explosive...

Ordnance...

Disposal...

You'd call him a bomb disposal expert. Or crazy. A guy with a death wish. He's heard it all before and he doesn't give a shit. He's the best.

They say he doesn't have blood in his veins, he has ice. They say he has no nerves.

All that's about to be tested.

Amira is recruited by the CIA to infiltrate a terrorist cell living in rural Pennsylvania. She's the perfect plant, no one would ever suspect her. Because her brother was killed when a bomb was dropped on the Syrian hospital where he was volunteering as a medic. And now hate burns deeply inside her. She's perfect.

That's what they tell James when he's told to train her to be the best damn bomb-maker there is. In a secret camp, deep in the woods, James teaches her everything he knows about building bombs. He's not a praying man, but now he's really hoping that he's doing the right thing.

Can he trust her? Will she ever trust him? Who is playing who? And who will pay the ultimate price?

Codename: Hansel and Gretel

TICK TOCK – the romantic suspense novel from best-selling author Jane Harvey-Berrick on Amazon

Swipe page for the prologue and first chapter...

We're born alone and we die alone.

I've never been afraid of dying. It's living that scares the hell out of me.

But in the bomb suit, I am utterly alone.

There is no today, no yesterday, no tomorrow.

Just here, right now.

There is no God, no Devil, no good, no evil.

Just me. And the sound of my breathing, loud and rhythmic.

Just me. And this bomb.

A bomb is a device that is designed to kill, maim or harass.

I'm not afraid. I don't have time to be afraid.

The sun burns down, the light is a white haze, sweat runs into my eyes. The longer I'm out here, kneeling in the dust, the more vulnerable the team watching my back.

I can't be quick. I have to be certain.

Because if I'm wrong, I die.

I am an EOD operator.

Explosives

Ordnance

Disposal.

Bomb disposal.

I am the Tick Tock man.

TICK TOCK, CHAPTER 1

James

Got him!

I raised my SA80 rifle and aimed at the man's chest. From 20 yards, I couldn't miss. But then again, neither could he.

He was driving an old Jeep, so battered that it looked as though string and chewing gum held it together. He revved the engine threateningly and I ducked behind a lamppost so he wouldn't be able to run me over. I couldn't see the driver's hands. What the fuck was he doing with his hands? He could be reaching for a weapon, or he could be arming a device that would blow a hole through the world.

Shit just got serious.

I gestured with the rifle, my voice harsh and gritty—a command.

"Raise your hands and place them on the steering wheel."

He didn't move, he just stared at me, his eyes narrowed with hatred.

"Raise your hands *now!*"

Still nothing.

The soldier next to me started to twitch.

"Staff! He's not doing anything! Does he even speak fucking English?"

He'd got a strong Geordie accent, so it sounded like, *Saj! Ees not dooin' ennyfink! Doos ee even spook fookin Eenglish?*

"I don't know. Do you?"

He gave me a quick, nervous grin. But my joke had helped him to relax. Or maybe he'd just stepped back from the edge of a big mistake.

I took a pace forward, jabbing my SA80 at the insurgent.

"Hands where I can see them!"

Even if he didn't speak English, my meaning was clear.

But I was distracted by the soldier next to me who was jigging from foot to foot like he wanted to piss his pants.

I glanced toward him.

"Calm down, it's alright..."

Suddenly, there was a loud bang, a flash of light from the Jeep, and a cloud of dust and blue smoke flared upward.

I lowered my rifle and swore.

"Staff Sergeant Spears!" bellowed Captain Elders, shaking his head. "If that had been a real device, you and your men would be very fucking dead right now. You should have made sure his hands were in sight. It's a good thing this is a training exercise in Wiltshire and not a real life situation in Ifuckingdontcareistan. I expected better of you, Spears. See me in my office later."

Then he strode away.

The Jeep driver grinned, tossed a V-sign with his fingers, racing off in a cloud of dust, the exhaust rattling asthmatically.

Wanker.

"Sorry, Staff," said my Lance Corporal, his expression crestfallen. "I fooked it oop."

"You, me, both," I sighed.

We joined the rest of the Troop and trudged back to the bus that would take us from the training ground to the barracks.

The pack on my back weighed 110 pounds: 50lb of basic Army shit; 60lb of EOD kit. It was 31°C and I was sweating my 'nads off. English summers weren't supposed to be this hot.

It was sheer relief to climb onto the bus and crawl to a seat at the back where I could dump my pack and drink some tepid water from my flask.

I looked around at my team that I'd been attached to, all from REME—the Corps of Royal Electrical and Mechanical Engineers. They were good lads, but young and inexperienced. At 29, I was the oldest. Next stop thirty. Fuck me. When did I get to be so old?

I leaned back against the seat and closed my eyes, letting the weariness take me. Within minutes, I was falling asleep. That was something you learned in this job: catch some ZZZs while you can. Hours in your sleeping bag can be few and far between on a deployment in a hostile environment. Over the years, I'd trained myself to sleep anywhere: in a hammock, up a tree, in a tank, or lying on a slab of concrete. Time and opportunity was all I needed.

Not that a nice soft bed with a nice soft blonde in it wouldn't be even better, but I took what I could get.

When the bus arrived back at base, I jerked awake.

Military bases are all essentially the same: red brick housing for families, low concrete barracks for unmarried personnel, ugly buildings, boring offices, hangars for planes or transport, tarmac parade grounds—grey, functional, depressing.

The Ministry Of Defence kept promising to tart up the living quarters, but I hadn't seen any sign of it lately. At least we all had single rooms now, except for recruits who hadn't passed basic.

Back at the Armoury, we returned our weapons and the ammunition was carefully counted. No one wanted ammo to find its way into the wrong hands.

"Well done, lads," I said, grinning despite my tiredness and our joint failure. "Not a bad op today—we were tight ... right up until we had a weapons-grade fuck up. Think about how it could have been improved so next time we'll be on it."

"Yes, Staff," came the muttered replies.

The smile slid from my face as I turned and headed toward the building housing the REME officers.

Not all officers are wankers. By the law of averages you occasionally come across one that you don't want to shoot. Elders was alright, not that I knew him well. I'd only been attached here for three weeks— barely enough time to find my way around base.

If I'd been overseas on ops, I'd have used the time to unofficially requisition some better kit for my men. There was always something they needed that the bastard of a Quartermaster wanted to keep tidied away in his nice, neat stores. Raiding his supplies could be a useful training op for my team. Unofficially, of course. But on a home base, it would be viewed as highly unprofessional and is career ending—amassing spares on ops was viewed differently.

Totally against regulations. But that was the thing about the men who were in my trade: ATs, Ammunition Technicians—bomb disposal officers—we made lousy soldiers, but we made great ATs.

Our minds worked differently from most soldiers—we were trained specifically for that reason. We had to see three steps beyond everyone else. We were taught to analyse, taught to think. And that made us independent—which most officers hated.

We were the opposite of fighter pilots: they have to tell everyone that they're a pilot and they say speed is life. I didn't tell anyone what I did, and speed is death.

Captain Elders accepted my salute briskly and waved me into a chair.

"Fuck up today, Staff. Not your finest hour."

"No, sir."

He'd seen what happened, I didn't need to apologise for it.

The Captain leaned back in his chair, tapping a cheap plastic biro against the scarred desk.

"I've had an unusual request come across my desk and someone at Division HQ thinks that you're the man for the job."

I stared at him warily. In my experience, a volunteer was someone who hadn't understood the question.

"It seems our friends across the pond need some help—someone with your skillset, as it turns out. Working with their own EOD teams —some sort of training exercise. You need to report to RAF Croughton tomorrow. Apparently the Yanks are so keen to have you, they're sending transport to pick you up. Be packed and ready by 0700."

I wasn't expecting that—a training exercise with American military?

Could be interesting: Americans trained hard. Fifteen years ago, they said they wanted to be world leaders in EOD within ten years, and maybe in terms of equipment, support, numbers and capability they had it all going for them. But it had come from throwing cash at the problem and not from operational need, so there was a knowledge gap. They dealt mostly with pipe bombs and there wasn't much interest in dealing with the full range of devices. In the British Army, we'd been trained for decades by learning how to neutralize everything the IRA could throw at us. There was a background of knowledge to draw on.

"Yes, sir. How long am I going for?"

He frowned and looked at the paperwork.

"Doesn't say. Best expect to be away for a few weeks."

Fuck!

"Yes, sir."

I took the orders that he handed to me and flicked through them as I headed back to my room, growing more and more confused.

The orders simply said when and where I'd be picked up: nothing about the training exercise, how long I'd been away, what I'd be doing, which regiment I'd be working with, or who'd requested me. Weirdly, the only contact was an email address that went to an office I'd never heard of at the MOD HQ in London.

I didn't know if Elders had been told any more than was in my orders, because otherwise he was just guessing at the job, as well as the timescale.

It wasn't completely unusual to do training exercises with our opposite number in the US Army; I'd even trained with Navy SEALs and EOD teams in the US Marine Corps—but this was definitely different.

For one thing, it looked as though I'd be travelling by myself rather than with the Unit I was attached to; and for another thing, there was nothing to say where I was heading. Besides, the logistics of these sorts of joint exercises always took months to plan. I should have heard something about it before now.

I pulled out my phone and Googled RAF Croughton:

"Royal Air Force Croughton houses the 422nd Air Base Group whose function is to provide installation support, services, force protection, and worldwide communications across the entire spectrum of operations. The group

is located in the UK and supports NATO, US European Command, US Central Command, Air Force Special Operations Command, US Department of State operations and Ministry of Defence operations. The group sustains more than 450 C2 circuits and supports 25% of all European Theater to continental United States (CONUS) communications."

In other words, spook work.

There was a story behind this deployment, I just didn't know what it was. Because it sounded like the sort of thing that would be staffed by the Special Forces ATOs. But since I'd been dumped in a dead end unit after that incident in Afghanistan, it gave me a chance to escape to something more exciting—and possibly save my career.

So there was nothing for me to do but pack my bags. Since I'd only been in Wiltshire for three weeks, I hadn't exactly made myself at home and I'd travelled light in the first place. Packing wasn't an issue: where to store my Ducati Sport 1000 was. I didn't trust those clumsy bastards in transport, the Royal Logistics Corps, not to damage it.

But as I was leaving in 12 hours, I didn't have a lot of choice either.

I decided to shoot a text to my mate Noddy, reminding him that he owed me, and asking him to look after my wheels until I got back.

He agreed, but also wound me up by threatening to ride it while I was away. Noddy weighed 300 pounds and had as much balance as a lame hippo: if he tried to ride my bike, they'd be taking him to A&E and my bike to the knackers' yard.

For a moment, I thought about texting Vanessa, but then remembered that we'd broken up because she didn't like being in a long distance relationship. As she only lived two hours away and that was already too far, there was no point telling her that I'd be in the US for God knows how long. She'd hated me being sent away all the time, bitching and moaning all the time about cancelled dates and missed birthdays; complaining when she found ants in her kitchen and I wasn't there to sort it out. But what the hell did she think the Army was? A holiday camp where you could go home when you wanted?

The Army was my home—the only one I had, so I did what I was told—mostly—and went where they sent me.

I tried not to think about what I was going to do when I'd served my 22 years. Returning to civilian life at 40 didn't hold any appeal for me. A few people stayed on after they'd done their full stint, but not many.

I shook my head: I still had 11 years before I had to face that horror story.

I settled down on my hard bunk with my hands behind my head and wondered what the Army had in store for me this time.

TICK TOCK – the romantic suspense novel from best-selling author Jane Harvey-Berrick on Amazon

MORE ABOUT JHB

"Love all, trust a few, do wrong to none"—this is one of my favourite sayings. Oh, and 'Be Nice!' That's another. Or maybe, 'Where's the chocolate?'

I get asked where my ideas come from—they come from everywhere. From walks with my dog on the beach, from listening to conversations in pubs and shops, where I lurk unnoticed with my notebook. And of course, ideas come from things I've seen or read, places I've been and people I meet.

Jackson Connor is a fictional character but some of the things he went through as a Marine are not. That's why I support these charities:

www.felixfund.org.uk – the UK Bomb Disposal Charity

www.nowzad.com – helping servicemen and women rescue stray and abandoned animals in former and current warzones

ACKNOWLEDGMENTS

If I truly had to ask everyone who's ever helped me, I'd have to start with thanking my parents for reading to me a lot of years back, my kindergarten teacher Mrs. Peck and ... well, you get the picture.

Wanting to write, being a writer, it's a lifelong lesson, and one that I'm still learning. But there are a number of people who have helped guide and sculpt *this* book. So, I'll start with these women, all amazing in their own rights, all different, all supportive.

To Sheena Lumsden for many things, but most of all, unwavering friendship.

To Sybil Wilson, Pop Kitty Designs for her cover artwork. Thank you for being prepared to try so many things to match the picture I had in my mind. You're fab!

To Amélie White Vahlé, who came up with some lovely French phrases for Marc.

To all the bloggers who give up their time for their passion of reading and reviewing books—thank you for your support.

To Kathryn Magyar who begged and pleaded for Maggie and Jack to get their HEA. Yes, she begged—and I do love that in a woman ;)

To Krista Webster for beta-reading at short notice.

And to Erin Spencer of the Southern Book Belles who asked me to write a short story for the Hard Rock Café signing in Tulsa, OK, back in 2015, and ended up with 20 chapters.

MORE BOOKS BY JHB

Series Titles
*The Education Series
An epic love story spanning the years, through war zones and more...
*The Education of Sebastian (Education series #1)
*The Education of Caroline (Education series #2)
*The Education of Sebastian & Caroline (combined edition, books 1 & 2)
Semper Fi: The Education of Caroline (Education series #3)

*The Traveling Series
All the fun of the fair ... and two worlds collide
*The Traveling Man (Traveling series #1)
*The Traveling Woman (Traveling series #2)
*Roustabout (Traveling series #3)
*Carnival (Traveling series #4)
*Gypsy (Traveling series #5)

The Justin Trainer Series
The bodyguard and the billionaire
Guarding the Billionaire (Justin Trainer series #1)

Saving the Billionaire (Justin Trainer series #2)

* The EOD Series
Blood, bombs and heartbreak
*Tick Tock (EOD series #1)
* Bombshell (EOD series #2)

*The Rhythm Series
Blood, sweat, tears and dance
*Slave to the Rhythm (Rhythm series #1)
*Luka (Rhythm series #2)

Standalone Titles
Contemporary Romance
The Lilac Cadillac
Battle Scars
One Careful Owner
*Lifers
At Your Beck & Call
The New Samurai
Exposure

New Adult
*Dangerous to Know & Love
Dazzled
Summer of Seventeen

Paranormal
*The Dark Detective: Venator (Book #1)
*The Dark Detective: Paukúnnum (Book #2)

Novellas
Playing in the Rain
*Behind the Walls

Anthologies of Short Stories

*The Year Book Volume 1
*The Year Book Volume 2
*The Year Book Volume 3

Audio Books
One Careful Owner
(*narrated by Seth Clayton*)

On the Stage
Later, After: Playscript
Trailer

With Alana Albertson
Father Figure

* These titles are published in languages other than English.
Please check Jane's website for details—and receive **a free short story every month** when you sign up for her newsletter :)

QR code for Jane's website

ROMANCE WITH STUART REARDON

My love co-author with these titles

Two book series - contemporary romance

*Undefeated

*Model Boyfriend

Three book series - romcom

*Gym Or Chocolate?

*The World According to Vince

*The Baby Game

Standalone

Survivor Love Island *(romcom)*

*Touch My Soul *(novella)*

WRITING AS BERRICK FORD

Police Thrillers, UK

Dead Water
Dead Man's Dive
Dead Reckoning
Dead Shore

www.berrickford.com